D1433774

SYKES

OF

SEBASTOPOL TERRACE

Above: 'I'll tell you what, we'll put this picture on the cover of the book.' – E.S.

SYKES

OF
SEBASTOPOL
TERRACE

ERIC SYKES

Virgin

DEDICATION

For my dear friend John Ballantyne, ENT Specialist,
without whose skill and care none of these programmes
would have been possible. We are still very close even
though we are now at the eight furlong marker.

First published in Great Britain in 2000 by
Virgin Publishing Ltd
Thames Wharf Studios
Rainville Road
London
W6 9HA

Copyright © Eric Sykes Ltd 2000

The right of Eric Sykes to be identified as the Author of this Work has been asserted by
him in accordance with the Copyright, Designs and Patents Act, 1988.

This book is sold subject to the condition that it shall not, by way of trade or otherwise, be
lent, resold, hired out or otherwise circulated without the publisher's prior written consent
in any form of binding or cover other than that in which it is published and without a
similar condition including this condition being imposed on the subsequent purchaser.

A catalogue record for this book is available from the British Library.

ISBN 1 85227 9850

Printed by Butler & Tanner
Insides designed by Design 23

CONTENTS

CHAPTER ONE
Windows

At about 7.30 p.m. on a damp, dark October evening, somebody heaved a half-brick through Mrs Polanski's front window; seemingly an act of mindless vandalism that began a chain of events that would be talked about for years to come. The half-brick crashed through the window, showering the table with broken glass just as the vicar sat enjoying his weekly tea visit. Unfortunately, the half-brick, at the end of its trajectory, bounced off the vicar's well-polished head whereupon he slumped, face-down, unconscious, into his bowlful of pineapple chunks.

Oblivious to what had just occurred, poor old deaf-as-a-post Mrs Polanski shuffled out of the kitchen with a fresh pot of tea. She didn't quite take it all in at first. She was refreshing the vicar's cup and, seeing him slumped over his bowl, her first reaction was outrage that he should be examining her pineapple chunks so minutely. Then she noticed the glass scattered all over the table and, when a gust of rain finally blew through the broken window ballooning the curtains, she understood what had happened . . . especially when she discovered the half-brick on the table was not a small brown loaf after all.

Shaking her head, she went back into the kitchen for a dustpan, thinking that England had many strange customs – Bonfire Night, Empire Day, Remembrance Day, the Maypole – perhaps today was to commemorate the abolition of the window tax. Who could tell, even so it was better than her native Poland.

Cluck-clucking, she gingerly placed slivers of glass into her dustpan. A normal housewife would have been hysterically dialling 999 for the police and an ambulance for the vicar but then Mrs Polanski was built of sterner stock. To be more exact, she was born into the Polish aristocracy and her life story could well have been scripted by Edgar Allan Poe.

Briefly, at the outbreak of World War II, her loving husband, Count Sergio Polanski, was killed leading a cavalry charge against a column of German tanks. She was informed of his death shortly afterwards by a high-ranking German officer of the Wehrmacht, and so impressed was he by the splendid magnificence of the old castle where the Countess lived, he promptly commandeered it for his headquarters. The Germans being an honourable nation, however, he paid her the courtesy of her title and Countess Irma Polanski was found alternative accommodation . . . in a little-known place called Auschwitz. Surviving all this, in 1945 she returned to her home to find it had been blitzed by our own Air Force. Eventually, after months of starvation, interrogation and degradation, she ended up in Sebastopol Terrace as plain Mrs

Above: Eric and Hattie enjoyed a bond of friendship almost as close as the bond between the TV 'twins.'

Opposite: 'Me phoning the admiralty to report the sinking of our boat. When asked, "What is your position?" Hat replied, "In here, standing up."' – E.S.

Polanski with just a few pounds in her purse. So really, a brick through her window was just a burp on the turbulence of her past existence.

Outside her house a small crowd cautiously approached from the darkness to stare uncomprehendingly into the well-lit room. A voice said, 'Is everything all right, Mrs Polanski?'

'Eh?' shrieked the old lady, desperately trying to adjust her hearing aid.

'Is he dead?' said another, pointing through the jagged opening to the vicar.

Another voice, an authoritarian one, came out of the shadows.

'All right, all right, stand back, everybody.'

It was Constable Turnbull. He leaned forward through the hole in what had, until five minutes ago, been the cleanest, shiniest window in Sebastopol Terrace. His eyes widened as he took in the scene before him . . . Mrs Polanski picking shards of glass from the table and putting them gingerly into a dustpan. He also noticed the vicar slumped forward with his face flattened into a bowl of whatever. He thought the vicar probably had sinus trouble and was sniffing Friars Balsam. He decided that levity was his best approach.

'Ah, ha,' he started, 'you two had a fight.'

Mrs Polanski turned towards this grinning oaf whose job it was to prevent this sort of thing happening in the first place. She didn't quite know how to reply to the inanity of his remark but she clucked her tongue with asperity when she noticed the rainwater was running off his cape onto her already desecrated carpet. Taking a step forward, she pushed him back into the darkness and smartly pulled the curtains together. Had she done this to begin with, things might have turned out differently. Constable Turnbull was embarrassed but with the drawing together of the curtains the darkness spared his blushes. He hurriedly shooed away the sensation seekers with the usual copper-speak, 'Come on, move along. Haven't you got any homes to go to?' And to the smaller ones, 'Hop it.' Nobody really wanted to hang about in the worst weather since '47 anyway, so they

Above: 'I've no idea what we're supposed to be doing, but at a guess I would suggest that Corky is trying to convince me that if he had a few more funny lines it could be a riot.' – E.S.

hopped it. Only then, when the street was cleared, did he turn to squelch his way to the police station. The weather was worsening and his shift had another hour to go. He wasn't patrolling in this lot; it was like crossing the Bay of Biscay in a public wash basin. His excuse at aborting his duty would be to write up his report on the events at Mrs Polanski's and thinking of her it suddenly dawned on him that there'd been glass scattered all over the table. So the brick had been hurled from the street, and this was not the heated domestic squabble that he'd first assumed. His spirits rose. After all, a domestic spat was commonplace but a brick hurled from the street at an unprotected window was front-page stuff.

He quickened his pace, mentally reviewing the incident. Then an extremely disturbing thought entered his mind and his spirits plummeted as quickly as they had risen. The villain could have been one of that crowd . . . he stopped in his tracks. In fact, with the wind against him, he staggered six paces back. He'd dropped a monumental clanger. He should have questioned the crowd before sending them off and taken a few names and addresses. It was more than likely that someone might even have witnessed the whole thing and could have given him the name of the culprit. What a fool he'd been. He ducked into the lee of a shop doorway. He needed the calm in order to think up a good excuse for his elementary blunder. But before he could reach for his fags, the solution flashed into his mind. It was simple – as soon as the crowd spotted his uniform they scarpered into the blackness. After all, his first duty was to check that Mrs Polanski was all right. This improvisation surprised him, it was brilliant . . .

'By golly,' he thought, as he prepared for the last lap to the station, 'There's a lot more to me than meets the eye.'

He lurched out of the doorway, shoulders hunched against the wind, walked headfirst into a lamppost and to make matters worse, he apologised.

In the charge room of the East Acton Police Station, Sergeant Ronnie Blinn stood behind his high desk, leaning on his elbows, sucking another peppermint and muttering 'Roll on retirement!' He was bored with his job, with the police force, the wife, the miserable street he lived in and he was just getting round to his unruly mob of offspring when the door burst open, a rush of sleet and wintry weather disgorging Constable Turnbull in its wake.

The sergeant's orderly stack of charge sheets sprang off his desk, scattered by the malevolence of the force seven from the Plains of Siberia. 'Shut that bloody door!' he shouted, desperately trying to grab the papers as they raced furiously past him.

The constable slammed the door shut with difficulty, and the charge sheets ceased their mad gambol, floating sedately to the floor like the gentle snow in Shangri La. Sergeant Blinn glared at Constable Turnbull who was known throughout the force as 'Corky.' Nobody knew why, and nobody questioned it; it was part of the folklore. But rumour had it that the nickname 'Corky' came about

Above: 'Spike Milligan and me in the Johnny Speight series Curry and Chips.*' – E.S.*

because he was so thick that, when he was bawled out, he'd smile modestly and take it as a compliment. So the Sergeant wisely held his counsel. He combed his hair before getting down on his hands and knees to pick up the charge sheets, many of which were now rain-soaked and, worse still, some of them bore the imprints of Corky's size fourteen boots.

It was some time before he had the sheets back on his desk and, with his handkerchief, tried to wipe away the marks of Constable Turnbull's passing. In truth, he hadn't passed far enough, he was sitting at a typewriter in a corner of the room and for the last half-hour had been savagely attacking the machine with two alternate stiff forefingers. The sergeant grimaced as another loud tap sounded from the corner where the aforesaid constable was having another stab at a cogent report. Sergeant Blinn wandered casually behind him to see what progress, if any, was being made. After all, it was no big deal; he knew all about the incident with the smashed window because Mrs Polanski had already telephoned him with her complaint. So what was the hold

Windows

up? He peered over the constable's shoulder and was appalled to see that he was having difficulty with the word 'proceeding', which was strange in itself because the hundreds of reports he must have submitted throughout his career invariably began with, 'As I was proceeding in an easterly direction' – or northerly or perhaps up or down or along, whichever, it was always preceded by 'proceeding.' Why didn't the fool just put, 'At approximately 19.25 a brick was thrown through Mrs Polanski's front window . . .' end of report. Why, for God's sake, didn't Corky just type that?

But he knew the answer. Sitting in front of a typewriter in a warm, cosy duty room was infinitely more appealing than a windswept shop doorway shielding a damp cigarette from the blustery sleet. And who knows, with the trouble the constable was taking over his report, he might be eligible for two or three hours overtime. The sergeant looked up at the clock on the wall and made a mental note of the time while the constable studied the keyboard as if it were in Urdu. Finally he stabbed at the letter 'A', missing it by such a wide margin that he actually struck the tabulator key, causing the carriage to shoot swiftly to the right, ending in the ting of the little bell.

'Congratulations,' declaimed Sergeant Blinn. 'You've won a coconut or you can have the teddy bear.' Twenty minutes later, the noise of the inexpert typist was beginning to exhaust his patience. He winced as the raspberry from the old machine conveyed to him that another report had been aborted. Then came another long pause and a rustle of paper before the next tap. He waited for some time for the tap of the next letter, instead there was the rab-a-dab-a-dab of the space bar, another pause then after a muttered 'sod it' from the corner, the whisk of the roller bar as yet another attempt was jettisoned. A pause and the ratchet ratched, ratched, ratched as a fresh blank report form was inserted. The sergeant's torture was about to end. At five minutes to midnight relief came as Constable Turnbull tappy-tappy-tapped on the dash key with a rapidity that belied his ignorance. Sergeant Blinn sighed with relief. What he'd just heard signalled the underline that would end the report.

Luckily, Constable Turnbull didn't bother to see the result of his tappy-tap-tap on the dash bar because if he'd done so he would have been perplexed to see that he hadn't underlined anything. It may have been his inexpert typing, or the fact that his eyes weren't too good, or his co-ordination was over the hill, but his underline turned out to be not an underline but three joined-up dashes followed by a full stop, then a semicolon and four more joined-up dashes, finishing off triumphantly with an asterisk. He stretched and handed his report over to the sergeant who scanned it with appreciative nods of admiration. 'Brilliant, brilliant as always. I'll see this goes upstairs immediately. A few more reports like this and you could find yourself in my job,' said the sergeant affably.

Corky smiled happily. 'Oh it's all part of the policeman's lot,' he said modestly. Then, putting on his helmet and adjusting the chinstrap, he reached for the door knob.

'Hang on,' shouted the sergeant, panic-stricken, 'before you open that door . . .' And he hurriedly grabbed the large pile of reports from his desk, put them on his chair and sat on them.

'Goodnight, Corky,' he said and Corky, bent double, fought his way out. As the door slammed behind him, the sergeant ran a comb through his hair again and, giving the constable's report a last glance, he crumpled it into a ball and tossed it into the waste paper basket . . . they didn't have a file marked 'fiction.'

The morning after the outrage at Mrs Polanski's, rumours sprouted like weeds on the M1; the vicar was dead; both he and Mrs Polanski were KGB agents; eye-witness reports claimed that the vicar was a drug addict; when the brick smashed the window he had his head in a bowl sniffing coke. All these rumours were very wide of the mark but whatever happened, the vicar could be sure of one thing – he'd have a full house at his church on Sunday. By lunchtime there was hardly a person in the street who had not passed by Mrs Polanski's house to glance furtively at the newly-installed window. And, pacing up and down in front of these residents, Constable Turnbull was in his element, saluting and answering any enquiry. Never at any time during the morning had there been less than two dozen sightseers gawping, whispering, clicking cameras, and if there was one thing Corky enjoyed above all else it was an audience. He was just about to slip up to the pie shop for a quick Cornish pasty when a group of Japanese tourists, each equipped with their obligatory cameras, hurried over to join the locals

wondering what all the fuss was about. Corky forgot his rumbling stomach and saluted . . . there could be a back-hander in this. One of them sidled up to him and, after several deferential bows, asked the name of the occupier. Corky glanced over his shoulder, smirked and said 'Winston Churchill.' The man's eyebrows shot up as he passed on this information to his colleagues whereupon they ooh-aahed, twittered and tinkled in Japanese. Then cameras came up and, after several blinding flashes, they all bowed to the constable, thinking what a wonderful place London was – and

Opposite: 'After a charity performance at Windsor Castle, an audience with Her Majesty Queen Elizabeth. Disaster at having mislaid my hearing aid, so unfortunately I cannot tell you what we talked about.' – E.S.

Below: 'Mr Brown is sitting in the back seat and however Hattie drives, you can be sure his face will always be in shot. Dear Charles Fulbright Brown.' – E.S.

Windows

Left: *This was a 180 yard fairway shot with a five iron and it landed six inches from the hole — or it would have done had there been a ball.'* — E.S.

reads because it's not written down. But the message is clear, drop your guard for a fleeting moment and bingo! There's one born every minute and your it . . .

And so it was on this bleak winter's twilight, only four days after Mrs Polanski's fifteen minutes of fame, there came an almighty crash of splintered glass, putting Mrs Polanski's puny window into the third division. Hat and I were in the middle of our tea when the whole plate glass window imploded over the counter of Madge's bread shop across the street.

'Good grief,' I mumbled through a mouthful of fried cod. 'That's the Crystal Palace gone.'

Hat, with a forkful of chip halfway to her mouth, stared at me in suspended animation. It was reminiscent of the war when the engine of a buzz bomb cuts out. Dropping her fork, she rushed towards the window and, cupping her hands round her eyes like a golfer lining up a putt, she peered into the gloom outside.

I was just behind her and I swear I jumped a foot in the air as she shrieked, 'Its Madge's!' Immediately, she hurried to the door but I beat her to it.

'Hang on a minute, Hat, you can't go out like that. It must be 40 below out there, you'll catch pneumonia.' She struggled to reach the door again. I blocked her path. 'Think woman, use your loaf. Do you want to die of hypochondria?'

Her eyes refocused on seeing the sense of my argument, or perhaps she was wondering if hypochondria was the correct disease. We both wrapped up warmly before rushing across the road to see if we could assist in any way. That was our intention but it was impossible. By this time the street was blocked with gawking wide-eyed idiots. I pulled Hat behind me pushing and shoving my way through the crowds until eventually we reached what was left of the sagging window. As luck would have it, Corky was standing guard in case of looters.

they still hadn't been out of East Acton. Corky watched them go, disappointed he hadn't been bunged a few yen. He sniffed. Of course, Winston Churchill didn't live in that crummy little house but neither, for that matter, did Mrs Polanski. She was two doors lower down.

All this excitement, however, was largely confined to Sebastopol Terrace. It had been ignored by the newspapers. In fact, not even a mention, in the local rag, the *Acton Bugle*, and television apparently had other fish to fry. So, without the life-giving breath of publicity, the street slumped back to its usual torpor . . . a big mistake because, as everyone knows, life is a very dodgy contract. Nobody asks for it, it's just dumped on us along with its small print, which nobody

'Ah,' he said when he recognised us. 'You've just missed Madge, she went across the street to your house.'

'Gordon Bennett,' I exploded, but there was nothing else for it. With head down, I dragged Hat back through the crowd. It was like fighting our way through a Wakefield Trinity Scrum, taking us several minutes to get across the street.

Mrs Blacktin from the launderette met us and said, 'Madge has been hammering your knocker trying to get in, but as you seemed to be out Mr Brown took her to his house.'

'Come on,' shouted Hat, but I ignored her. I wasn't going into Mr Brown's house. I'd had enough excitement for one day.

She was off like a flash and, with a feeling of a job well done, I fiddled in my pocket for my front door key. With any luck the chips might still be warm and a drop of whisky wouldn't do me any harm, either. I reached into my starboard jacket pocket . . . nothing. But I wasn't unduly worried, I had many more pockets to go through. In fact, what with overcoat, jacket and trousers I went through seven other pockets . . . and still no key. Finally, I put my hand in my back trouser pocket. I was right the key wasn't there, the only thing that goes into my back trouser pocket is my wallet.

Suddenly, I froze . . . then frantically I thrust my hand into my back pocket so violently I went through to my underpants, and my worst fears were realised; I knew with a dreadful sinking certainty that my wallet had been nicked when I was pulling Hattie through the crowd. I sank down on to the bitterly cold front door step and it was there that Hat found me over an hour later. I explained through chattering teeth what had happened.

'You should have come to Mr Brown's house,' she said.

I shook my head sadly. I couldn't explain to her that it was impossible to go into Mr Brown's house without a tie on.

Madge's window was the second in only four days, but it was still ignored by the TV, the national press and even the *Acton Bugle* seemed unaware of the drama in Sebastopol Terrace. To be honest, it was no big deal to them. After all,

there were more windows smashed every Saturday night after the football matches and nobody bothered to splash them over the front page. Five days later, however, Mr Motson, the butcher, had his window smashed. By the end of November, six more windows had been given the same treatment and still the media ignored it. And what a marvellous headline it would make. 'Serial window smasher still at large!' Even the police seemed unable to find the perpetrator, their excuse being that they were too short on manpower to patrol the Terrace in strength. Some people had begun to board up their windows before dark and quite a few householders put Sellotape strips on their windows as

Above: Clowning for the cameras in 1977.

they used to do in the wartime blitzes.

In spite of all this, Mr Brown was very smug and sanguine about the whole thing. He maintained that whoever was responsible for these outrages had to be someone who was settling old scores, and as he hadn't an enemy in the world, his house would be sacrosanct. Mr Charles Fulbright Brown wasn't such a bad fellow really, he was just born 300 years too late. Live by the sword and you die by the sword – he was always coming out with garbage like this. Why couldn't he get with it? Get modern . . . live by a nuclear pile and you die by the fallout, or play on the railway

Left: Eric in Sykes And A Mission, 1961.

line and its good night Vienna. In any case, it has nothing to do with having your window smashed.

Hattie and I were discussing him one evening as we were watching the *Epilogue*. I wasn't listening to the man smiling into the television camera, I was regurgitating in my mind Mr Brown's attitude. Suddenly I had the answer, I was on my feet like a shot and switched off the TV.

'Oh,' said Hat, disappointed. 'What did you do that for?'

'I know who the window smasher is.'

But Hat didn't seem too interested. The *Epilogue* was her favourite programme next to *Songs of Praise*.

'It's Mr Brown,' I declared triumphantly. She stared at me as if I'd suddenly caught fire and with a wave of her hand she stood up and went into the kitchen. Over her shoulder she said, 'I'm going to make some cocoa, and I suggest you put something in yours.'

I followed her quickly. 'No listen, Hat. There's only one person in this street who is so confident about his window, and that is the smasher himself.' I stabbed my finger pointedly next door.

Hat took the cocoa into the other room as if I'd just mentioned it was time we had a bit of rain, or the traffic was bad today. The more she didn't say anything, the more certain I became that I was right . . . it was while she was washing up the cups she broke the silence.

'What are you going to do about it?' She said, by which time I had concocted a plan.

'First thing I'm going to do,' I said, 'I shall follow him every night to see where he goes.'

'What about Madge and Mrs Pickering?' Hat asked.

'What ABOUT Madge and Mrs Pickering?' I said.

'It's Thursday,' she said, with some exasperation.

I thought for a moment then I said, 'OK, I'll start my surveillance on Friday night.'

And with that we went upstairs.

Thursday night was our Monopoly night. I enjoyed Madge's company and that of Mrs Pickering, who owns the flower shop. She was in the same class at school with Hat and it seemed only natural she should be the fourth player. She wasn't bad, either. In fact, had Monopoly been an event at the Winter Olympics, she would have won at least a bronze. But tonight, for the first time since we started these get-togethers, I was the favourite. I was dickering whether I should buy Park Lane or another two hotels when the whole evening exploded with the dreaded sound of breaking glass. It was so loud that Mrs Pickering jumped up with a shriek, scattering the board, the money, the boot, the racing car and my three hotels. They all rushed out to see who was the latest victim. I couldn't care less; for the first time in months I was winning, and if I could have acquired Park Lane and Mayfair I could have cleaned up. I reckoned that knee jerk and scream of Mrs Pickering was deliberate. After all, she had no chance of winning . . . she only had Water Works and Fenchurch Street Station.

Hat came in white faced. 'It's Mr Browns,' she said, breathlessly.

'Oh, dear,' I said, trying to keep the jubilation out of my voice.

'He's alright,' she said. 'He wasn't in the room.'

I nodded sadly and sighed, 'Live by the sword and…'

Hat rounded on me. 'You're glad, aren't you? Have you no human pity in you?'

I replied with the same amount of asperity. 'What are you suggesting, we have a whip round?'

I continued to place the pieces on the board.

'You can forget that stupid game,' she said. 'I'm going into Mr Brown's to make him a cup of tea.' And with that she slammed the door behind her.

I sprang to my feet and yelled at the door, 'It might only be a game to you but it's important to me.' I stopped suddenly. The door couldn't care less. I cheered up, especially when I thought of Mr Brown's window. At least it had removed him as the prime suspect, for which I was heartily glad. I didn't relish traipsing through the cold, dark, wintry streets at night after Mr Brown.

I put away the Monopoly game and finished off their wine. Then I went to bed – knowing Hat she'd be picking up all the pieces of glass, vacuuming the carpet and I wouldn't put it past her to put up some new wallpaper.

Sitting at the breakfast table the following morning, I was rifling through the local paper to see if there was anything about Mr Brown's window because, knowing him, he would have been up half the night contacting the BBC, all the national newspapers and even Reuters, concerning the mystery window-smasher. Our usual daily newspaper was the *Acton Bugle* and it lay demurely folded by my plate but that didn't fool me. Hat had already been through it; I knew that because pages four and five were stuck together by a lump of porridge. I was mildly annoyed because I've told her before that I want to be the first to scan the newspaper. As head of the house it was my duty and I wanted to read

a balanced report on the window outrage, rather than the garbled rumours that had dominated the gossip of the last couple of months.

Hat was in the kitchen bustling about with my breakfast and I wondered what was taking so long. It wasn't as if my breakfast dishes covered the sideboard – kedgeree, kippers, chops, eggs and bacon. No, unless it was my birthday or something special it was usually two slices of toast with a smear of Bovril. I was just about to find out what was happening when the flap on the letterbox on the front door clattered and printed a handbill sashayed onto the carpet. I rose . . . immediately there was a blur from the kitchen and Hat passed me on the way to the door.

Snatching up the leaflet, she was back in the kitchen leaving me reeling in the backwash of her passing. If the kitchen door hadn't still been swinging wildly I might have doubted what had just occurred. There was only one way to find out what it was all about. I pushed the kitchen door, but it only moved a foot before it struck a heavy object, and I heard Hat cry out. I waited a moment or two for her to

Right: Hattie in Sykes And A Burglary, *1972*

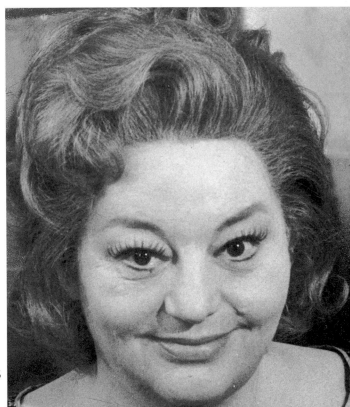

regain her composure and to try finish reading whatever it was, then I gently pushed the door and entered the kitchen.

When I entered the kitchen Hat was pretending to be busy examining a slice of bread. A slice of ordinary bread, for God's sake. You'd think she was entering it in the Ideal Home Exhibition! I said coolly, 'What's it all about?'

Hat stared at the bread and I could almost hear the grinding of her brain as she desperately searched for something plausible to come out in speech form. I saved her the trouble. It was so pathetic. 'What's so important about that slip of paper?' Hat reddened. 'What piece of paper?' she said with a show of indifference.

I pointed as I spoke. 'That piece of paper sticking out of your apron pocket.'

'Oh this,' she said. 'Oh, it's just a piece of stuff they send around all the time.' It was pitiful. If this was the audition the director would long ago have said, 'Thank you very much. Don't ring us, we'll ring you.'

Hat tried to laugh it off. 'Oh that, I was just on my way to throw it in the dustbin.'

I considered her with one eyebrow raised but before I could speak, the doorbell rang, well, it more than rang, and it was an imperative jangling insisting on entry and without delay. It could only be one person, Mr Charles Fulbright Brown. Hat's hand flew to the paper in her pocket and I immediately jumped to the right conclusion. In some way Mr Brown and that paper were connected.

'Good morning, Sykes,' he grinned, as I opened the door. He appeared to be full of *bonhomie*, which usually boded ill for yours truly. Without turning, I heard the door squeak softly as Hat entered the room behind me.

'Good morning, Mr Brown,' she said over my shoulder and I heard the rustle of paper as she held it up jabbing it with her finger, and shaking her head vigorously. I sensed all this signalling to Mr Brown behind my back. Hat and I are identical twins and our e.s.p. is extraordinary. I'm sorry — forget about that last bit. I could see what was going on behind me because to the right of Mr Brown is a large mirror and that's how I could decipher Hat's antics.

Mr Brown obviously didn't understand her or else he's just a born-again troublemaker.

'Ah,' he beamed, 'I see you've got my leaflet.'

I looked in the mirror as Hat handed it to me over my shoulder. I felt really sorry for her; Mr Brown had dropped her in it from some considerable height. I took a step back and put my arm around her shoulders whilst I read the piece headed 'The Window Smasher', a meeting called by Mr Charles Fulbright Brown. Oh God, I thought, Mr Brown held more meetings than they had at Sandown Park. Most of his lectures were sparsely attended, some not all, but it never satisfied his lust for power in Sebastopol Terrace, which he obviously considered his fiefdom. He was a self-made politician – arrogant, devious, and firmly convinced the world would be a better place if only it would listen to him. Mr Brown's agenda was admirably worded:

'Who is the window smasher?

What are the police doing about it?

Should we take matters into our own hands? Etc., etc., etc.'

'Very public-spirited of you, Mr Brown,' I said. 'I only wish I was free, I'd be at your meeting like a shot.'

I looked at him and didn't particularly like the self-satisfied smirk on his face. I can only describe would be similar to Charles Dickens' Oliver falling into a vat of lukewarm mulligatawny. I turned to Hat uncomprehending; she looked away and said in a small voice, 'Read on.' I skimmed through five, six and seven of the agenda. 'Meeting to be held next Wednesday, seven o'clock prompt' and it gave the address. I was about to shrug when it hit me like a number six bus; something about the address sounded familiar . . . it was mine!! I threw the leaflet to the floor.

'Oh, no it isn't,' I yelped. 'This is our home!' I thrust my face close to his. 'OUR HOME,' I repeated. 'It's not a meeting place or assembly room or a seaman's mission. This is our house and my name's on the rent book to prove it.' I strode angrily over to the sofa glancing at Hat who stood there wringing her hands. 'NO! NO! NO! I pounded the sofa cushions to emphasise each 'NO.' Hat sidled across and snatched the cushion from me in case Mr Brown noticed the dust. I whirled around on him.

'Listen,' I said through clenched teeth, Humphrey Bogart sprang to mind but I quickly postponed the thought. 'Listen,' I said again, 'the last time you had a meeting here I said never again . . . and I mean it!'

'Oh, come on, Sykes,' grinned Mr Brown, 'that was almost a year ago.'

'Yes,' I replied, 'and we're still paying for it – over 50 quid for booze, tea, coffee, biscuits, cake.' I was counting off all the times off my fingers. 'Hospital fees when Dobson hit his wife with an ashtray.'

Hat nodded and put her fourpence in. 'Yes, and that ashtray was a souvenir from Cleethorpes.'

Both of us ignored her. I was still holding out my hand but I'd forgotten what finger I was on. Anyway, before I could recover my train of thought Hat broke in again: 'Structural damage to the stairs when Constable Turnbull was pushed over the banisters.'

Mr Brown stared goggle-eyed. 'You're making this up,' he blurted without conviction.

I snorted, 'No, you'd gone by then. Oh yes,' I went on, 'you left when Madge threw a bottle at Mrs Tomlinson.'

'I don't remember that,' said Hat.

'Well, you were probably ringing the police.'

Madge hadn't really

Above: Eric in the film You'd Better Be In Disguise.

thrown anything at Mrs Tomlinson but I felt a little exaggeration wouldn't come amiss in the situation. I didn't want to overdo it, however, so I decided to wrap it up. 'So all you have to do, Mr Brown, is draw a large cardboard hand with a pointing finger on my front gate indicating the meeting has been changed to your house next door.'

Mr Brown opened his mouth, in two minds whether to speak or breathe again – but before he could come to a decision I cut in. 'Now if you'll excuse me, it's time I got dressed.' And with that I climbed the stairs without a backward glance. What an exit!

Half an hour later, shaved and smartly dressed, I bounced downstairs in a happy frame of mind, although I was already late for work for the third time that week and it was only Wednesday. But what a day – I had certainly put Mr Brown in his place. Oh, yes, I wasn't the patsy he took me for. After all, I'm British through and through . . . quiet and reserved normally, but once we're roused it's stand fast the front line . . . oh, yes you can twist the lion's tail once too often. Mr Brown would think twice before he crossed swords with me again. Exhilarated by my fantasies I strode down the main road to the bus stop, but I was high on euphoria and disdained the 48 bus and decided to take a taxi instead. Some ten minutes later, a cab swerved to the kerb in front of me, depositing a fare, an old lady with a handbag as deep as a shrimping net. It was pathetic to see her counting a handful of small coins. I stood behind her looking at my watch several times, then at the cabby who sat patiently waiting. I caught his eye and we both shrugged and gazed heavenwards, at last she handed over a jingle of coins which he didn't even bother to count. And as she moved painfully away, I was about to open the door when an awful thought struck me. It may have been triggered by the sight of the old

17

Windows

Left: In two minds in Sykes And Two Birthdays.

lady's loose change but with a deafening thud, it hit me. I'd left my loose change on my bedside table; it was an understandable gaffe in my state of exhilaration but obviously I couldn't ride to work in a taxi penniless, so I slammed the door shut and, leaned towards the driver.

'What time is it?' I said. It wasn't brilliant but I couldn't think of anything better.

'Hop in,' he said cheerfully, 'I'll run you to the town hall so you can look up at the clock.' He released the brake and, with a bellow of laughter, he disappeared into the exhaust fumes of rush hour.

Strangely enough, this little incident brought me back to earth with a bump. I was mortal again, and my triumphant exchanges with Mr Brown were completely wiped from my memory as I concentrated on a different excuse for my lateness at work. I needn't have worried, though – it was my lucky day or Virgo was passing through Sagittarius or whatever, all I know is I didn't need an excuse anyway. Fortunately, that morning my boss, Mr Hackensmidt, had been knocked down as he was crossing the road. As it turned out, he'd be in hospital for at least a week so I could be late a few more times with an easy conscience.

In fact, when I returned home that evening I'd completely forgotten about Mr Brown's meeting . . . it was only when

I walked past his house and noticed that it was in complete darkness that I remembered all too clearly my instructions about Mr Brown placing a large cardboard hand with a pointing finger indicating the meeting would be held at his place. Hurriedly, I pushed through my own gate and as I made my way towards the door I spotted a chink of light through the curtains. Crouching to look through into the room, I was appalled to see at least a dozen people lolling about the place. It was reminiscent of the departure lounge at Gatwick Airport, and judging by their faces the flight to Malaga was already three hours late . . .

Obviously, someone was speaking to them and I would have to bet any money that it was Mr Brown, although the gap in the curtains wasn't wide enough for me to make a formal identification. I staggered over to the door, shaking with anger, so much so, that I couldn't control my hand enough to put the key in the lock. But the door was opened from the inside by Mr Brown, with a glass of wine in his hand and a smile of welcome on his face. 'Ah, Sykes,' he said, 'so glad you made it. Come in, come in.'

I stood in the doorway, rooted to the spot at his audacious effrontery. I glanced at the audience, who were shivering and rubbing their arms as the cruel winter leapt in gleefully to enjoy the warmth. Hat, who was over the other side of the room, said, 'Well close the door, Eric or we will all freeze to death.' I back-heeled it and as it slammed shut, it triggered in me a different attitude to the situation. I decided to play it cool, real cool. I threw Mr Brown a scout's salute and said 'Dib, dib, dib,' helloed Madge, nodded to the rest of them and passed through to the kitchen followed by Hat. I'd no doubt she would be able to explain why my orders had been so blatantly disobeyed. I took off my overcoat and scarf and held them out but she walked past me as if I wasn't there. It was deliberate. It was definitely a visual 'Who was your servant last year?' So I threw them over the back of a chair whilst I decided how to regain the upper hand. I stared out the window, trying to frame my method of attack but before I could come to a definite conclusion Hat said, 'Come and get it while it's hot.' I turned round and she was filling a plate with my favourite – mincemeat with a nice flaky pastry crust on it. 'Sit down, Eric, we'll continue in there while you have your supper here.'

I dithered. It was a mistake. I should have walked in the kitchen with dilated nostrils and said, 'I'll give you five minutes to get 'em all out.' That's what I should have done, but that steaming plate of mince pie was too much. I was already salivating and when Hat took an open bottle of wine out of the fridge and produced a glass it was a game, set and match to my darling sister. While I shovelled down the best meal I've had in years, Hat explained why the meeting was being held here in spite of my strict orders. Apparently, Mr Brown had convinced her that the arrangements could not now be changed because he'd already invited the Mayor of East Acton, the superintendent at the local police station and for some unknown reason the vicar, whose head was now back in shape.

I swallowed and pointed with my knife to the other room, but before I could speak Hat anticipated with, 'Of course, they're not here yet but Mr Brown said there was plenty of time before they made an official entrance.'

I couldn't quite believe my ears, my sister must be the most gullible person in the world. I now realised what the carpet was laid out for laid out from the gate to the front door. It was a red carpet as well and I had a sinking feeling the stairs would be bare.

I shook my head. I couldn't speak, my mouth was fully occupied.

'Not only that,' she went on, 'Mr Brown has given me a cheque for some of the expenses incurred at the last meeting.'

I had stopped eating in amazement. 'How much?' I gurgled washing down a belch with a gulp of wine.

'Five pounds,' she said in an awed whisper. I stared at her,

Right: Even animal stunt extra 'Patch' left Eric in the dog house in Sykes And A Window . . .

the tone of her voice was the same as if it had been two million not a measly fiver. 'By jingo,' I said. 'He shouldn't chuck his money about like that.'

Hat was refilling my glass. 'There's no need to be sarcastic,' she said and in a whisper she added, 'that's Mr Brown's bottle from his own cellar you're drinking from. And for your information the price of that one bottle of Chablis was £65.' And with that she made her way back to the meeting.

I shook my head in disbelief as I looked into my glass. £65 a bottle. Then it dawned on me – Hat had been liberally splashing my glass at about a tenner a throw. Mr Brown would have a fit when he came in for a refill only to find I'd been at it.

Windows

Quick as a flash I was on my feet and in a minute I was holding the bottle under the cold-water tap to replenish what Hat had so generously bestowed on me. Then I replaced the bottle in the fridge – and not a moment too soon.

Mr Brown pushed through the swing door into the kitchen and made his way to the fridge. Filling his glass, he took a great gulp. I held my breath, praying that he wouldn't notice the dilution in the taste. He was a great wine buff but as he took another gulp, closing his eyes with ecstasy, I began to suspect that he wasn't as great a wine buff as he would have everyone believe. His next move put the matter beyond a shadow of a doubt. He went over to the table and, to my horror, he picked up my half empty glass. At first I thought he was going to drink it but he only lifted it to his nose and sniffed. 'Ugh!!!' he gasped with a pained look on his face. 'I would have offered you some of my Chablis '57, Sykes, but you wouldn't appreciate it.'

'Oh, that must be expensive,' I replied. I can never resist a chance to send him up.

''57 is *the* year, Sykes,' he said icily. 'Actually,' he went on, 'it costs over £100 a bottle.'

I whistled. It had certainly gone up in value since Hat told me about it, but then what do I know about wine?

'What's that stuff you're drinking?'

Quick as a flash I said, 'It's Korean Riesling.'

Mr Brown shuddered. 'There's no accounting for taste, Sykes.' And his parting shot was to remind me not to be too long as the meeting was at a crucial stage. As the door swung behind him, I looked into my now empty glass, trying to decide on a refill. Then I chuckled. I'd just had a glass of '57 Chablis. Why should I pour myself a glass of Mr Brown's watered-down imposter? Thinking about Mr Brown, I shook my head ruefully. One had to admit he didn't let the grass grow under his feet. This made me smile. He could probably do with some on his head, I thought. It was a weird thought and I put it down to his '57 Chablis . . .

But you had to hand it to him. Two weeks had elapsed since his window had been replaced, and one would think that after his previous widespread boasting of his invulnerability, he would want to hide himself from the public gaze. At least a pair of dark glasses or a false beard. Some people might even want to cower under the bed for a week or two until the dust settled. Not he, not a bit of it – quite the opposite, in fact. He was now an engine of activity. His vigilantes now numbered eight, well nine, if you counted old Jack Dimbleby. He wasn't really useful as he had to be pushed up and down in a wheelchair, but it got him away from his wife for an hour or two . . .

My thoughts were interrupted as Mr Brown's head shot round the door. He wasn't calm and supercilious, this time he was rattled.

'What are you waiting for, Sykes, a round of applause?' And he disappeared back into the room.

It was only then I realised that, being so introspective, I had failed to notice that the mumble of voices was now several octaves higher and the polite murmur was now an angry babble as everybody tried to talk at once.

When I entered the room all conversation ceased abruptly, so suddenly that for one horrific moment I thought I'd been struck deaf. A cold panic surged up in me, but before I could faint I heard the plaintive barking of a dog, and with a great sigh of relief I knew my hearing was not impaired. Surprisingly, it might even have improved, since I distinctly heard the rumble of someone's stomach, a sound not unlike the pulling of a plug to empty the washing-up water. Still no one moved, it was like stocktaking at Madame Tussaud's.

Mr Brown clapped his hands together and said, 'Would you return to your seats everybody please?' and, as if he'd released them all from a hypnotic spell, they became human again. Dutifully, they all resumed their perches, leaving me standing, just standing there on my own hearth rug like a new boy at school. A rush of anger engulfed me; who did high and mighty Brown think he was, ordering me about in my own home?

Defiantly, I strode into the kitchen and returned immediately with a chair, which I slammed down facing the television set with my back to the meeting. At nine o'clock there

Right: Eric indulging in his favourite pastime at a Pro-Am tournament at Sunningdale.

was a boxing match from the Apothecary's Hall. And I didn't want to miss that. I switched on the set and settled back. The weatherman faded in smiling as he pointed to his chart, arrows every which way, more like the Battle of Hastings. Never mind, the boxing was after this . . . suddenly a hand the size of a small dustbin lid reached out and grabbed the front of my shirt, lifted me off the chair and I found myself staring slightly down into the face of Mr Oswald Motson, family butcher. He was holding me up with a strength that could sling a whole carcass of beef onto a meat hook with less effort than it took me to hang up my jacket.

'Put my brother down, Mr Motson.' It was Hattie in a voice I hadn't heard since she was running the Girl Guides. The eager light went out of the butcher's eyes. With his left hand, he swivelled the chair and deposited me behind it, my hands on the chair back as if I was in the dock.

'Thanks Hat,' I mumbled as I tucked my shirt back into my trousers. A few months ago it wasn't Mr Motson, it was Oswald this and Oswald that. I suspected things were hotting up between them when I had lamb chops six days in a row. I also noticed Hat went shopping dressed as if she was going to the Royal Garden Party.

So one evening, as I helped myself to mint sauce, I casually mentioned that Mr Motson was a bit of a lad, married, and his wife lived in Portsmouth. I didn't look at her but I knew she'd heard me, so for good measure I added another wife in Northampton. Still no reaction from Hat, although I noticed she'd stopped eating. Not another word was said. The following evening we had fish fingers, for three months Hat became a vegetarian and Oswald was *persona non grata*.

Mr Brown spoke. 'Now, Mr Sykes I'm sure that you're aware that we are gathered here tonight in order to draw up a list of suspects for the smashing of our windows.' He paused to let this sink in, then he continued in a grave voice, 'And I'm afraid, Sykes, that you are very high on the list.'

I had visions of myself being carted up a French street on

a tumbril on my way to the guillotine. Mr Brown's voice brought me back to England, and I caught the gist of his question. 'Where were you between seven and seven thirty on the evening of the first window outrage?'

Dry-mouthed I replied defensively, 'Good grief, that was in October last year! How should I know where I was between seven and seven thirty?'

I turned and appealed to someone on my right; unfortunately it was Mr Motson crouching on the edge of his seat, watching me intently like a Rottweiler waiting for the command 'Kill!' Behind me I heard the roar of the crowd in the Apothecathy's Hall and half-turned towards the set.

Windows

Motson was on his feet in an instant, as if I'd asked him for a dance. 'I was only going to switch it off,' I said and did so. Turning back to the Kangaroo Court, I said, 'On the night Mrs Polanski's window was smashed I didn't get home till after ten o'clock because the bus broke down and we all had to get off and wait for another one.'

Hat broke in, 'No, Eric, don't you remember you had to work late that night because I telephoned you at your office and there was no reply?'

'Ah, yes,' I said lamely. 'I was upstairs stocktaking.' It was all fantasy, of course; we didn't have a stockroom, but I couldn't walk in late and tell her I'd spent the evening in the billiard hall.

Mr Brown nodded at us both. 'Well,' he said urbanely, 'when you have your alibi sorted out we'll continue.'

Hat put up her hand. 'May I ask you a question, Mr Brown,' she said in a tone of voice I knew only too well. It was the soft seductiveness of a landmine floating down on the end of its parachute just before it hit the ground. Even Mr Brown was wary as he gave his assent.

'Where were *you* on that night Mrs Polanski's window was shattered?'

All heads now swivelled to Mr Brown; it was now the centre court at Wimbledon. Hat's question was a corker, obviously hours of *Perry Mason* on television hadn't been wasted. However, Mr Brown was equal to it. 'I am not on trial,' he said suavely, 'and may I remind you I, too, have had my window smashed.'

'We all have,' said Madge and everybody nodded their agreement.

Mr Motson jerked his thumb over the shoulder at me. 'Except him,' he said, struggling to be let off the leash. Mr Brown nodded, 'That is the main reason for his presence at

Left: Publicity shot from the movie Village of Daughters, *1962.*

this investigation.' He then held his lapels as if it was his court gown. 'Now, leaving aside Mrs Polanski, we come to the second outrage.' I sighed; I was back on the ducking stool. Mr Brown was consulting his notes, which he had placed on our telephone table. 'The window of the bread shop, which as you will know is just across the street . . .' Bill Bottomly the postman shuffled his feet and waved the order paper. 'Yes,' snapped Mr Brown peevishly, he didn't like being interrupted.

'May I ask a question?' said Bottomly, unabashed by Mr Brown's obvious distaste.

'Of course,' replied Mr Brown, 'but later when I will be inviting questions from the floor.'

Bottomly was adamant. 'I'd like to ask a question now,' he said.

Unruffled, Madge intervened. 'Good for you, Bill,' she said. 'Ask away, it's a free country.'

Mr Brown sighed, 'The chair gives way to the floor,' he extended his hand to the postman, indicating it was OK to go ahead. Bottomly nodded curtly.

He cleared his throat. 'How long is this pantomime going on for? I've got a home to go to.'

'I agree,' said Madge. 'I vote Ricky is innocent, all those in favour.'

Mr Brown was panic-stricken when some of them were hesitantly raising their hands. 'Let the chair speak,' he squealed, waving his arms as if to wipe out any of the votes already cast. He could see his whole night of glory crashing about his ears. Those who wanted to get home reluctantly put down their hands. Mr Brown mopped his brow. 'Before we put it to a vote, I would like to sum up.' Somebody groaned. As if he hadn't heard it he continued, 'Therefore I must ask Mr Sykes to withdraw to the kitchen whilst I bring the meeting to an end.'

I wasn't going in the kitchen; there wasn't a telly in there so I stood fast.

Mr Brown sighed. 'Mr Motson, would you show Mr Sykes the kitchen.'

The butcher licked his chops but before he could rise I was on my way. I didn't need Motson or anyone else for that matter to show me the kitchen. I knew exactly where it was, I lived here for God's sake, and with as much dignity as I could muster I pushed open the door followed by Hattie.

Constable Turnbull, who had been at the meeting more as an observer than as a jurist, took his helmet from the hat stand and, turning to the assembly, he said importantly, 'Well, I'll be off. I've got my own work to do and whatever happens you can all rest easy. There'll be no windows broken tonight on my manor.'

He adjusted his chin strap and was about to salute the assembly when there was the heart-stopping twice-weekly crashing sound of shattered glass. For a moment there was stunned silence then everyone rushed to the stack of clothing, overcoats, scarves, caps, etc. It was a welcome adjournment to a useless evening. I cautiously pushed open the kitchen door to squint through a blue haze of tobacco smoke being madly chased upstairs by the blustery wind – the front door was wide open.

'Are you sure it was a window smashing?' asked Hat.

'Course it was. I'd know that sound anywhere.'

I made my way through the debris of the tribunal and peered out of the front door.

'Yes,' I said, 'There's a crowd outside Jessie Warburton's.'

Hat collapsed on to the sofa. 'Not another one,' she wailed, close to tears. 'Why don't the police do something?'

I closed the front door. 'Poor old Jessie,' I said. 'Her husband left her six months ago, her eldest son's in Wormwood Scrubs, and now this.'

I looked towards Hat and she was smiling, I did a double

Below: Eric with Jimmy Edwards and Ernie Wise at The Stage *centenary celebrations at The Savoy, 1980.*

take. Two minutes ago she was ready to bawl her eyes out. Had she snapped? Was she going doolally? 'It's nothing to smile about,' I said.

Hat's smile broadened and she rose to her feet. I stood back a pace, wishing I hadn't closed the front door. I would have been out like a shot.

'Don't you see, Eric?' she said softly, 'don't you see what this means?'

I was backing up the stairs.

'You're in the clear,' she laughed and clapped her hands in a burst of sheer joy.

I decided to humour her. I clapped my hands as well. 'I'm in the clear,' I shouted, happily running around the room punching the air. I vaulted over the sofa, then suddenly I stopped. 'Hat,' I said a little breathlessly, 'how am I in the clear?'

She looked at the ceiling in exasperation. 'Because,' she said, as if talking to a halfwit, 'you were here with the accusers and a window is broken. It couldn't possibly have been you.'

When the penny finally dropped, I let out a shout of joy and continued my lap of honour. It was a mistake – remember the life contract? I had overlooked the small print again in my pathetic expressions of relief. Finally, I slumped exhausted in the armchair and Hat let in the straight-faced jury led by Mr Brown.

'Come to apologise, have you?' she crowed, dropping a curtsey.

Mr Brown turned to his posse. 'I told you they'd try to wriggle out of it.'

Hat was puzzled. She looked incredulously at the accusing faces of Mr Motson, Mrs Crabtree and Mr Brown. 'How could Eric have smashed that window? You were here all the time. He would have had to pass you and you would have seen him.'

Mr Brown raised his eyes. 'You've got a back door, haven't you?'

Hat snorted in derision. 'If Eric had gone out the back he'd have had to run like the clappers to get round to the front, smash the window and come back here.'

Mr Brown's eyes lit up his glasses. 'Exactly,' he snapped. 'Just look at him.'

I was slouched in the armchair, sweat pouring down my face, breathing as if I'd just done a four-minute mile. Why, oh why don't we read the small print?

When they'd gone, Hat was all for opening a bottle of wine. She was so happy I couldn't refuse, especially when I remembered there was a couple of glasses left in Mr Brown's bottle but, unlike Hat, I wasn't convinced that I was off the hook. There would be other meetings behind locked doors. I didn't really believe Mr Brown thought I'd smashed the windows, but he was driving the bus and the brakes had gone. Motson the butcher was the real danger. He'd never forgiven the break up of the cosy relationship with my sister and Hat as Mrs Motson was unthinkable. Also, I couldn't face the rest of my life with a brother-in-law called Oswald.

Nothing happened during the next two days and by the third day their plan of action was revealed. The bus I caught every morning accelerated past me – didn't stop – although the driver and I used to be in the scouts together. I was perplexed, but not unduly worried. I went to get some cigarettes but as I was about to enter the shop I saw a hand through the glass door turn the sign round from 'open' to 'closed.' I rattled the door for a minute, but nothing happened. What the hell, I could always give up smoking. I brightened when Jessie Warburton came up the street. As she approached, I wanted to tell her how sorry I was with regard to her window but a strange thing happened. When she recognised me, she stopped in her tracks then crossed to the other side of the street. It was pathetic. If they thought for one moment that sending me to Coventry was going to reduce me to a gibbering confessor, owning up to everything, they were wrong. In fact, when I got home that night I told Hat what had transpired and we had a good laugh.

How wrong we were. After a week of being sent to Coventry I was a changed man. It affected me to such an extent that I stopped going out, refusing even to look out of the window. I just stared at the wall for hours. Hat was marvellous.

Above: Eric and Hattie uncovered in the Thames TV spectacular, Sykes With The Lid Off, *1971.*

She was marvellous and so was Peter the cuckoo clock, but you can't discuss anything deep with him. It's difficult to appreciate the feeling of being a pariah. On second thoughts, it's not a very good example because nobody ever speaks to a pariah anyway and for all we know they may enjoy being ignored, but I like to think I'm gregarious – a good mixer – so it probably had more effect on me. It was driving towards me: an A1 mega breakdown. I'd even looked forward to dialling the time so that I could hear another voice besides Hat's. Eventually, it was all too much – I finally cracked. I was on the verge of insanity. I was even contemplating ending it all. Hanging was too brutal, in any case it might hurt. Jump off Beachy Head? No that was out. I'd probably be half way down suddenly wishing I hadn't jumped.

Hattie brought me a cup of tea with a little drop of malt whisky to cheer me up, but I was too far gone. Then Hat said something that altered the whole ball game. She was about to go back into the kitchen when she stopped and addressed the ceiling, 'Why doesn't the window smasher do us, then we could all be back to normal?'

The kitchen door swung behind her and I thought about what she had just said, then it dawned on me like an African sunrise. That was it, the answer to all our problems.

'Oh, wonderful, wonderful Harriet. Out of the mouths of babes and sucklings.' I was on my feet bubbling with excitement. I shouted, 'Hat!!!'

She was back like a flash. 'What is it?' she gasped, 'what's happened?'

'You've just given me the solution,' I yelled.

'Oh, that,' she said, collapsing in a chair with relief. I thought the telly had gone off again.

'Listen, Hat,' I said eagerly, 'you just said if our window was smashed, I'd be in the clear.'

Windows

'Did I?' she said, a frown creasing her forehead.

I ignored this. Her memory isn't what it was. 'I'm going outside to chuck a brick through our window.'

She looked at me in horror, then after a time she said, 'You'll do no such thing.'

'Hat, listen.'

But she interrupted me. 'Just supposing you're caught, they will all assume you did all the other windows as well.'

'I won't get caught, Hat,' I said, striding towards the window to pull the curtains aside. 'Look at that, Hat, it's pouring out there. Look, it's black as the coalman's earhole.'

She came to the window and peered out. The she fearfully turned to me. 'Eric, I'm scared.' She wrung her hands but I could see she was weakening.

'Listen, Hat,' I said as inspiration swept though me. 'You go upstairs now and run the bath. When it's full come down and go into the kitchen.'

'The kitchen,' she said, looking as if she'd forgotten where it was.

'You don't want flying glass all over you, do you?' I said.

'Eric,' she blurted.

But I interrupted her in case she changed her mind. 'I'll go out and chuck the brick, and as soon as you hear the window go, come out of the kitchen, open the front door and let me in . . . then shout upstairs, "Eric, somebody's thrown a brick through our window."'

She looked at me with concentrated eyes as she tried to take in her instructions.

'Shout this a couple of times so that somebody will hear. Madge is still open across the street, she'll hear you and anybody near will come and see what it's all about.' I shrugged into my raincoat before she could spot any flaws in my plan. It was obvious that all the 'wheres' and 'what ifs' and 'supposings' were whirling round her mind like a spin-dryer.

'Eric,' she said finally, 'why do you want me to run a bath?'

I tapped my nose and gave her a long, knowing wink. 'That's my alibi,' I said triumphantly. 'When you let me in, I'll dash upstairs, take my clothes off, lie in the bath just long enough to get wet, and when the crowds come round I'll be coming downstairs in my dressing gown drying my hair.' I spread out my arms to illustrate my genius.

She brightened. 'And they'll think you were in the bath when it happened.'

I put both hands on her shoulders and looked at her seriously. 'There's not a lot gets past you, Hat. I knew you'd grasp it straight away. Now off you go and fill the bath. I'll go down to the boiler room for a piece of coal.'

'Oh,' she said airily, 'don't worry about the coal. There'll be plenty of hot water.'

I looked at her coolly. 'I want the coal so that I can chuck it through the window.'

'Ah,' she said, 'I never thought of that'. Then she started upstairs to fill the bath and I was about to go down to the boiler room when she stopped half way and said, 'Do you want me to put any bath salts in the water?'

'No, Hat, just plain water will do,' I sighed. Sometimes I think I overestimate my sister. However, in ten minutes we were all set. Bath filled, coal in hand, heart in mouth, I cautiously opened the front door and with a thumbs up I stepped out into the night. Hat hurried into the kitchen and crouched with her ear to the door. A few moments later she heard the familiar crashing of glass. Stage one complete.

Immediately she ran to the front door and opened it, but nothing happened. She timidly whispered, 'Eric?' There was a definite hiccup in stage two. By now Eric should be upstairs and in the bath. Perhaps he was. Hat wondered if I'd passed her so quickly she'd missed me. She hastily ran up the stairs into the bathroom, where steam was rising gently from the water, which was placid. As she started back down the stairs she heard a loud commotion outside and she also noticed that the front window was still intact. With a sinking feeling, she realised that another of my brilliant schemes had turned out to be full of holes and I was up to my neck in one of them.

Corky pushed his way in holding my arm, and taking up the rear was Mr Brown, an overcoat covering his dressing gown and an old sou'wester that kept slipping down over his eyes. He wasn't wearing his glasses so his ranting was wasted as he wagged his finger under Corky's nose and

Above : Corky continued to pursue his enquiries when Eric and Hattie's misadventures transferred to the stage.

shouted, 'I knew all along you were the window smasher.'

Then he whirled round to me and said, 'Perhaps you'll believe me now, constable. Not once,' he spluttered, ' but this is the second time he's broken my window.'

'I'm sorry, Hat,' I said in a low voice. 'It was an accident.' There were tears rolling down her face and it nearly set me off, too.

Corky said in an officious voice, 'I saw it all.'

I swung round on him, 'It was you that caused it.'

'That's right, blame someone else,' sneered Mr Brown.

'I'll admit that I was about to throw the lump of coal, and as my arm went back, Corky leapt forward. "What d'you think you're doing?" he shouted, or something like it.' I paused and turned to Hat. 'I'm sorry, Hat, the lump of coal was just leaving my hand when he shouted and it went right through Mr Brown's window.'

'Did you get all that, Mr constable?' demanded Mr Brown.

Hat swung on him. 'Yes, Eric did throw a lump of coal but he was aiming for that window.' She pointed dramatically to the window now plastered with wet white faces desperately trying to hear what all the fracas was about.

Corky then stepped towards me and, like an extremely bad repertory actor just before the curtain, he produced a set of handcuffs and said the immortal lines, 'I arrest you in the name of the law and I must warn you . . .'

Outside they were applauding and whistling as Corky led me out with a raincoat over my head, although it had stopped raining five minutes ago.

When I appeared in the magistrates court there were two drunks, three traffic offences and a wife-beater before me, and as I took my place in front of the bench there was a definite rustle of interest from the audience as if I was the major attraction – hardly surprising – they were practically all the residents from Sebastopol Terrace. The magistrate was very nice, I thought, and seemed sympathetic towards me. Constable Turnbull wasn't too bad. As he stepped up into the witness box, he looked self-assured and fully conversant with procedure. After all, he'd been doing it since before the war. He gave a good account of the incident, starting with, 'As I was proceeding north up Sebastopol Terrace ...' I didn't correct him. I mean, he wasn't proceeding anywhere. When I was about to throw the lump of coal, he dashed out of Madge's bread shop. I remembered this because as he was putting on the handcuffs there was jam on his finger, and the bottom of his moustache was frosted with sugar. We both liked Madge's doughnuts. This, however, is all irrelevant. Corky ended by saying that I had no previous convictions and he added that he had known me for several years and had always considered me to be honest and upright.

At this I saw Hat start to applaud, but she was the only one. Mr Brown then gave his version of events and he was really quite complimentary in a way. Perhaps I am a little eccentric; in any case I really thought I was going to get off, at least no more than a small fine. A caution would be quite acceptable. I was already thinking of fish and chips for tea and maybe a bottle of Chianti – we might invite Mr Brown and Corky.

I was so wrapped up in my daydream of my coming out part that I missed most of the summing up. It was only when I heard the magistrate ask me to stand that I came back to the real world. In fact, he had to ask me twice. Corky, who was sanding by me, lent towards the bench and in a soft voice addressed the magistrate, 'I'm afraid he suffers from deafness, your worship.'

I nodded and cupped my ear; it was my undoing, I shouldn't have nodded. Why, oh why don't they publish the small print? The magistrate had a whispered conversation with the cronies either side of him. Clearing his throat, he started loudly as if I wasn't only deaf, but had difficulty with the language. The upshot of it all came as a shock. I was remanded for seven days pending a medical report.

Corky took my arm gently and led me down to the cells.

'Don't worry,' he said, 'we did well there. He's a tough old bird is Mr Blenkinsop, nobody likes to come up before him. Six months – at least.' Corky was in his element. 'Oh, yes, he sent Billy Bigknuckle down for two years, for contempt of court. All he said to the beak was, "You're a stupid old git."'

I wasn't really interested; all I was concerned about was my own gloomy future. As if he could read my mind, he said jovially, 'Oh, don't worry about your future.' Then he whispered confidentially, 'You won't get sent down ... just convince the psychiatrist or whoever gives you a medical that you're ... err ...' he struggled for words that wouldn't offend me. 'Well,' he went on, 'that you're a bit slow, you don't remember breaking those windows.'

I looked at him levelly for a moment. 'What you're trying to say, Corky, is convince the psychiatrist that I'm a nutter.'

Corky was embarrassed. 'Well, in a way, yes. It shouldn't be too hard for you. I mean ...' he stopped, realising he was stuck in the middle of a minefield. Lamely, he continued, 'Well, it'll be better than being slammed up in the Scrubs.'

'What will be better?' I asked, all my relief ebbing fast. Corky took me by the elbow and said in a low voice, 'Well, Broadmoor or Rampton.'

'Broadmoor!' I yelped. 'Shush,' hissed Corky.

I was aghast. ' I don't want to be locked up in a criminal asylum for the insane.'

'It's better than Wormwood Scrubs,' he said laconically. 'That's for the hard men, they're professional villains, and there's one thing they hate more than slopping out: an amateur like you.'

He had me now bordering on the panic stage. He relented as my dead white face, relieved only by two staring eyes, reminded him of a suet dumpling with two prunes stuck in it, and the fact that he hadn't eaten for over an hour.

'If I went to Broadmoor,' I said in a quivering voice, 'Would I be in with people like Myra Hindley and Ian Brady?'

He patted my arm reassuringly. 'Of course not, Myra's in a woman's prison. Ian Brady might be in Broadmoor, but he'll bc in a separate wing.'

I wasn't totally reassured and was about to ask him

regarding visiting times, when he suddenly stopped. 'Hey,' he said, then softer so that he wouldn't be overheard, 'You might meet Brady, you know; in the mess hall or the billiard room.'

'Billiard room?' I echoed.

'Whatever,' he replied, waving his arm dismissively. ' If you do meet him, do you think you could get his autograph?'

I was staggered.

'No, no,' he said, 'it's not for me, it's for Sergeant Blinn.

intently as a wartime submariner noting the pings of an approaching destroyer, finally finishing with the obligatory offering up of my urine in a plastic container covered by a cloth? The whole farce became apparent when he said, 'You are remarkably fit for a man of you age, Mr Wilson.'

I looked at him strangely, perhaps I'd misheard. Eventually I said, My name isn't Wilson, I'm Sykes.'

There was an awkward silence while he perused his diary.

His dad was a young copper on that case.'

The medical, as it turned out, was a joke. In my naivety, I'd believed psychiatry was a science of the mind. So why did I have to go through the indignities of knee-tapping, a cold stethoscope to my back and chest while the doctor's concentrated eyes gazed at nothing and he listened as

Above: At the launch of Eric's film The Plank *with Tommy Cooper, Anna Carteret and Clovissa Newcombe.*

'Are you sure?' he asked inanely.

I didn't bother to nod. He pressed a button on his intercom and a tinny female voice asked, 'Yes Mr Kasper?'

'Jennie,' he replied, 'didn't we have Mr Wilson down for Tuesday?'

'Yes,' came back the voice, '11 a.m.'

'Jennie,' he said, speaking slowly and deliberately, 'Mr Wilson is booked in for 11 a.m. Tuesday.' He paused, then he asked, ' Is this correct?'

'Yes,' came the metallic answer. He gazed at me implying that he was surrounded by idiots. Then, getting a grip on his feelings he said, 'Then why is this gentleman called Sykes sitting before me?'

A sigh filtered through the intercom. 'Quite right, his appointment is for today.' There was a pause, then her patience snapped. She yelled, 'Tuesday is tomorrow!' and there was a swift click as she severed communication. He looked at me with a sickly grin, then we moved on to the blots and what they reminded me of, followed by inserting different-shaped pieces of wood into identical spaces. But his mind wasn't really on it, the sun had gone out of his day. We both perked up when the telephone rang, at least there was a little more sanity than the gobbledegook rubbish we'd played together. He picked up the phone and tapped the pieces of wood; meaning I should continue to fit them into spaces while he talked. I picked up the star-shaped bit. It was only then that he said, 'Hello, Dr Kasper speaking.' He listened for a moment or two then he frowned. He looked across at me and said, 'Yes, he's here with me.' There was another silence as he listened before he finally ended the conversation with, 'Well, it's your decision but I'd like it in writing because I think you're wrong.' He banged down the phone, took the star-shaped piece of wood and tapped it firmly into place.

'Ah well,' I said, 'you've done this before.'

He shook his head and spoke as if drained, all his enthusiasm gone. 'You can go,' he said apathetically.

'Go?' I echoed, not fully understanding.

'Yes, go. You're free, you've been released.'

There was a tap on the door and Constable Turnbull entered with my belt and shoe laces.

'I'll see him now, doctor,' he said. 'Where do I sign?'

'See my secretary as you go out,' he mumbled disinterest-edly, 'she's got all the official papers.'

And as I left I couldn't help feeling sorry for him and hoped he had better luck with Mr Wilson on Tuesday.

I waited in the charge room while Corky went into the locker room and changed into his sports jacket, then we made our way to the Dog and Partridge, where he filled me in. Apparently, the real culprit had walked into the police station and given himself up voluntarily, admitting all the window smashing offences and signing a statement to that effect. His case will be up before the bench tomorrow.

I wasn't really listening, I was too overwhelmed by the sudden freedom. It's amazing how precious our liberty is. Here I was with a pint of best bitter, free as the wind. I felt like breaking into 'Rule Britannia'. In fact, I started softly but Corky nudged me and nodded to a notice on the wall – 'No Singing' – so we drained our mugs and set off towards home.

When we walked up to Sebastopol Terrace I didn't quite know what to expect. Perhaps people lining the streets, smiling and clapping as I passed, maybe the sound of the Salvation Army. Flags round the front door and a huge 'Welcome Home, Eric' on a banner across the street. It was nothing like this. In fact, it was almost as bad as being sent to Coventry.

Home was a let down. The welcoming committee mustered by Hat no doubt sat around glumly staring into glasses of warm champagne. Only Hat, bless her, came and kissed me. There was no response from Mr Brown, the postman, Motson the butcher. I certainly didn't relish a kiss from this lot, but they might at least have apologised for the ordeal I'd been subjected to. Even Madge only gave me half a smile. Hat, however, was determined to get the party going. There was a loud pop behind me followed by a deluge as half a pint of champagne shampooed the back of my neck. It didn't seem to bother Hat, though; she laughed gaily as she refilled the proffered glasses and then she raised hers and asked them all to drink to my homecoming.

'Good health, Eric,' she said. Together they all muttered

Opposite: Eric dreaming up new ideas in his Bayswater office, 1965.

something similar and tossed back the champagne. Then, avoiding my eyes, they made their way to the door.

'Thank you very much,' I said in a loud, sarcastic voice.

Mr Brown stopped. 'Just a minute everybody.'

They hesitated for a moment then turned to face him.

'May I have your attention, please,' he said. 'Firstly, I think we owe Sykes an apology for any inconvenience this whole affair may have caused him and I'm sure I answer for us all when I say sorry.'

'It's all very well,' I began, but he held up his hand.

'I haven't finished yet,' he said sternly and turned to Hattie. 'Your brother has not even a word of thanks or shown the slightest feeling of gratitude to Mr Blackwood, who voluntarily gave up his freedom to prevent a miscarriage of justice.'

'Who's Mr Blackwood?' I whispered to Hat, but obviously I didn't whisper quietly enough.

'Mr Blackwood,' said Brown, 'is the father of six children, and incidentally we are to make a house-to-house collection so at least they will enjoy Christmas, although nothing will compensate them for the absence of their father.'

I was aghast. 'I can't believe it,' I blurted. 'He's been smashing windows since October.'

Mr Brown raised one eyebrow. 'I notice he didn't break yours,' he said.

'Poor little mites,' said Madge, 'can't you find a little pity for them?' And with that they all trooped out.

Motson, being the last, leered at me. 'I don't suppose you could make a donation for the Blackwood Christmas fund?' he asked as he slammed the door behind him.

I was dumbfounded and stood staring at the door like a retarded zombie. Then my blood rushed madly to my head – I had a flush of anger so strong that I was no longer human. Grasping the neck of the champagne bottle I rushed to the window and, with a savage lunge, hurled the bottle at it.

'ERIC!' screamed Hattie, but she was too late. There was a jagged hole where the glass had been and still in the grip of incandescent rage I thrust my head through it and yelled, 'Now do I qualify for my good citizen's badge?' In that moment normality returned and I was almost surprised to

find my head sticking out of the jagged hole in the window. Hat helped me in, carefully avoiding the shattered window, which could have severed my jugular.

This done, she collapsed on the sofa. 'Why did you have to do that?' she sobbed, the tears pouring down her face.

'I'm sorry, Hat,' I said humbly, now ashamed and embarrassed. I wasn't a violent person but the last week or two had driven me perilously close to the edge and my behaviour was the culmination of the suspicion and humiliation showered on me. A couple of pints too many with Corky in the Dog and Partridge contributed to my unforgivable outbreak.

'I'm really sorry, Hat,' I said again, hoping she would be magnanimous and understanding, but I keep forgetting she's a woman, a different species, and that in her concern for what the neighbours would think she had completely forgotten me. I decided to break the *impasse*. 'Hat,' I said, 'what's done is done, but it's not the end of the world. It's still early – I'll ring the glazier and by four o'clock at the latest we'll have a brand new window.'

More tears rolled down her white cheeks and in between wiping her eyes and nose she gasped, 'It's no good, Eric, Mr Blackwood *is* the glazier. He smashed the windows so that he could make a little money to buy his children Christmas presents.'

Now I understood. We'd never had occasion to have a new window – so how was I to know who Mr Blackwood was? Then a new thought struck me and I went to the telephone table and took out the Yellow Pages. 'He's not the only glazier in the southeast of England,' I said. But my optimism was premature, as I discovered after several phone calls. The glaziers were either engaged or those who answered the phone cut me off with remarks such as, 'Sorry, I can't help at the moment, we're up to our eyes.' And some of these as far afield as Tunbridge Wells. I thought it odd but I was soon to find the answer.

We were huddled in overcoats and scarves while we watched the six o'clock news on television – the cardboard I'd Sellotaped across the hole in the window was useless and it might have been better for us to watch the six o'clock news through the hole in the window while sitting in the

Above: Eric celebrates landing a job in a TV commercial in 1975.

garden. Suddenly, Hat nudged me. 'Eric, look.' She pointed at the screen, where throngs of people, some carrying banners, all chanting something, were besieging our local magistrates court.

A cold, white-faced announcer spoke to the camera: 'These extraordinary scenes in East Acton are the result of a spontaneous protest by thousands of glaziers and the local residents of Sebastopol Terrace.' There was a shot of another section of the crowd.

'Oh, look,' cried Hat, 'there's Mr Brown!' And sure enough, there he was waving a union jack.

Then we were back with the reporter: 'Traffic has been at a standstill for the last two hours and the glaziers' union have requested that one of their members – a Mr James Blackwood – be released on humanitarian grounds. This is Julian McNemeny for BBC News.'

I switched off the set and we went into the kitchen where it was a few degrees warmer. 'Would you believe it?' I said. 'No wonder I couldn't find anyone to put our window in.' We watched the news again later that night and it was vir-

tually the same, except that gifts and donations for the Blackwood children from all parts of the British Isles were flooding in to the appeal fund.

The upshot of it all was Mr Blackwood got off with a small fine and they are now rich enough to live in Mayfair. Mrs Polanski landed very nicely on her Polish feet when the BBC discovered she was the Countess Polanski and contracted her for her life story, to be broadcast on *Panorama* over six weeks. Mr Brown managed to get his name in the *Acton Bugle*, although it appeared as Mr Charles Filbert Brawn, lumped in with all the other Blackwood customers.

As for Hattie and me . . . nothing. Nobody interviewed us, photographed us or offered us a walk-on part on *Coronation Street*. In fact, we didn't even get a new window until the spring . . . the hole in the window remained stuffed with an old duvet throughout January and February.

As I have said many times, life is a very dodgy contract . . .

CHAPTER TWO

Postmen

Millions of people post letters every day without incident, and I suppose most postmen are reasonable, ordinary, everyday people, but there's always the awkward one, and when I set out to post a letter you can bet your sweet life that it's the awkward one who is emptying the box at that moment. It was. As I dashed up the street, he was just locking the box with an enormous bunch of keys that would have given a normal man a hernia. He turned to face me and I held out my letter.

'What's that for?' he said, slinging the bag over his shoulder.

'It's a letter.'

He paused to light the remains of a fag; then he said: 'I can see it's a letter. I've been on the job for nearly two years now and I can spot a letter immediately. What are you giving it to me for?'

'Well, you're a postman.'

'What's that got to do with it?' he said.

I didn't really know how to answer that – after all, it wasn't as if I'd asked him for half a dozen lamb chops – so I just stood there looking at him.

'All you have to do,' he said, as if he was talking to an idiot child, 'you put your letter in that little slot . . .', he paused to let this sink in, ... in the side of the box. OK?'

Now inevitably, when I find myself in a spot like this, a crowd always seems to gather, and there they were – two scruffy little urchins who'd obviously heard the postman's last remark because one of them pointed helpfully to the

slot. I could feel myself going red, especially as the other little ratbag tried to take the letter from me in order to post it. I pulled away from him.

'I know how to post a letter,' I said. The two lads looked at each other and giggled. The postman waited patiently. He said, 'It won't bite you.'

'Yes,' I said, 'but you've just emptied it.'

'Well then,' he replied, 'there'll be plenty of room for yours, won't there,' and with that he started to stuff the bag into his van.

At this point I should have tossed the letter into the box, winked at the lads and made some kind of sarcastic remark about the post office, but I never seem to think of the obvious. I certainly wasn't going to be humiliated by this spotty herbert in a postman's uniform – a typical youth of today with a few sparse hairs on his top lip which I suppose he thought made him look macho; it was pathetic. I've had girlfriends with a better growth than that.

Anyway the thing had gone too far for me to back down in front of these two kids, but what was I to do? Perhaps if I handed him the letter with a pound note, in such a way that they couldn't see it . . . but I rejected that idea straight away, I didn't have a pound on me, and even if I had he'd probably hold it up for all the world to see, and say 'What's this, then?' . . . He was still sorting stuff out in the back of his van, and I thought of leaning in to tell him confidentially

Above and opposite: Eric and Hattie at a press call for the final series of Sykes in 1979.

that it was an urgent letter to my mother in hospital who had only a few days to live. No, I wasn't going to grovel, also the two kids had moved forward with their ears hanging out and I didn't want them to know about my mother. In any case she'd been dead for twenty years. I looked at the post-

Above: Perhaps the script needed a pause for thought . . .

man. What I should do was shove him up against his van, and say 'Now listen Buster', but he wasn't all that small, and with my luck he'd turn out to be a judo black belt. So I appealed to his better nature . . .

I smiled, 'Come on lad, you could just slip it into your bag.'

He slammed the door, and locked it. 'Yes, I suppose I could, and supposing everybody started giving me letters, what would happen to these pillar boxes, they'd be useless, no good to anybody apart from the odd dog.' Then he got in his van and started the engine.

I bent down to the window. 'Where's the next box?' I shouted.

He leaned across. 'The next one's in Balaclava Road.'

'Balaclava Road,' I said, 'that's just around the corner. Give me five minutes' start.'

'Hop in,' he said. 'I'll give you a lift', and he opened the door.

'Thanks,' I said, and looked triumphantly to the lads, but they were already racing down the street.

'We have regulations, you know,' shouted the postman over the noise of the engine, 'and we have to abide by them.' He didn't seem to be a bad fellow after all.

'I appreciate that,' I shouted back. 'If we didn't have rules we'd be all over the place, so I can see your point of view, and I wouldn't have bothered you like this, only this letter is rather important . . . . It's to my mother in hospital, and I only hope it reaches her in time.

'What you on about?' he said, and I realized he hadn't heard a word . . .

It's a sad world, it really is. Here's this young fellow: he's got his health, a good job in the post office, and a nice little van to run around in, so he couldn't care less about the elderly. But I cared. I could see them dashing to the bedside . . . a letter from your son . . . I knew he would not let me down, and a tear would trickle down the wrinkled old cheek . . . I blew my nose, looked down at the envelope in my hand, and came back to earth with a bump – 'Goal of the Month, c/o Grandstand, BBC' – I shoved it in my pocket in case he saw it.

We pulled up at the pillar box just as the two kids arrived, red and breathless but eager to watch developments. I

Above: On screen, Sykes never knowingly lost an argument.

nipped out and pushed the letter into the box. He was still in the van, leaning across to watch me.

'There you are,' he said. 'It's easy, isn't it?'

I waited by the box, and he went to wind up the window.

'Hang on,' I said, 'aren't you going to empty it?'

'No,' he said, 'I did that one first.' And with that he drove off.

For a moment there was stunned silence, then the kids turned and dashed off in high glee to spread the news round the neighbourhood.

CHAPTER THREE

The Last Time I Saw Bogsea

Every year my sister and I spend a week's holiday in Bogsea. Its not the greatest watering hole in the western hemisphere, but it's on the coast, and apart from the east wind, and the fairly constant rainfall it's quite pleasant if you wrap up well.

We neither like it nor dislike it. It's become a habit, and we know our way around, which is important – for instance you can spot the first-timers; when they're turfed out of their digs after breakfast if it's fine they're OK, but more often than not when it's raining they waste the whole morning scurrying about looking for somewhere to keep dry. Hat and I, being regulars, know the ropes now; if it's raining, no messing about – straight out of the front door, across the road and into the bus shelter. It's not quite as warm as Marks and Spencer's, but it's a whole lot cheaper.

We always stay at Mrs Webb's boarding house. The food's good and there's plenty of it if you like cabbage, and being regulars we get certain perks. We have a very good table in the dining room for instance, also, if the weather is very bad we're allowed to stay indoors with use of the ludo and draughts, and of course we're like one of the family now – Mrs Webb calls us Eric and Hattie, and we call her Mrs Webb. This year before we left on our annual pilgrimage we went through the checklist as usual: milk cancelled, papers cancelled, gas off and an out-of-order sign on the bell to fool casual burglars.

We caught the usual train to Bogsea at Victoria. Everything was normal except for one big difference – we had Mr Brown and Corky with us. I was dead against it from the start. I told Hat that we see Mr Brown and Corky practically every day of our lives, and the idea of going to Bogsea is to get away from them for a week. I mean I can understand Hat wanting Mr Brown along; she could visualize herself showing him round the place, taking him to the novelty gift shop, collecting shells on the beach for him to take home and perhaps be reminded of her every time he took one out to polish it . . . but Corky – that was something else. I told her that the reason we'd always been able to relax at Bogsea was that Corky was keeping an eye on our house, but Hat said that was precisely why we were taking him. The last time we'd left him in charge the place was a shambles when we got back. Empty bean cans, furniture all over the place. Corky pleaded ignorance and said it had been very windy, which I couldn't quite figure out, but under pressure he admitted he'd had a couple of friends round. Hat picked up a pair of corsets and said:

Above: Out in the cold again in Sykes And A Camping, 1963.

Opposite: 'And I'm telling you, constable, it's the only unicycle in existence with two wheels . . .' – E.S.

Above: 'Hat and I in a fog. It was created in a studio using a smoke machine and it was very effective. In fact, it was so thick, this is us looking for the camera.' – E.S.

'What kind of friends?'

Corky gulped and said: 'That pair of corsets belonged to Harry Pangbourne. He had to wear 'em because he had a bad back.'

Straightaway Hat snapped: 'He had a bad front as well,' and threw a bra in Corky's face. The only reason she didn't prefer charges was that we got quite a bit of loot on the empties.

So this year Hat decided it was safer to bring Corky with us.

Anyway the journey down to Bogsea was the longest it had ever been. Apart from the fact that we were two hours late Mr Brown was at his condescending best. 'First time I've travelled second, quite comfortable really,' and 'When is the first sitting for lunch?' Hat coughed apologetically and I explained it didn't have a dining car; we were only going to Bogsea and it was not the midnight train to Istanbul. That shut him up. Corky didn't care; he'd brought a stack of food with him and ate steadily throughout the journey. I'll bet he had more provisions with him than they had in the buffet car. Hat tried to liven things up with 'I spy with my little eye,' but Mr Brown snorted and looked out of the window, so that was the end of that. By the time we got off the train I was already homesick, and you know what a crummy place we live in.

Unfortunately we had to walk from the station because it was just starting to drizzle, and taxi drivers don't like hanging about in the rain. Mr Brown was moaning all the way. I didn't see why he should be so upset at having to walk – after all I was carrying one of his suitcases, and Hat was carrying his other two as well as ours. It was a pitiful procession: me leading because I knew the way; then Corky, holding a parcel over his head; then Mr Brown with the one umbrella; and a furlong behind came Hat, loaded down like a bundle of

40

sherpas. Suddenly the heavens opened, and it poured.

Straightaway I was in the bus shelter, hustled by Corky. Mr Brown took his time, because after all he had the umbrella; then we watched as Hat struggled the last few yards. Gone was the Margaret Thatcher bouffant golden hairstyle she set out with – three hours at the hairdresser's and now in five minutes she looked like a cold suet pudding with custard. We stood in a miserable line watching the rain belt down. Corky looked out of the side window and there was a poster glistening in the rain with the top corner peeling off. It showed a dolly bird lying on the beach with the sun beaming down, and underneath it said 'Come to sunny Bogsea.'

Corky sniffed. 'The bloke who painted that wants locking up.'

Hat quickly took up the cudgels. 'It's not always like this. We've had some marvellous summers here, haven't we, Eric?'

I blew a raindrop off the end of my nose. 'Oh yes,' I said. 'What about that Wednesday in 1952?'

'Oh come on, Eric. Look at the year before last – the sun was so strong you had to buy a hat.'

'Nothing to do with the weather though was it? It was on account of the seagulls.'

Mr Brown's lip curled. 'Very funny,' he said. 'Trust you to start the holiday with a coarse remark. Do you know any more jokes like that?'

I looked him straight in the eye. 'As a matter of fact I do. If you want seagull stories, I've got a million of 'em.'

Hat straightened up from wiping Mr Brown's suitcases with her hankie. 'Eric!'

'It's OK, Hat, it's the one about the man selling seagulls. You know . . .' and I whispered it to her.

Below: 'When asked by the Swiss landlord what we thought of the views, I replied that we hadn't seen anything because of the mountains. The beer was cold as well.'
– E.S.

'Oh yes, that one. Oh, it's funny this one, Mr Brown. There's this man on the beach selling seagulls, you see, and I stepped in before she could ruin the joke. 'Hang on,' I said. 'I'll tell it. He asked me.'

Hat just giggled, so I turned to Mr Brown. 'There's this man selling seagulls, you see. He's on the beach shouting "Seagulls one pound each – get your lovely seagulls here, one pound each".'

Mr Brown broke in: 'Just get on with it, Sykes. We don't require all the character voices.'

'OK,' I said. 'Anyway he's selling these seagulls for one pound each, and a bloke came up to him, gave him a pound and said "I'll have one." "Right," says the man, and put the pound in his pocket, and goes on shouting "Seagulls one pound each." The fellow who gave him a pound said "Hang on, where's my seagull?" And the man pointed to one flying past and said, "There's your one"'.

Well, Hat fell about laughing, and I was a bit chuffed because I'd told it well, and even Corky was smiling, but Mr Brown was looking at each of us in amazement.

'Why on earth did he want a seagull?'

Corky shook his head sadly. 'Don't you get it, Charlie. It's a joke – "There's your one," and the man has to try and catch it.' Then he laughed as if he'd told the joke.

I looked at Mr Brown. 'Get it?'

Mr Brown's forehead puckered up in concentration. 'What I don't understand is, why did he want a seagull in the first place? It isn't as if they're edible.'

He looked at Corky for support, but Corky shook his head sadly and leaned across him to me. 'The penny hasn't dropped yet.'

The ran had now eased off, and Mr Brown stepped out of the shelter to shake his umbrella. But Corky hadn't finished with him; he tapped him on the arm and, as if speaking to a child, he said: 'You see, Charlie, there's this man on the beach, and he had a lot of seagulls for sale.'

Hat broke in: 'Well, they're not his, actually.'

Corky stopped dead in his tracks and turned to Hat. 'And he's selling them?'

Hat wished she hadn't said anything but she tried to pass it off. 'Well, yes. But seagulls are seagulls – I mean they belong to anybody, don't they?'

Corky squared his shoulders and put on his policeman's face. 'They do not belong to anybody, madam. They're crown property.'

By this time I was getting cold, and wishing I'd never started it, sol picked up my bag and said, 'It's only a joke.'

Corky looked at me gravely. 'It's against the law.'

'Oh, for goodness sake, Corky. You're on holiday, just forget you're a policeman for one week.'

'Never mind that, lad,' he said. 'If I catch him selling seagulls, he'll be inside so fast his feet won't touch the promenade.'

Hat shook her head ruefully. 'Don't tell any more jokes, Eric.'

Mr Brown turned his head. 'I second that, and before I die of pneumonia can you tell me when this bus is due?'

I looked at Hat, then at him. 'What bus?'

Mr Brown clucked in exasperation. 'The bus to take us wherever this lodging house is.'

'We don't need a bus. It's right there across the road - Mon Repos.'

Mr Brown's voice went up an octave: 'Well, for Pete's sake why are we standing here in this freezing cold, like a bunch of wet nanas?'

'It's your fault,' I said. 'You asked me if I had any more jokes like that and I told you one.

'That's right,' chirped Hat. 'You did ask him, Mr Brown.'

'Yes, I know I did, but I didn't think he was going to tell one, did I.'

Corky slapped him on the back. 'Oh, come on, Charlie. We're on holiday. Where's your sense of humour? Smile . . . let's all have some fun.'

Mr Brown wasn't so easily consoled. 'You can have some fun if you wish,' he snapped. 'You can pedal up and down

Opposite: Constable 'Corky' Turnbull and his wife shared a caravan holiday with us - never again shall our two caravans meet. The world is too small.' – E.S.

the prom on a unicycle whistling the *Marseillaise* for all I care, but I intend to get indoors for a large whisky and a hot bath.' He prepared to cross the road.

Hat restrained him. 'Mrs Webb doesn't allow alcohol in the house.'

Mr Brown's face fell. 'Oh, for goodness sake,' he said. 'Well, I'll just have to make do with a hot bath.'

This time I stopped him. 'What time is it?'

Mr Brown glanced at his watch: 'Twenty past twelve.'

why I let you talk me into coming here in the first place.'

Well, I wasn't letting him get away with that. 'Me talk you into it? You practically begged to come with us. "I'm sick of the Bahamas," you said.'

Corky snorted. 'The Bahamas? He's never set foot in the Bahamas.'

'Oh really, constable. It's not necessary to go to a place to be sick of it.' And with that he stepped into the road, narrowly missing the horse-drawn tram.

Above: Eric and Hattie often made public appearances together to promote the show. This one was in 1964.

'Oh, what a pity,' I said. 'You've missed it by five minutes.

Mr Brown looked helplessly from me to Hat. 'I can't even have a bath?'

'It's not the Ritz Carlton, you know.'

'I knew it,' he said. 'It's going to be a disaster. I don't know

We were about to follow when Corky stopped us. 'Hang on a second,' he said, and we saw a young policeman approaching.

'Now what?' I said.

Out of the corner of her mouth Hat whispered: 'Think he wants to report the man selling seagulls.'

Corky approached the young constable, and gave him a perfunctory salute. 'Morning, constable. Everything all right?'

The young policeman looked at us in turn, then leaned forward slightly towards Corky to see if he could detect the smell of alcohol. Satisfied, he stepped back a pace. 'Yes, sir. Can I help you?'

Corky beamed at him. 'No, no, lad. But when you report in you might inform your superior that Turnbull's in town.'

Hat and I exchanged glances. The young PC's eyes narrowed. 'Turnbull?'

Corky took out his identification card. 'Constable Turnbull F Division East Acton. If you need any assistance while I'm down here I'll be at Mon Repos,' and he winked.

The young PC smiled. 'Oh, I get you. Thanks very much. I'll let the sergeant know, and if a spate of murders breaks out we'll be round for you like a shot.'

I looked at the young PC. 'Murder?' I said. 'He's not exactly head of the CID. He specializes in stray dogs.'

The young PC smiled. 'Ah well, then. I'll see what I can do, we'll let a few of them loose and he can round 'em up.'

Corky tapped the PC's chest: 'Listen, sonny, when I was your age I was in the Flying Squad. Oh yes, when the East End of London was known as Hell's Kitchen. There was one particular time – '

The policeman started to move off. Corky held his arm. 'Look at me when I'm talking!'

Hat picked up the suitcases. 'We're going to get the Siege of Sidney Street again. I'm off.'

'So am I,' I said. 'Otherwise we'll miss lunch.'

That was it. At the mention of lunch Corky's eyes glazed over and he picked up his brown paper parcel. He turned to the policeman: 'Aye well, lad, bear it in mind – Turnbull. And if I can be of any assistance don't hesitate to let me know.'

The young constable came to attention and saluted. 'Thank you, sir. The chief will be easier in his mind now he knows you're here.'

The sarcasm was lost on Corky, who just nodded. 'All right lad, carry on.'

As the young constable watched us struggle up the steps of Mon Repos he rubbed his chin thoughtfully and contemplated three things: (a) they were so worked to death in London that Constable Turnbull was old before his time; (b) he was in disguise; and (c) that ID card had been out of date since about 1965. He turned away and strolled down the prom, hoping to spot a stray nude.

Now one thing about Mrs Webb's boarding house is that it's run on strict lines, and one or two of our prisons should take a leaf out of her book. As we stood nervously in the hallway among the coats and umbrellas and buckets and spades, Hat and I knew we were off on the wrong foot. We

Above: 'Hat and me dancing the tortilla - meaning we're doing the omelette.' – E. S.

were late. Corky was already rubbing his hands together as the smell of lunch hung heavy on the damp air.

'Right,' he said. 'Which is the dining room?'

I was standing with my ear pressed to the door. Hat mouthed: 'Have they started?' and made the motion of using a knife and fork. I shrugged and Hat pushed me aside and listened. 'It's all right,' she whispered. 'She's reading the regulations.'

'Oh,' I said. 'Shall we go in, or shall we wait till she's finished?'

Above: Hattie in Sykes And A Gamble*, 1962.*

Hat looked at her watch, but the decision was made. Corky, unable to resist the smell of food, boldly opened the door and entered. He looked round, nodded at the room in general, and was joined by Mr Brown. Hat and I followed, trying to look as inconspicuous as possible.

Mrs Webb's eyes followed us over the rim of her pince-nez, and she looked pointedly at her watch. I smiled weakly but she pursed her lips and returned to the regulations. 'Rule 37,' she said. 'No ladies in gentlemen's rooms, unless married. Rule 38. All boarders will be in by eleven sharp, and lastly all boarders must vacate the hotel by 9.30 each morning and return at 12 noon for lunch unless I have been notified to the contrary in writing twenty-four hours previously. Now is that clear?'

She looked round the room. There was a general murmur of assent, then Mr Brown coughed to gain her attention and spoke up.

'Mrs Webb.'

'Well?'

'Er, Mrs Webb, with regard to the bathrooms – , She held up her hand. 'You may use it freely, except when the weather is fine – then I prefer you to go down the yard.'

Mr Brown looked at me perplexed for a moment. Then he turned to Mrs Webb and smiled: 'No, no. You misunderstand me – for a bath,'

Mrs Webb's eyebrows went up a notch. 'A bath,' she said. 'What day will you require one?'

Mr Brown looked at me again, but I pretended to be examining the cutlery. He turned to Mrs Webb. 'Well, every day, naturally.'

At this all the heads swivelled round to look at him. Mrs Webb, unperturbed, was writing on her clipboard: 'Room 14 every day.' Then she looked up. 'You'll find the bathroom available from 6 am to 6.15. You follow Captain Thompson.' And with that she swept out of the room.

Mr Brown swung round towards us and hissed: 'This is intolerable, Sykes. Can't even have a bath when I want one.'

'Don't look at me,' I said. 'You should have had one before you left home.'

Hat leaned forward. 'In any case, Mr Brown, that geyser in the bathroom is a bit suspect. When you turn the hot on get back against the wall. If it rumbles nicely you'll be quite safe, but if it starts shaking and clanging get behind the wash basin, or the best thing of all is to stand on the fire escape and reach in through the window and turn it off.'

The look on Mr Brown's face was worth a couple of quid, but I knew Hat was laying it on a bit thick. 'Come on, Hat. It's not as bad as that.'

'How do you know?' she said. 'You've never used it.' Corky chuckled. 'I'd give anything to see Charlie here on the fire escape with his bare – Hat banged the table. 'Please, constable,' she said.

'You're not down at the station now.' Then she looked across at Mr Brown, who was a picture of abject misery, and the mother in her came to the fore. 'Cheer up, Mr Brown. It's not as black as it's painted – for instance, here you are on table number six with us.'

Mr Brown shrugged. 'What's so special about table number six?'

'Ah well, you see, it's your first visit. The new ones have to sit over there in the corner where there's a draught and you can always smell cabbage. Then over the years you move up towards the window – that's the plum table. You can watch the traffic while you eat, and see the little table over there under the aspidistra.' She pointed discreetly, and Mr Brown looked at it with distaste.

'Well, we were on that table four years running, weren't we, Eric?'

I shuddered.

Mr Brown shrugged. 'It looks perfectly all right to me.'

I beckoned him closer. 'It looks all right,' I said, 'but things used to drop out of the aspidistra.'

Mr Brown looked quickly across to the plant.

'You'd be getting stuck into the soup – you look away for a second and plop.' When I said 'plop' Mr Brown jerked back and gulped noisily. I went on: 'All right if it was clear soup, but with brown windsor you could never be sure.'

Mr Brown paled and his eyes widened. Even Corky frowned, and if he was hungry he would have drunk a bowlful of the Limpopo.

Hat slapped me playfully, then addressed Mr Brown:

'He's having you on, Mr Brown.'

'I didn't think for a moment he was serious,' he said sternly; but during the week that followed he never passed that plant without holding a hankie to his mouth.

'Anyway,' said Hat, carrying on where she had left off, 'we were at that table for four years running.'

Right: With Fiona Guant as Louise Plunkett-Taylor in
Sykes And An Engagement, *1973*

I nodded. 'Four years, and we'd have been there yet if Mr Bottomley hadn't fallen off the pier.'

Hat kicked me under the table and I realized that the other boarders were listening. Mr Bottomley's body had never been found, and the boarding house was always rife with speculation. Some boarders thought he'd run off with Mrs Webb's maid; others that Mrs Webb fancied him and that both Mr Bottomley and her maid were buried somewhere on the beach. But whatever the solution Mr Bottomley's name was taboo at Mon Repos and more than one boarder foolish enough to broach the subject had been sent packing the same day, and no refund either.

Above: Keeping up with current events, 1976.

Luckily the tension was broken as Mrs Webb poked her head round the door; she was smiling at me. Well, it's hardly a smile – it's as if she has her foot in a bear trap and she doesn't want anyone to know. She beckoned me and disappeared again.

Hat grabbed my wrist. 'Do you think she heard?'

'No, of course not. This happens every year.

I looked round the room, then leaned across the table. 'Every year she tries to mark my card.'

Mr Brown affected indifference. 'She does what?'

'Mrs Webb. She finds me a nice girl with a view to matrimony.'

Mr Brown snorted and I was about to elucidate when Mrs Webb looked in again.

'OK, Mrs Webb. I'm coming,' and I followed her into the kitchen.

Corky nudged Mr Brown. 'You know, Charlie, it's time you found a wife and settled down.'

Mr Brown was horrified. 'Me?' he said.

Corky turned to Hat. 'Is there a Mr Webb?'

Hat shook her head. 'No, she's a widow.'

Corky stared at Mr Brown. 'You know, Charlie, I think your ship's come in. From what Hattie tells me she's a marvellous cook. It's a nice going concern here, and you could have a bath every day.'

Mr Brown glared at him. 'Me and Mrs Webb? What a

horrid thought! And in any case if I ever did consider marriage I certainly wouldn't be a widow's second husband.'

Hat patted his arm. 'It's better than being her first,' she said, and she nearly fell over backwards laughing.

That's when I returned with this girl, Mrs Webb's latest protégée for the marriage stakes. I mean the last year's filly was a non-starter, but this one would have found it hard going to parade round the paddock. To call her hair mousy would have sent the mice dashing off to the Race Relations board. She wore thick pebble glasses – or they may have been cracked – and she was much too thin.

I walked her to the table and introduced her. 'This is Miss Palethorpe. My sister Hat, Constable Turnbull and Mr Brown.'

Above: Tommy Cooper in The Eric Sykes 1990 Show *in 1982. The rope is a kimeer. When anybody wanted Tommy they just grabbed it and shoted 'Kimeer!'*

She smiled awkwardly at everybody, and I coughed discreetly, hoping she'd go, but instead she sat down in my chair. Mr Brown looked up at me and chuckled. I looked across to the window and said: 'It's clearing up a bit.' Everybody looked out. Then once more it went quiet and I was still standing there like a pork chop at a vegetarian convention, but before I took root Mrs Webb bustled in with a chair, and I smiled my relief as I sat down.

Mrs Webb chucked my cheek and whispered: 'Don't be shy, her name's Jocelyn.' Then she clapped her hands and the maids came round with the brown windsor.

Normally the food at Mrs Webb's is one of the highlights of the holiday, but that first meal was a disaster. I could feel everybody's eyes on me and Jocelyn. Once we reached for the pepper at the same time and our hands touched.

'I'm sorry,' I blurted, and as I went to hand it to her the top came off. She sneezed and her glasses fell into her soup. I immediately reached for my napkin to wipe them; unfortunately it wasn't my napkin but the tablecloth, and I dragged my soup into my lap. Luckily there wasn't much left in my bowl, but as I took my fork to scratch out the stain I dropped it. When I bent down to pick it up Jocelyn had the same idea, and wallop – the crack of our heads made Mrs Webb look in from the kitchen.

I couldn't excuse myself and go to my room, because nobody leaves the table at Mrs Webb's before the meal is finished without a doctor's certificate. But eventually the pudding was cleared away, and Corky said it was the best meal he'd ever had, especially the cabaret. Even Mr Brown was so amused by watching me and Jocelyn that he never sent anything back to the kitchen.

Jocelyn had got round to calling me Ricky, and Mr Brown leaned over to me and said: 'That's your week taken care of, Ricky.'

I was just about to tell them all to take a running jump when Mrs Webb walked in with a pile of local newspapers, and I remembered that this was the annual ritual of 'Find the Lady'. Mrs Webb placed a paper on every table, then she came to us and pointed to the picture.

'That's her this year,' she said, 'Her name is Tillie Truelove.'

I looked at the side view of a blonde girl, but she wasn't very recognizable.

'It gets tougher every year,' I said. 'Look at that picture - you can only see part of her nose.

Hat leaned across. 'Well, at least we know she's blonde.'

Mrs Webb sniffed. 'It's time you won it. You've been trying long enough.'

Corky glanced at the photo. 'What is it, a competition or something?'

Mrs Webb looked at him as if he was a foreigner. 'Oh, I forgot. You're new, aren't you? Oh well, you're in for a very hectic week, isn't he, Eric?'

I nodded with a sickly smile, because Joycelyn's knee was pressed so hard against mine that I feared for my cartilage.

Corky looked at Mrs Webb. 'Well, what happens?'

She tapped the newspaper. 'The rules are all there. You see, every day this girl is in a certain area at a given time – see, it tells you where underneath. Well then, all you have to do is spot her, then you say –' Mrs Webb lifted her pince-nez and read: 'You are Tillie Truelove. I read the *Daily Bugle* regularly and I claim the five pounds.'

Mr Brown's lip curled.

'Is that all you have to do?' said Corky.

'Ah yes, but you have to be carrying a copy of the paper with you. And if you're right she hands over a fiver.'

Mr Brown fitted a cigaretta to his holder. 'Sounds rather facile to me.'

Mrs Webb glanced at him sharply. 'It passes the time, doesn't it? You ask young Eric here.'

Corky chuckled. 'Young Eric?'

I squirmed with embarrassment. Why did she have to keep calling me 'young Eric' in front of people? I'm not all that young. Hat says it's the way I behave, which is ludicrous – just because I happen to like donkey rides, and what if I do sometimes wear a cowboy hat? Good grief, it's only made of paper, and we are supposed to be on holiday enjoying ourselves.

'Isn't that right, Eric?'

I jerked out of my reverie. 'Sorry, Mrs Webb.'

Mrs Webb folded her arms. 'I said you've been searching for her every time for at least twelve years, haven't you?'

'Any luck?' said Corky.

Hat broke in: 'He's never actually won the fiver, but he's had umpteen dates, been arrested twice, and had his face slapped several times.'

Corky leaned back in his chair. 'I begin to see now why you invited me down here,' he said.

Hat and I looked at each other. In the first place we

hadn't invited him, as he put it. As far as I could see he'd just tagged along without so much as a by your leave; and secondly an invitation seemed to imply that he was our guest, and I hoped he wasn't expecting us to pick up his bill. I decided to step on it right away.

'It's the first I've heard of inviting you,' I said. 'When you came to the station with us I thought it was just to wave us off. I didn't know you were actually coming with us.'

Hat put her hand on my arm. 'I did make the reservation for him,' she said.

'Yes, but that doesn't mean we've adopted him. He pays for his own holiday.'

Corky tapped the table with his finger. 'It's lucky for you, my lad, that I am here though, isn't it, with this newspaper competition of yours.'

'What are you talking about?' I said.

Corky's eyes glinted. 'It stands to reason. Oh yes, I'm highly trained for this sort of work. With my background I'll have her challenged in no time.'

'Oh, really,' I exclaimed. 'It's not that simple, mate. I know – I've been at it for twelve years. "You are Doris Pureheart . . . you are Sue Sweety . . .you are Alice Heart-throb." If anybody's trained for it, it's me.'

Corky smirked. 'Trained for it? Twelve years and you haven't copped once – and they even tell you in the paper where's she's going to be and at what time! Good grief, if we lads in the force had the same record as you Dr Crippen'd still be running around today.'

Hat laughed and tried to change the conversation, but I wasn't letting Corky come out on top.

'All right, Mr Constable Sherlock Holmes, if you're so certain I'll have a little bet with you. Never mind the five pounds you win, I'll give another five pounds for every time you spot Tillie Truelove. Mind you, if you don't spot her you pay me five pounds.'

Hat shot me a warning glance.

Right: Eric in Yorkshire Television's production of Charley's Aunt, 1979.

'It's OK, Hat, no problems. He couldn't spot her if she was fifteen foot tall with bells going and a light flashing on her head.'

Corky looked at me quizzically. 'Every time I spot her and claim the fiver you will also give me a fiver.'

'That's right,' I said. 'But she's in about six different locations at different times, and if you don't spot her once you owe me thirty quid.'

Corky grabbed the newspaper and stared hard at the photo, then he sat back. 'Done – it's a bet.'

Hat dabbed at her nose with a hankie. 'Well, that's it, then. That's our holiday money gone.'

'Course it isn't. Listen, Hat. This way I don't even have to waste time looking for her. Every day he comes in and gives me thirty quid.'

Jocelyn touched my knee again. 'That'll give us more time together, Ricky.'

Mrs Webb smiled fondly at us both and I knew in my bones this was going to be the worst holiday I'd ever had, and I've had some crummy ones.

Being our first day, we were allowed to stay indoors after lunch in order to unpack, so at least I could have a little privacy in my room. Usually I hung my stuff up, then memorized the words, 'You are Tillie Truelove, I read the *Daily Bugle* regularly, and I claim the five pounds.' It doesn't sound much, but I'd heard that if you got one word out of place when you

Above: Eric and Hattie embarking on a spot of counter espionage in Sykes And A Suspicion, *1961.*

Opposite: Cornered by office siren Anna Carteret in Big Bad Mouse, *Shaftesbury Theatre, 1966.*

challenged her you weren't entitled to the fiver, and it would be stupid to pick her out, then lose the money on a technicality.

However, I was just unwrapping my plimsolls when there was a knock on the door. I froze, then there was another knock and the door handle rattled. 'Eric, are you in there?'

Thank goodness, it was only Hat. I let her in. 'Why did you lock the door?'

'I thought it might be Jocelyn.'

Hat snorted. 'I don't think she's that hard up.'

'Oh no? You should have seen what she was doing to my leg under the table. I'm surprised I don't walk with a permanent limp.'

Hat raised an eyebrow.

'Oh, come on, Hat. I know I'm not Clint Eastwood, but if I want a girl I'll go and get one, so why does Mrs Webb do it? Every year the same – she always throws a girl at me. You'd think she was running a marriage bureau.'

'Oh, she doesn't mean any harm. She probably thinks its time you settled down. Anyway, forget it. Put your coat on.'

I looked at her. 'Where are we going?'

Her face lit up. 'We're on holiday. We're in Bogsea. I thought we might have a stroll down to the lifeboat house.'

'Hallelujah', I said. 'The lifeboat house. Every year we walk down to the lifeboat house, put 10p in the box, then back to the digs.'

The Last Time I Saw Bogsea

Hat was unabashed. 'All right then, we'll go down to the novelty gift shop.'

'We're not going down to the novelty gift shop either. We've got more plastic shells at home with "Bogsea" on 'em than they'll ever have.'

Hat waved her arms about. 'Well, we don't have to go to the novelty gift shop. We can – well, we can walk right past it.' She started twiddling one of the brass knobs on the bedstead, then she smiled. 'Why don't we go to the beach?'

'In this weather?'

That seemed to be the whole gamut of Bogsea. Hat made for the door. 'I'll go and find out what's on at the pictures.'

'You do that,' I said, and sat on the bed. The pictures – that was a laugh. Last time we went it was *Lives of a Bengal Lancer* – well, it was until the film broke. What a way to spend a holiday – leave a comfortable home and travel forty-odd miles to walk round a lifeboat house. Every year the same: we migrate like a flock of drunken starlings, and I was heartily sick of it. Sick of these digs, sick of Mrs Webb and her annual wedding fodder, sick of the view from my

window – another boarding house. I got up, walked to the window, and gazed idly across at Dunrovin. My eye caught a movement in one of the windows and suddenly the adrenalin hit me. There was a gorgeous blonde in just bra and pants and she appeared to be unpacking. Like a flash of sunlight through the clouds I knew it. It had to be. It was Tillie Truelove. I rushed to my suitcase, grabbed my binoculars, and had a good old shufti. Then I checked it with the picture in the newspaper – it was remarkable: she had the same hairstyle, and when she turned in a certain way it was without a doubt Tillie Truelove.

I felt somebody at my elbow, and I turned to see Hat and Jocelyn looking over my shoulder.

'What is it this time, Eric?' asked Hat in a cold voice. 'A red-crested plover?'

'Eh? No, Hat. It's her. It's Tillie Truelove. Here, have a look.'

Hat ignored the binoculars and drew the curtain.

Jocelyn sighed. 'I wish I was blonde like her.'

'A walking goldmine over there,' I said. 'All Bogsea on the alert, and I know where she is before the contest even starts.'

Hat folded her arms. 'And what if she isn't Tillie Truelove?'

'She's got to be, hasn't she – blonde, good-looking? She wouldn't be on holiday in Bogsea, not a girl like that. She'd be in the South of France. So she's got to be here working, and even if it isn't Tillie Truelove it's going to be great chatting her up. "You are Tillie Truelove." "No, I'm not." "Oh, I thought you were." "Fancy a drink." "I'd love one." Bingo!'

Hat put her arm round Jocelyn's shoulders. 'He always talks like this, Jocelyn, but he doesn't mean anything.' She took hold of my arm. 'Come on, Eric. Jocelyn's going to take us up on the cliff.'

I shuddered. 'Sorry, Hat. I'd love to come but – er – I'd sooner get my unpacking finished.'

'You can look down at the sea and ships and things,' said Jocelyn.

'Some other time.'

Hat buttoned her coat. 'Well, we'll go, Jocelyn. I'm sure

Left: Drenched again, but his trusty cigar stayed lit, 1976.

•

Above: Sykes And A Phobia saw Eric seemingly start to lose his marbles in 1963.

Eric won't mind us borrowing his binoculars.'

My face fell. 'Oh, for goodness sake. I might as well come with you.'

Hat smiled and opened the door. We were just in time to catch a glimpse of Mr Brown in his dressing gown with a towel over his arm, stealing up the corridor on tiptoe. He jumped like a scalded cat when Hat called him.

'Mr Brown, you can't go for a bath in the afternoon. You know Mrs Webb's rules.'

Mr Brown looked over his shoulder, then whispered:

'Mrs Webb's gone to her room for a nap. She'll never know,' and he gleefully crept towards the bathroom.

Hat shook her head, saying: 'She'll know all right.'

Jocelyn looked alarmed. 'You won't tell on him, will you?'

I put my finger to my lip. 'Just wait,' I said, and sure enough five seconds later there was a rumbling, clanking, gurgling cacophony. Mr Brown shot by like the electric hare

at White City, and Mrs Webb could be heard above it all asking who was responsible. Luckily as we got to the front door the rain started pelting down again, so I was able to go back to my room and cogitate.

Monday was day one of the Tillie Truelove operation. Corky was off early with his newspaper to case the South Esplanade, which was Tillie's first venue. My plan was not so complicated. I watched Tillie from my bedroom window, the idea being when she went I would follow. What could be simpler than that?

Mr Brown was casually pretending to read *The Times* in the bus shelter opposite the front door of the digs. He had overslept and missed his bathtime, but the minute Mrs Webb left to buy the daily provisions he intended to be in that tub like a shot. Poor old fool, I thought, little does he know that Mrs Webb always takes the plug with her.

Across the way I could see the blonde girl putting on her make-up. It was an hour yet before her first appearance on the esplanade, but I had to keep watch in case she went early, and it was no hardship although she was fully dressed – I must have missed that while I was having breakfast. Suddenly she grabbed a bag and made for the door. Straight-away I was downstairs, just in time to see her crossing the road to go to the beach. Once there she spread out her towel and slipped out of her dress – what a beauty – then came the ritual of the suntan lotion, even though the sun was weak. I figured the lotion was more for protection against the cold. I sauntered past her casually, then I sauntered back, then I skipped a couple of pebbles across the waves.

There was still half an hour before she had to go to work, so I decided to have a paddle. I wasn't over-keen, but taking my shoes and socks off would take some time, and I would be less conspicuous than standing there skimming pebbles out to sea; in any case my arm was getting tired. As I stepped into the water I glanced towards her out of the corner of my eye. She was talking to a well-built young man but, worse still, she was pointing at me. I looked round but there was no one else in sight, so it must have been me. I smiled and waved, and the man started walking towards me. He didn't look too friendly so I went slightly further into the sea, but he kept coming on and I struggled a little further out until the water was up to my knees. He stopped on the edge, and she came up and joined him.

'That's definitely the man that has been watching me through binoculars,' she said.

'Right,' he said, and started struggling with his belt.

There was nowhere for me to go except out, and I went. I'm not a bad swimmer, and I thought if I got far enough away he wouldn't follow me, but I was wrong, for he was already stripped and striding through the surf. I struck out for all I was worth, thrashing away in a mad panic towards America. After a few minutes I eased off. Gasping and retch-ing I looked back: the beach seemed miles away, but there

Above: Eric, Hattie and John Bailey up a gum tree up an Alp in Sykes And A Mountain*, 1965.*

was the tiny figure of Tillie, and wading towards her was the big guy. He'd given up and I was safe.

After the first warm flood of relief panic struck me again – the beach was getting further away, and I realized that the tide was going out. I kicked my legs and tried to swim back but my strength had gone. I was being tossed about in the swell, and thinking what a stupid thing I'd done. I shouldn't have swum out to sea, I could have fallen down at his feet clutching my heart and saying, 'Where's my pills?' He wouldn't have dared touch me then. I thought about Hat, and a wave of remorse came over me. I thought if I ever got out of this I'd be kinder to her, perhaps take her a cup of tea on Sunday mornings. At one point I thought I heard a hel-icopter, but it was only my teeth chattering. I went to touch my nose but I couldn't feel anything at all. I thought I'd missed, and strangely enough I was past caring. The sea gently raised me up and I caught a glimpse of Bogsea, then down I went into a trough, up and down, up and down, and I began feeling drowsy. I felt I could float like this for ever. A seagull hovered above me, mewling and floating on the wind. I thought to myself, some poor sucker's paid a pound for that one. I never heard the boat engines approaching. I had already committed myself to the vast deep.

However, my number hadn't been called because when I opened my eyes I was in bed at Mrs Webb's. I noticed I was in my own room, but there was something different about it. Then I saw that there was a fire in the grate. It must have been late because the light was on, but there was something else – the window was boarded up. I thought about it: my watch said quarter past five, but that could have been either one of the quarter past fives in a day; and why board up the window? Then I remembered the blonde across the way. I

decided it didn't really matter following Tillie anyway. All I had to do was lie back and collect thirty quid a day from Corky, who'd never spot her in a million years. I've known him walk right past his wife in an empty car park. Mind you, I don't blame him for that. Poor old Elsie – his eyes must have been bad when he married her; nobody could go off that much in forty years.

I quickly wiped her out of my mind and stared at the fire. It was a good fire. I hadn't had a fire in my bedroom since I fell asleep with a lighted cigarette – that was a narrow squeak, it could have been very nasty if the eiderdown hadn't been damp. I began to take stock of the situation. The first thing was to find some excuse for floating outside the three-mile limit in flannels and a sports jacket. I fell off the pier – no, that wouldn't do, since there was a large wire fence to keep idiots like me from falling off. Perhaps I dived

Below: 'She's only got two aces, I have three . . .' – E.S.

off the pier to save a drowning child? This idea appealed to me until I examined it. Where was the child now, and how had my shoes and socks come to be neatly lying on the beach a mile away? Then I thought of my shoes and socks and the blonde and the muscular young man. Of course they'd blown the gaff – it was probably them that had rescued me, then they'd brought me back here and told the whole story. Of course that was it, and that was why the window had been boarded up. I knew I'd never hear the last of it from Corky and Mr Brown.

Speaking of the devil the door opened, and he popped his head in. 'Ah, Sykes, so you're back in the land of the living,' he said, chuckling. 'We thought we'd lost you.'

Then Hat followed him in. 'Oh, you're awake. You had us all worried – the lifeboat, then the ambulance and crowds and everything.'

'The lifeboat?' I asked. 'The lifeboat came out for me?'

'Only just in time too,' said Mr Brown. 'The coxswain said another five minutes and it would have been too late.'

'The lifeboat,' I muttered and turned my head away. 'I call that ironic.'

Mr Brown and Hat looked at each other.

'What d'you mean "ironic", Eric?' Hat said.

I turned to her. 'For twelve years I've been coming down here, and every year I walk round the lifeboat shed and religiously put 10p in the box. I've contributed pounds to that boat, and the only time in living memory it's put to sea I'm the only one who's missed it.'

Mr Brown raised one eyebrow. 'Luckily it didn't miss you, Sykes.'

Hat was indignant. 'You should be jolly grateful, Eric, to everybody for risking their lives to save you – the boat crew, the ambulance men, Mrs Webb put a fire in your room, Mr Brown here – I looked at her for a second. 'When did Mr Brown risk his life?'

'He didn't exactly risk his life, but he helped to save yours. He gave you a hot bath.'

I struggled to a sitting position. 'He did what?'

'When they carried you indoors he asked Mrs Webb to get a hot bath ready. Then he had them take you into the bathroom, then he gave you a hot bath, and lucky he did otherwise you might have got exposure.' I looked at Mr Brown and shuddered. I mean, I'm not a prude or anything like that; I didn't mind doctors seeing me with nothing on, or even a nurse if she's old enough – but Mr Brown, with no qualifications! Hat was exasperated. 'Well, at least you can say thank you.'

'Thank you,' I mumbled.

Mr Brown turned his head away, a little shamefaced, and I thought that was out of character. I was expecting him to come out with something like: 'Typical of your brother, you save his life and that's all the thanks you get.'

But here he was smiling weakly. 'It's only what anybody would have done,' he said, and in a flash I got the picture. They'd carried me into the bathroom, then he'd locked the door and nipped into the bath himself – luxuriating in a nice hot bath while I was stretched out stiff as a board on the floor.

I glanced sharply at him and he blushed, and I knew I'd hit on it. I'll bet he took a book in with him as well.

'I'll go and tell Mrs Webb you're awake,' said Hat. But as she spoke Mrs Webb, Jocelyn and Corky came in. They trotted out the usual platitudes.

Then, having ascertained that I was well enough, Mrs Webb said: 'I'll have to charge you extra for the fire and the electric light –' she looked meaningly at the boarded window and sniffed. 'Then there's the bath.'

I looked at Mr Brown; he was nodding in agreement.

Then Corky leaned over the bed rail. 'Here's something else to cheer you up,' and he took out some fivers. 'What a day I've had,' he chuckled. 'Tillie Truelove: Esplanade 11 a.m., Winter Gardens 12 a.m. This afternoon 2.30 Floral Clock.' He held out the fivers. 'I spotted, challenged and collected at every location,' he beamed, 'so that's thirty quid you owe me.'

Hat looked at the ceiling in anguish. 'Thirty pounds, and there's still four days to go.' Then the dinner gong went and so did everybody else.

The following day I felt pretty chirpy, and I was about to

get up when Jocelyn popped her head in. 'How do you feel today?' she said.

I just smiled bravely and shrugged, and she went on: 'If you're up to it you can come with me. I'll look after you.'

'Great,' I said, and made to get up, then pretended to slump back on the pillows as if exhausted.

She shook her head. 'You're not up to it yet, are you? Never mind. I'll be in every now and again to see if you want anything,' and thankfully she left.

So I was stuck with lying in bed bored to the back teeth, and because of the expense Hat had cancelled the fire, so I couldn't even look at that. But being here was marginally preferable to having to talk to Jocelyn, and besides that I had to think of a way of queering Corky's pitch – break his leg so he couldn't get out, or better still smash his glasses. But then knowing him and his knowledge of the National Health he'd probably have a dozen spare pairs on him and a boxful of false teeth. Since she'd brought my breakfast

Above: With Jimmy Edwards and Ernie Wise at The Stage*'s Centenary celebrations, 1980.*

up I hadn't seen Hat, and of course Mr Brown was too embarrassed to face me.

I stared up at the light. Normally I wouldn't look directly at a lighted bulb, but Mrs Webb knew how to make a boarding house viable – it couldn't have been more than five watts. I thought about it idly, and decided that in all probability we were all being charged for 100 watts, so on lights alone she was making a 95 per cent profit. After a time I noticed that it was swinging slightly, so we were either in the middle of a slight earth tremor, or Mr Hackensmidt had somebody in his room. Then I decided it was a draught. My door was open and it was Jocelyn again. I groaned and turned my head away.

'You have a good rest,' she said, and I heard the door close behind her.

I wasn't so lucky the next time she came. I didn't hear her come in and she caught me trying to bore a hole in the boards covering the window, but she was a simple soul and believed me when I said I was merely trying to let a little light in.

'You poor thing,' she said, and I had to restrain her from taking the boards down altogether – I didn't want that much light, just enough to see whether Tillie was still there. As Jocelyn was about to leave she pointed to the boarded window and said: 'By the way, she went home this morning.'

At lunchtime Hat came in with a bowl of soup. I looked at it with complete apathy. 'What did you have for lunch?' I asked.

'Ooh, we had avocado pear with shrimp, lovely roast beef, Yorkshire pudding and cabbage.'

I held up my hand. 'Where's mine, then?' I said. 'I'm sick of this muck.'

'It's good for you. It'll build up your strength.'

'So will roast beef and Yorkshire pudding, but you can

skip the cabbage.'

'I'm sorry, Eric, but I can't stop now. I have to go,' and she hurried to the door.

'Wait a minute, Hat.'

She stopped and turned. 'I'm late,' she said.

'Never mind that. We've paid for full board, and broth isn't full board. So if Mrs Webb's going to charge me for the bath, which whether I had one is questionable, and the fire – see that she makes a discount for the roast beef. OK?'

There was no answer, so I looked to the door and she wasn't there. She'd gone. Never even had the courtesy to say 'I'm off now.' I ate the broth reluctantly and was overwhelmed with self-pity. My one week's holiday – one miserable week, that's all – not a lot to ask to be able to enjoy the air and the beach and the novelty gift shop, and here I was bedridden, incapacitated, forcing down lukewarm broth, while everybody, even my own sister, was out enjoying themselves. All the year round at work I'm hale and hearty – just my luck to be struck down in my own time. On top of that I was thirty pounds in debt to Corky and the chances were that thirty pounds was only the tip of the iceberg.

I was right. At about six o'clock there was a smart rat-a-tat-tat on the door and Corky walked in, beaming. 'Evening, all,' he said. 'And how's the geriatric ward?'

I picked up the newspaper. 'Not now, Corky,' I said. 'I'm having a relapse.'

He sat on the bed. 'Don't be so soft. There's nothing wrong with you that a hard day's work won't cure.' He reached out for one of my sandwiches and I slapped his hand. 'I was only looking,' he said. 'And seeing as how your strength is coming back there's another thirty quid you owe me.'

I turned my head away, feigning indifference.

'Money for jam,' he chuckled, and I heard the door close. As he left I turned round, and would you believe it my sandwiches had gone and an apple. I was out of bed like a shot, I was going to get those sandwiches back if I had to hold him upsidedown and shake 'em out. The door burst

Left: At the breakfast table, 1967.

open just as I reached it, and I went flying back over the bed. It was Hat, breathless and so excited she didn't seem to notice I was getting up off the floor.

'Eric, oh Eric, I've got something to tell you.' Then she hurried to the door, and looked up and down the corridor to see if anyone was listening. 'Do you know what I did today?' she waited. It always exasperates me when Hat asks fatuous questions like that. How could I possibly know what she'd done apart from bringing me gruel at lunchtime, and belting me with the door? 'Listen, Eric,' she said. 'I followed Corky and I watched him challenging Tillie Truelove.'

'That's a big help, that is. Now he's got proof that he challenged Tillie.'

'Oh, no,' she went on. 'He didn't see me.'

A sudden thought struck me: 'You actually saw Tillie Truelove?'

'Yes,' said Hat, 'and saw her pay out the money.'

I looked at Hat in a new light. 'You know, Hat, I've underestimated you. You're a genius.'

She flushed with pleasure.

'Let's have it,' I said.

She looked puzzled. 'Have what?'

I made the money sign with finger and thumb, 'Thirty quid', then said: 'As soon as you saw Corky challenged, you waited till he'd gone, then you challenged her.'

Hat looked blank.

'You did see Tillie Truelove, didn't you?'

'Yes, I saw her all right. It was definitely Tillie Truelove. So what?'

I stared in disbelief. 'And you never challenged her and copped the fivers?'

Hat put her hand to her mouth. 'Oh dear,' she said. 'I never thought of that.'

I fell back on the pillows. It couldn't be true. It would be a kindness to have her put down.

She recovered herself and chuckled. 'That isn't what I wanted to tell you,' she said. 'I've found out how Corky does it.'

'You didn't follow him into the gents?'

Above: Eric in The Return of Sherlock Holmes *for Granada, 1986.*

'Of course not. I only . . . . ' Then she stopped, and blushed. 'Oh, Eric. Don't be so rude. I found out how he knows where Tillie Truelove is.'

I sat bolt upright.

She pulled a chair up to the bed and leaned forward. 'You know that young policeman we met on the first day?'

'Policeman?' I asked.

'In the bus shelter. Corky got chatting about the – '

I cut her off. 'Yes, I remember. What about him?'

'Well,' she said. 'His job is to keep an eye on Tillie Truelove, in case there's trouble.'

'What sort of trouble?'

'I dunno, Mrs Webb told me. She said somebody might think she was – well, that Tillie Truelove, well, was, being a girl and just hanging about, you know.'

'On the game,' I said.

'Yes.' She looked down. 'It's not easy being a woman. I mean if you're a man you can just stand there and nobody comes up and says "How much?" But if you're –'

Again I stopped her. 'Never mind Women's Lib, Hat. The young policeman who keeps an eye on her.'

'That's right,' she said. 'Well, all Corky had to do was look for him, don't you see – you can't miss a policeman in uniform – and when the young policeman stood near Tillie he took out his handkerchief and blew his nose. Then Corky knew it was Tillie.'

I thought for a moment. 'He could have a cold.'

'No,' she said. 'He blew it in all the different places that Tillie appeared and immediately Corky stepped up and challenged her.'

I stared at her in disbelief. No wonder he was so sure of winning – of all the crafty, low-down tricks to pull on a mate. I could feel my temper rising and I looked round the room for a weapon. 'I knew it,' I grated. 'I knew he was cheating somehow. He couldn't find her on his own – not Corky. He couldn't find a piano if it was tied to his leg.'

'Exactly,' said Hat. 'And that's where we've got him.'

'I'll have him all right,' I said, struggling to get out of bed.

'No, no. Listen,' she said, hardly able to contain herself. 'That young constable won't be on duty for a bit. He got knocked down by a taxi while he was directing traffic, and Mrs Webb says they're so short-staffed Tillie will be on her own the rest of the week.' She sat back, eyes shining, and a grin from ear to ear – and that opens up a lot of face.

I suddenly felt better. All right, he'd won on two days, but there were three left, and I knew Corky – underneath that carefully cultivated look of experienced reliability, intelligence and steadfastness he was useless; and what's more, tomorrow I would be in the hunt for Tillie. I was already thinking of how to tackle the problem.

On the following morning I asked Mr Brown, Hat and Jocelyn to my room after breakfast and I outlined my plan. On the bed was a map of Bogsea, and I'd ringed all the places where Tillie Truelove was to appear.

'Operation Find the Lady,' I said.

'Oh, not that stupid game,' said Mr Brown. 'Really, Sykes, if you're so hard up for five pounds why don't you ask me?'

'All right, then,' I said. 'Can I have five pounds?'

'Certainly not,' he replied indignantly, 'and if I'd known that you'd asked me here in order to borrow money, I would never have come.'

Hat put her arm through his. 'Oh, come on, Mr Brown. It's just Eric's little joke, and he knows how we can spot Tillie.'

Mr Brown disengaged his arm. 'I'm sick of your brother's little jokes', he said. 'I had enough with the seagulls, and as for Tillie, I don't care if you spot her, stripe her or paint her all over in Dulux.'

'So you're not coming with us?' I said.

'No, I'm not. I have other things to do. Mrs Webb has to go to Clacton this morning.' Then he chuckled and took a bath plug out of his pocket. 'See you at lunch,' and he was gone.

'Well, there's only three of us now,' I said. 'That leaves a certain element of chance, but we might be lucky – now here is Tillie's first venue. The vicinity of the pier at eleven o'clock, right?'

They both nodded.

'OK so far. Now she may go on the pier or not, but that's easy. I'll watch the entrance – there's only one – so if she goes in or out I'll have her.'

Hat and Jocelyn looked at each other. 'Now to get to the pier vicinity you approach either from the South Promenade, or from the north. The only other way is across the road, in which case she'd have to go through the miniature golf, right?'

They both nodded again.

'So I'll be watching the pier in case she passes in or out of that. You, Jocelyn, will watch the North Promenade, and you, Hat, from the south. I was hoping that Mr Brown could

have done the miniature golf, but that's a chance we'll have to take. Now is everything all clear?'

'What happens if one of us spots her?' said Hat.

'Challenge her, and if you're right we nip over and challenge her in turn. That's fifteen quid for a start. The other venues will be a piece of cake – we just follow her. OK?' They stared down at the map for a few moments, deep in thought. Well, when I say deep in thought I was paying Hat a compliment – she was probably wondering how Mr

Above: Captain Sykes in The Bargee, *1963.*

Brown had got the hang of the boiler so quickly.

Jocelyn broke the silence. 'But wherever Tillie is there are always lots of people. If one of us spots her how will we contact the other two?'

I was waiting for that. I smiled. 'We'll each have a balloon.'

Hat looked at me quizzically. 'A balloon?'

'Yes, a balloon,' I said. 'There's a balloon man on the cor-

ner and he sells them.'

Hat laughed. 'You give him a pound and he lets one go. "Where's my one?" you say, and he points to it disappearing up in the air, and says "There you are"',' and she laughed so much that I feared for her dress.

Above: Ronnie Barker and Harry Corbett starred with Eric in Galton and Simpson's The Bargee.

Jocelyn just looked on, perplexed.

'It's OK, Jocelyn. It's a private joke about seagulls,' I said, and waited till Hat was ready. She'd stopped laughing, but it takes some time for the rest of her to subside.

'Go on, Ricky,' said Jocelyn.

I winced. 'Well, we'll have three balloons, each on a six-foot piece of string, but we hold the balloons under our arm. Then when one of us spots Tillie whoever it is lets their balloon rise. The rest of us can't miss a balloon hovering six feet over the heads of the crowd.'

'What a good idea,' said Hat. 'Just like a marker buoy.'

'Exactly,' I said, and straightened up. The briefing was over.

Just as we left the digs we heard the clanking and thumping from upstairs, and as we stepped into the street I couldn't help laughing. There was Mr Brown on the fire escape, with a towel flapping round his thin, white legs, peering in through the bathroom window.

At a quarter to eleven we were in position. So far so good, except that I felt such a fool holding a balloon under my arm, and whenever anybody looked at me strangely I said: 'You haven't seen a little boy, have you?' Pretending to have lost my little boy also gave me the excuse to search around for Tillie, then I had another piece of inspiration. I approached the lady selling tickets for the pier.

'You haven't seen a little boy, have you? He's with his mother, a blonde girl.'

The ticket lady shook her head. 'I haven't seen a little boy or a blonde girl. If I had I'd have challenged her. Tillie Truelove's round here somewhere.'

'Oh,' I said. 'Is she?' and wandered away.

I realized that it was going to be more difficult than I thought. The place was milling with people. There were one or two blondes, but I discounted them – one was pushing a pram while another was eating candy floss, and I didn't think Tillie would have done that. In any case they all carried copies of the Daily Bugle, so they were obviously looking as well. Then at about ten minutes past eleven the balloon went up literally and hovered six feet above the crowd, about fifty yards away. I was off like a shot, shoving and elbowing my way through till I got to the balloon. Hat was standing there, but her balloon was still under her arm,

and she was staring at a little boy who was holding the balloon and staring back at her.

The little boy tugged my jacket, and said, 'Hey mister, would you like to hold this balloon?'

'No thanks, sonny,' I said. 'I've got one of my own.'

'It's not mine. A woman asked me to hold it for her, and I have to go now.'

Hat stepped forward. 'Was she a medium-sized, with glasses and brown hair?'

'Yes, she's gone to the ladies.'

'I'll go and get her,' said Hat. 'Hold this, Eric', and she handed me her balloon. Then the kid handed me his and ran off, and I looked a right idiot standing there with three balloons. My luck was in, however, because before Hat came back I'd sold them.

'She's not in there,' said Hat.

'That's typical, that is,' I muttered. 'Went in and had one, then completely forgot about the lad when she came out.'

'Never mind,' said Hat. 'She'll soon find us when she sees the balloons.' Then she did a double take. 'What happened to the balloons?' I told her, and we went off and had a drink at the Metropole.

The only good to come out of it all was that Corky without his contact hadn't spotted Tillie either so at least I got thirty quid back. Oh, and there was another ray of sunshine – when we got back for lunch we learned that the bathroom window had jammed. Mr Brown had been stuck on the fire escape clutching his towel to him for over an hour before somebody spotted him and opened the window. The bathroom was flooded and water had gone through the ceiling into the dining-room, and if Mr Brown hadn't been put to bed with suspected pneumonia Mrs Webb would have had him on the two o'clock train for sure.

Mercifully the week came to an end and the time came to pack our bags. Mr Brown was in a shocking state but insisted he was well enough to travel – Mrs Webb had given him such a rucking he'd have hitch-hiked home with blackwater fever rather than face her again.

The Last Time I Saw Bogsea

Corky was looking down in the mouth. The young policeman had hobbled in with his foot in plaster to claim his half of the Tillie loot, so that put Corky more in the red because he'd already paid me thirty quid; and by the time he'd settled his bill with Mrs Webb he looked like a broken old man. I brought one of my cases down and there he was, sitting on a chair in the hall, gazing vacantly into his purse.

'Cheer up,' I said. 'It's only money.'

He looked up at me. 'It's all right for you, you get yours on the social security. I have to work for mine.'

I ignored it and went back to my bedroom. It was only then that I realized there'd been something odd about him – it suddenly struck me that he'd been so shocked by having to pay out money, he'd only remembered to black in the right half of his moustache. Viewed from one side he still bore a faint resemblance to Ronald Colman, but when he turned the other way it looked as if he had a thin strip of plaster on his top lip.

Anyway, one thing was for sure – this would be our last communal holiday and I wouldn't be sorry. I was just tying the string round my other suitcase when Jocelyn and Mrs Webb popped in. I looked up, then went on with my packing.

'Just came in to say goodbye, Ricky.'

'Goodbye, Jocelyn,' I said, without looking up.

'You've been avoiding me all week, haven't you?' It was as if she was talking to someone slightly backward.

'I haven't been avoiding you,' I said. 'A couple of days I was bedridden and the rest of the week you were always off somewhere.'

Jocelyn giggled and looked at Mrs Webb. 'Only at certain times,' she said. 'For instance: 11 and 11.30 Esplanade, 11.30 to 12 Winter Gardens, Floral Clock.' She stopped and waited.

I hoisted my suitcase off the bed, then I flung it back on again, startled. 'You are Tillie Truelove,' I blurted.

She shrieked with laughter. 'Yes, but you're too late now. You are a silly boy.'

I slumped down on the bed. What a turn-up for the book!

I'd been searching and scheming and walking my feet off and she'd been right here under my nose. Sixty quid a day touching my knee under the table every mealtime, and I didn't know it. I turned and looked at her. She thought it a big joke.

'Wait a minute,' I said. 'Tillie Truelove is blonde.'

'A wig, silly,' and she took it out of a carrier bag and swung it round. 'Well, 'bye Ricky. Better luck next time,' and she blew me a kiss and was gone.

I sat there dejected. It was clear now about that day with the balloons. No wonder Jocelyn didn't come out of the toilet. She went in all right, but Tillie Truelove came out in a blonde wig. I sat bolt upright – and good grief, while I was standing outside holding those three balloons she'd bought one of them and I hadn't even recognized her. What an idiot I was. What a great mark one super-de-luxe berk I was. I realized that Mrs Webb was still standing by the door.

'Well, I'll be off now, Mrs Webb.' I shrugged philosophically. 'There's always next year.

'Not here there isn't.' She folded her arms.

'Eh?' I looked at her blankly.

'Well, it wouldn't be fair, would it?' she said. 'Now that you know that the girl from the Daily Bugle stays here, you'd be able to spot her easy. I mean, I bent over backwards for you with Jocelyn, introducing you, and putting her at your table.'

'Yes, but I thought you –' I broke off and the enormity of it all hit me. 'Mrs Webb, every year for the past twelve years we've been coming here and you –'

She nodded. 'And every year I've been introducing you to the girl, and every year you've avoided her like the plague while everybody else in Bogsea has been cashing in.'

I just stared at her, haggard and sick. 'You haven't got a couple of aspirin, have you?'

Well, that was our last holiday in Bogsea. We haven't been back since, and it's a few years now, but I still wake up sweating some nights when I think of all the fivers I threw away.

Opposite: 'I think this was our first contract.' – E.S.

66

CHAPTER FOUR

Sykes and a Stranger

"SYKES" No. 13

By Eric Sykes

EXECUTIVE PRODUCER	DENNIS MAIN WILSON
ASSISTANT	FREDA BARRATT
P.A.	BILL WILSON
A.F.M.	GAVIN CLARKE
FLOOR ASSISTANT	JOHN JAMES
DESIGNER	PAUL ALLEN
COSTUME	BOBI BARTLETT
MAKE UP	JUDY CLAY
T.M.1.	BERT POSTLETHWAITE
T.M.2.	NORMAN BREIRLEY
SOUND SUPERVISOR	PETER ROSE
GRAM OPERATOR	IAN TOMLIN
VISION MIXER	TONY ROWE
ERIC	ERIC SYKES
HATTIE	HATTIE JACQUES
TOM	PETER SELLERS
LADY	JOAN YOUNG
1st SHOP ASST	MARY MILLER
2nd SHOP ASST	CHERYL HALL
MANAGER	FRANK GATLIFF
P.C. WALK-ONS	DERYCK GUYLER
P.C.s WALK-ONS	GREG POWELL
	DINNY POWELL

EXTRAS IN STUDIO

BOB HOOPER (in dress shop), TESSA LANDERS, WIN McLEOD, PEARL HAWKS, VIRGINIA JONES,

JOANNA HARKNESS, PATRICA GORDENA, LENNIE WARD

SETS

INT. ERIC'S LIVING ROOM, BEDROOM (1), INT. DRESS SHOP

Above: Eric with Harry Locke in Sykes And A Following, *1963.*

SCENE 1 LIVING ROOM

(HATTIE WITH CROSSWORD ON SETTIE, ERIC SITTING BESIDE HER,
BORED, WITH STRING)
Motto: If you feel that your
Life is dull, humdrum
And grey …. be
Thankful (animated)

HATTIE: Four down, animal, three letters.

ERIC: Eh? Could be anything, animal, three letters er – cow.

HATTIE: It says feline.

ERIC: Oh well you didn't say that did you – dog.

HATTIE: Cat.

ERIC: Pardon?

HATTIE: It can't be dog, it starts with a 'C'.

ERIC: It could be cow then.

HATTIE: With an 'A' in the middle.

ERIC: If you'd given me the facts: three letter word, starting with CA – CAR.

HATTIE: A car isn't an animal, is it.

ERIC: That one of ours is, it's a pig.

HATTIE: That starts with a 'P'.

ERIC: That's not *The Times* is it?

HATTIE: No, you remember six across – brother & sister born at the same time – five letters – well, it's twins.

ERIC: I put that in –

HATTIE: No, you put twits –

ERIC: I was thinking of us.

HATTIE: Eric.

ERIC: Well, I'm fed up Hat, bored

(GOES TO GOLDFISH BOWL)

HATTIE: I fed them.

ERIC: You fed them - it's Thursday – it's my
         day to feed them. If I'd known you
         were going to feed them, I wouldn't
         have stayed in, would I?
         I've got nothing else now till eleven
         fifteen, have I?

HATTIE: No, it's my turn to lock up.

ERIC: Well, that's it then (HE PICKS UP
         PHONE AND DIALS) – go on –

HATTIE: Ten to nine.

ERIC: Ten past nine. (LISTENS) Ah quarter to six.

HATTIE: Is that all?

ERIC: It's dragging Hat.

HATTIE: Peter says ten to nine.

ERIC: Oh, him. You can't believe him, it takes him all his time to open the door.

HATTIE: Well he isn't getting any younger, you know.

Above: Eric and Hattie on the buses in Sykes And A
Following, *1963.*

(ERIC GOES TO CUCKOO CLOCK)

ERIC: Neither are we – tick, tock, tick tock
Life's oozing away from us.

(HE BLOWS SMOKE IN CLOCK – PUTS FIN-
GER IN, CLOCK COMES OUT WHEEZING)

HATTIE: Oh Eric.

ERIC: It's only a piece of wood. Hattie our
life is humdrum, dull and grey, and it
should be pink and frothing.

DOORBELL

HATTIE: Rent man.

(GETS BOOK FROM SIDEBOARD. GOES TO
DOOR)

ERIC: Rent man, - milk man – paper boy –
young Conservatives – penny for the
guy – The first Noel – same people,
year in year out, same thing.

(HATTIE AT DOOR)

ERIC: (CONT)   Why doesn't something
different happen?

(MAN AT DOOR PUSHES HATTIE TOWARDS
SETTEE & GIVES HER A KISS)

ERIC: Same thing day in, day out.

HATTIE: Eric have you got a moment?

(ERIC – REACTION)

Above: The Sykes show worked just as well when it transferred to the stage . . .

(TOM KISSES HER AGAIN)
(ERIC GOES ROUND SETTEE. HE PULLS TOM OFF)

ERIC: If you don't mind, we'll pay the rent in money.

(TOM THROWS ERIC OVER SETTEE)

TOM: Ah now, who're you, Ernest, Herbert? Eric – that's it, Eric. (SLAPS ERIC ON THE BACK) You're both changed, so you have.

HATTIE: Would you mind telling us who you are?

(TOM GOES TO HATTIE KISSES HER AGAIN)

ERIC: (STOPPING TOM) Don't do that again, you'll give her nettle rash.

(TOM THROWS ERIC OVER SETTEE)

TOM: Sorry to keep throwing you about but – well don't you know me?

ERIC: Weren't you in *Peter Pan*?

TOM: Tom Grando, little Tom Grando we were at school together.

ERIC: Little Tommy Grando, come off it, he didn't have a beard.

TOM: He didn't have money either.

HATTIE: Wait a minute, didn't you run away to sea?

Above: . . . Eric's skill as an entertainer was all the more in evidence when he had an audience to work with . . .

Sykes and a Stranger

TOM: That's it – you remember as kids we used to play by the old bakery.

ERIC: Of course, Tommy Grando.

TOM: Yes, you were always hitting me.

ERIC: Well – a – yes – and look at you now – it's done you good hasn't it? I wish somebody had taken the time to hit me more often.

TOM: It's never too late.

ERIC: Ha Ha. (GULPS)

HATTIE: Well er, would you like a cup of tea?

TOM: Tea – ha – (GETS BOTTLE OUT OF HIP POCKET, TAKES CORK OUT WITH TEETH DRINKS OUT OF IT)

TOM: Go on me China – this'll blow the back of your shirt up.

(ERIC DRINKS)

TOM: No, you ain't doing it right. You've got to do it like this. (DRINKS AGAIN)

ES : (COUGHING) Thank you. What's in this?

TOM: Scotch, gin, aftershave lotion, and boot polish.

ERIC: It's poison.

TOM: It's good for you – see how your eyes shine – It's the added boot polish does that. Now then d'you remember one cold winter night standing against the wall of the bakehouse?

ERIC: We used to stand there every night.

HATTIE: Not Sunday.

ERIC: Where did we stand Sundays?

HATTIE: Well I think we used to stand in different places.

TOM: I never.

ERIC: Where did you stand then?

TOM: You're asking a lot of questions aren't
you.

ERIC: No, no it's just that we missed you.

TOM: It couldn't have been Sunday 'cos I
used to pump the organ didn't I? You
remember that, five years I pumped
that organ.

HATTIE: Five years

TOM: My one regret is that I didn't carry on
with my music.

HATTIE: You always were musical.

TOM: Best organ pumper they ever had. All
by ear; 23 slow pumps for 'Abide with
Me', 48, 'Rock of Ages', not a lot of
people know that.

ERIC: I didn't.

TOM: It's in the *Guinness Book of Records*, and
the Hallelujah Chorus – I used to go –
made – my little arms were just a blur.
It was Tuesday.

ERIC: What was Tuesday?

Above: . . . and being on stage is always something he has enjoyed.

TOM: We were standing against the wall of the bakehouse. You had your back to the warm wall and it
was my turn to stand under the window and sniff the bread.

HATTIE: That was the best place.

TOM: Yes, well I looked up at the stars and said, 'When I'm 14,' I said, 'I'm going to sea,' I said.

HATTIE: Oh yes, I remember you said that.

TOM: I said, 'When I come home from the sea,' I said, 'I'll be rich and I'll marry you.'

HATTIE: (LAUGHS) Those silly things we do when we're kids.

(ALL LAUGH)

TOM: Ah....how about Friday?

HATTIE: Pardon?

TOM: A Friday wedding.

HATTIE: Friday's a bit tricky for me. I help Mrs Thompson on Friday.

TOM: Don't you realise lovely when I was lost (PAN TO TIGHT) for three days in the Gobi Desert, it was (2S WITH HATTIE) your face that kept me going.

HATTIE: It couldn't have been my face. I've never been there.

TOM: Just because I'm a common sailor, I suppose.

HATTIE: No, I like common sailors.

TOM: You do, do you?

HATTIE: What I mean is I've got nothing against common sailors as such.

ERIC: Yes (LAUGHS) No.....You see I'm sure . . .

TOM: You're not (ERIC TRYING TO PULL HIM OFF) getting out of it now even if I have to carry you to church, tie you to the rail and pump the Wedding March myself. (CLINCH)

HATTIE: Ooo...No Eric!

Above: The usual suspects were rounded up for the stage perfomances.

(ERIC GETS CHAIR: HOLDS IT OVER TOM'S HEAD & IS ABOUT TO HIT HIM WITH IT
WHEN TOM TURNS AROUND SO ERIC SITS IN CHAIR)

     ERIC: Let's talk this thing over.

   HATTIE: Well the thing is I cannot marry you and that is that.

     TOM: Give me one good reason.

   HATTIE: Give him one good reason. Eric.

ERIC: Well, well a good reason, eh? I'll give you a good reason, apart from Mrs Thompson, um, Because she's already married.

TOM: If you're married where's your husband?

HATTIE: Tell him…

ERIC: Oh…he's…er…wouldn't you like to know?

TOM: Well if he's dead that's alright. And if he isn't I'll make arrangements.

ERIC: He's not dead no – no he's pulsating away, he's not a foot from your face. Guess who? It's me – I'm her husband.

HATTIE: Eric…

TOM: Come orf it you're brother and sister!

(GRABBING ERIC'S COAT)

ERIC: She's a sister but I'm not her brother…my sister, she's, oh I don't know where she is. This is my wife.

TOM: But you've got a sister Harriet and they told me she lived here with you.

ERIC: But she's out.

TOM: When's she coming in?

ERIC: I don't know…today, tomorrow, she's a funny girl. Well, wife we musn't keep this gentleman from his ship. Bon voyage, fair wind.

TOM: I'll wait.

(HE MOVES ROUND SETTEE & SITS)

HATTIE: Wait oh…. but you never know when she'll be in – it may be today, tomorrow, any time.

TOM: I'm in no hurry.

ERIC: She may have emigrated today, she was always keen. She was having lessons in Australian. She used to wear her hat pinned up on the side .

TOM: Well then I'll wait for her first letter, I've set my heart on marrying Harriet. Kept me going through the deserts of Arabia. From the doldrums to the horse latitudes.

ERIC: But supposing she doesn't write for a month?

TOM: Fine, in that case you'll have a spare room for a month.

ERIC: Spare room!

TOM: Don't get excited mate, I'll pay you for it. I ain't skint. I could work you a score if you're a bit borasic lint.

HATTIE: Borasic lint?

Below: Eric and Hattie with Melanie Parr as Amanda in Sykes And A Menace, *1964.*

ERIC: Rhyming slang for being broke.

(HATTIE – REACTION)

ERIC: Supposing she comes back in the middle of the night?

TOM: She's gonna get a lovely surprise ain't she!

SCENE 2. BEDROOM (1)

(HATTIE IS SITTING IN CHAIR, DRESSED WITH BLANKET AROUND HER)

SLOW ZOOM INTO

HATTIE: What are we going to do Eric? Eric this is the fourth night without sleep.

(ERIC SNORES)

HATTIE: Eric…

ERIC: What, what, what?

HATTIE: Wouldn't you be more comfortable if you got right inside the bed?

ERIC: No thank you Hattie, this is your bed. I don't want to deprive you of it…(LIES DOWN)

HATTIE: What are we going to do about him?

ERIC: Him – it is a problem isn't it? It wouldn't hurt you would it just to marry him in the first place.

HATTIE: What? I'd never sleep again. If you hadn't said I was your wife I could have told him I didn't want to marry him and that would have been that.

ERIC: That would've been that. Yes the way he was carrying on, you don't know men hat, after years in the horse latitudes he'd be a menace I can remember when we were confined to camp for three days…

HATTIE: I don't want to hear about Ginger Purvis. Again.

ERIC: He was like a thing possessed. 'You're a pretty little barmaid,' he said.

HATTIE: Eric!

ERIC: He's in a monastery now.

HATTIE: You don't know about women either. If a woman says she's not going to marry a man – that's that.

ERIC: You said that didn't you and he give me one good reason. Wait a minute. (SITS UP) Supposing my sister turned up tomorrow and refused him?

HATTIE: You haven't got another sister.

ERIC: Haven't I? I'm a twin remember.

Above: Eric experimenting with flower power and Max Bygraves, 1982.

81

Sykes and a Stranger

HATTIE: Not you – oh Eric no.

ERIC: Who better? I'm more identical to me than anyone I know.

MUSIC LINK 2

END PRE-RECORDING

SCENE 3
DRESS SHOP

CRAB R. as MANAGER enters.

MANAGER: I hope everything is alright Mrs Hackenshaw?

LADY: If it is it'll be the first time.

MANAGER REACTION

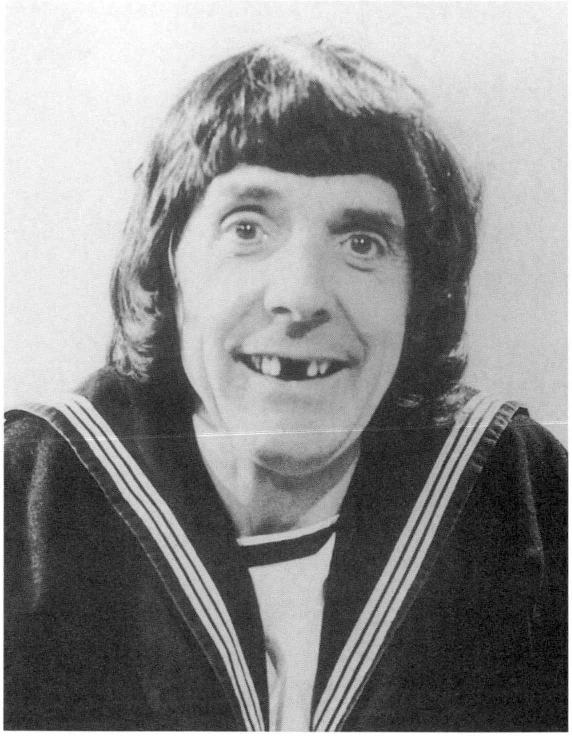

ERIC ENTERS AND APPROACHES DUMMY

Above: Sykes With The Lid Off *(1971) gave Eric the chance show his verstility . . .*

ERIC: Morning Madame. Oh I'm sorry
(SEES LADY AND 1ST SHOP ASSISTANT) I thought it was real.

LADY: I'd like to try it on.

1ST ASST: Certainly Madam. In the cubicle.

LADY: It won't run will it?

ERIC: Not if you keep a firm grip on the collar. Ha, ha.

1ST ASST: Is this gentleman with you?

LADY: Good heavens I hope not.

ERIC: Just a joke Madam.

LADY: It's a pity you don't have more to do with your time than wandering around the ladies underwear department. In order to titillate a jaded appetite.

ERIC: If I had a jaded appetite I'd go to a restaurant.

(TAKES DRESS OFF RAIL)

LADY: You see he's a toucher.

ERIC: For heaven's sake. What's so strange about a man in a dress shop?

LADY: That's what I would like to ascertain. I shall certainly speak to the manager.

ERIC: He's a man.

LADY: That's a matter of opinion.

ERIC: I wouldn't say he was exactly feminine

*Above: That sneer – Panzer Commander or Elvis Presley? (*Sykes With The Lid Off*).*

(TURNS AND HANGS THE DRESS BACK UP BUT THERE IS A SECOND ASSISTANT BEHIND THE RAIL. HE HANGS ON THE TOP OF HER DRESS)

2nd ASST: Do I look like a dress rail?

ERIC: I'm sorry I didn't see you..

1st ASST: Now can I help you?

ERIC: I'm looking for a dress – a lady's dress.

1st ASST: We don't stock any other kind sir.

ERIC: Actually I saw one when I came in rather like this one.

Sykes and a Stranger

(HE TURNS AND LIFTS UP THE SHOP GIRL'S
DRESS. SHE TURNS AND CLOUTS HIM)

1st ASST: Now er, (CALMLY) are you sure you
want a dress?

ERIC: Why else would I come here?

1st ASST: I don't know, I'm not a psychiatrist.

ERIC: Are you as saucy to all your customers?

1st ASST: All our customers don't go lifting up
the assistant's dresses. Sir, what are your
measurements?

ERIC: I don't know exactly. One that will fit
me.

1st ASST: Would you like to sit down a minute.
I'll get you a cup of tea.

ERIC: Listen Miss, er, well what's happening
you see –

(LADY SCREAMS) (ERIC AND LADY OUT OF
CUBICLE)

LADY: How dare you! You Peeping Tom. Just
looking at a dress isn't enough.

(ERIC GOES TO DRESS RAIL)

ERIC: That's more than enough.

ERIC: I'm sorry – I'll change behind the dresses.

*Above: More fun in uniform for Guardsman Sykes
(Sykes With The Lid Off).*

(WHIPS DRESS. WOMAN SCREAMS. ERIC CLOWNS WITH RAIL: FLICKS UP RAIL. WOMEN IN
UNDERWEAR COME THROUGH RAILS, ERIC RUNS OFF)

(SHOP ASST SCREAMS)

(ERIC TURNS TO APOLOGISE AND KNOCKS CENTRE MODEL OVER)

    1ˢᵗ ASST: I'll get the manager.

    ERIC: I'll get him, I know him.

(ERIC UPSTAGE L. COLLIDES WITH 2ᴺᴰ ASST. WHO IS CARRYING A PILE OF BOXES)

    2ⁿᵈ ASST: What's up Annie?

(MANAGER ENTERS)

MANAGER: What's going on here?

    1ˢᵗ ASST: Look at that, Mr Carstairs. There's a strange man in here.

MANAGER: Really? (LADY COMES OUT OF CUBICLE) I humbly apologise Mrs Hakenshaw.

    LADY: It's a disgraceful exhibition. He's run off with my dress.

MANAGER: Are you sure –

    LADY: I did not walk from Kensington Gore like this.

MANAGER: Terribly sorry, Madam. We'll catch him.

    LADY: In the meantime, what about my dress?

MANAGER: Yes, what a shambles.

Above: Popping out for a quick bite (Sykes With The Lid Off).

LADY: After today, I shall never set foot in this store again.

MANAGER: Promise? I mean, I'm sorry, I didn't know what I was saying. Deidre, inform the store detective – watch all the doors – I should never have left haberdashery. (PAN & ZOOM) All right, watch all the doors, Miss Jones. Down to the front hall, Miss Wilkinson.

(THE STAFF EXIT. MANAGER DUSTS MODEL – ERIC IS MODEL. MANAGER EXITS)

(ERIC SNEEZES)

(2ⁿᵈ ASSIST GOES TO PICK ERIC UP FINDS HE IS REAL. SHE SCREAMS)
(MANAGER COMES BACK)

MANAGER: What's the matter?

2ⁿᵈ ASSIST: That man!

MANAGER: Hey! What's going on? (CHASES ERIC OUT OF SHOP)

MUSIC LINK 3

SCENE 4:
LIVING ROOM
(TOM LYING ON SETTEE WITH STRING)

HATTIE: (UP AND DOWN BEHIND SETTEE) Look, Mr Grando, why don't you go to a hotel.

TOM: Tom? Trying to get rid of me, ain't you.

HATTIE: No – it's just – well – you won't like Harriet.

TOM: What, after all those years – I'll like her. I even fancy you myself.

HATTIE: Thank you very much. Well let me tell you, my sister-in-law is a lot worse looking than I am.

TOM: You're joking.

Right: Hattie with a moving problem in Our House, *an ABC TV series in which she appeared in 1960.*

HATTIE: No I'm not, I'm very serious. If you don't like her, will you promise to leave us?

TOM: I might, – then again I might not.

HATTIE: Suppose I telephone the police?

TOM: (RISING) That would be very foolish.

(HATTIE – REACTION)

TOM: I'm an artist with this. They would be around here and find two little bodies all lying…

(HATTIE – REACTION)

            . . . there and I would be halfway to the Spice Islands. So don't try anything funny Missus.

HATTIE: Just a joke – can I get you something to eat?

TOM: No I'll get it, you might put something in it. I'll get my own egg and chips.

HATTIE: I could taste it for you first.

TOM: I know your tasting, I'd be left with one chip. Now sit down and behave. (GOES INTO KITCHEN) I've seen your type before.

(HATTIE GOES TO PHONE AND STEALTHLY DIALS/TOM COMES BACK)

TOM: Hello.

HATTIE: Hello.

TOM: Police?

HATTIE: Yes, ha ha. three-thirty precisely. (4 CUCKOOS)

(PUTS PHONE DOWN)

TOM: Does he always do that at four o'clock?

Above: Another moving experience – collecting a plank for some D.I.Y. repairs in Sykes And A Plank, *1964. With Eric and Hattie in this picture is Richard Shaw.*

HATTIE: No but you fluster him.

(TOM GOES BACK TO KITCHEN)

(HATTIE GOES TO DOOR)

(ERIC DRESSED AS A WOMAN RUSHES IN)

HATTIE: Is it you Eric?

ERIC: Course it is – who'd you think, Miss Britain 1923?

HATTIE: Well I....

ERIC: Oh dear, I've had a fellow following me all the way from the high street.

HATTIE: Rubbish.

ERIC: You're jealous.

HATTIE: Of course not Eric, but have you seen yourself?

ERIC: I did catch a glimpse in a shop window – and d'you know I nearly whistled. HA HA.

(WALKS AROUND THE SETTEE IN AGONY)

HATTIE: Bear up Eric, once he sees you in that rig-out he'll be out like a shot.

ERIC: If he isn't I will....

HATTIE: He's in the kitchen.

(TOM COMES FROM KITCHEN)

HATTIE: Oh Mr Grando, this is my sister-in-law, Harriet.

TOM: Eh?

ERIC: Oh and who is this gentleman?

TOM: Grando – Tommy Grando. So you're little Hattie?

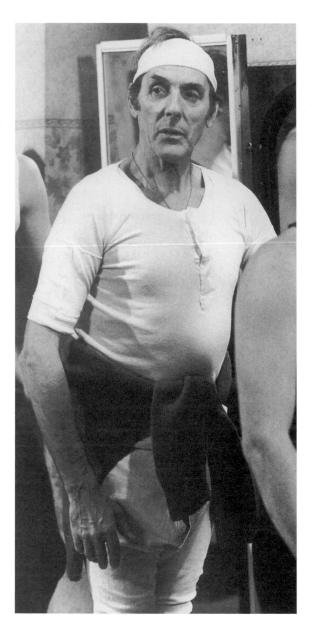

Above: The new Nureyev? Eric training for a new career in a commercial in 1975.

90

ERIC: Yes, little Hattie.

TOM: Let me take a look at you – oh you're lovely ain't you?

(ERIC – REACTION)

ERIC: Eh? Are you sure?

TOM: Just the sort of woman I've been looking for – you're different.

(ERIC – REACTION)

ERIC: You're right there –

TOM: I said I was going to marry you, and I always keep my promises.

HATTIE: Look er….Hattie couldn't do anything unless Eric gave his consent. He's sort of her guardian.

TOM: Yes? When I set my mind on a
thing I usually get it. (PUTS HIS
ARM AROUND ERIC) You're
no twiggy.

ERIC: Twiggy? Get off me – you great
short-sighted nit. Where are you
going?

(TOM MAKES TO GO UPSTAIRS)

TOM: I'm going to get your brother's
permission.

HATTIE: Wait a minute, I had a word with
Eric and he says he'd never consent to
his sister marrying a man with a beard.

*Above: Miss Applerod's school of Drama, Elocution and
Movement had never seen such grace, poise and elegance.*

TOM: Well in that case…(TAKES OFF
BEARD)

ERIC: False beard, that's dishonest.

TOM: I'll see if your brother thinks so.

ERIC: No no, I'd better have a chat with him first.

TOM: Bring him down here.

ERIC: It might be a bit difficult (GOES UP OOV) Eric, oh Eric, are you up? (OWN VOICE) What is it? He wants to marry me. Well he can't. Thank you. (ERIC AS WOMAN COMES BACK) I'm sorry…

TOM: (FLICK KNIFE) I heard. I'll get him down here.

ERIC: No no, I'll ask him to get up (GOES UP) Eric, Eric, the man wants you to come down. Oh right ho.

(COMES DOWN IN DRESSING GOWN & SLIPPERS)

    What is it?

HATTIE: Oh Eric, you're up. Feeling better?

ERIC: Yes thanks – a little lie down helps. Now what do you want?

TOM: What I have to say will wait till your sister comes down.

ERIC: Well she's lying down.

TOM: You're a right lot of layabouts. I'll get her up.

ERIC: No, no. Hattie can you come down?

(ERIC GOES UPSTAIRS)

TOM: I bet you 50 nicker, they won't come down together.

ERIC: Well make up your mind (POPS OUT AS ERIC) Anything you have to say you can say it to me. (POPS BACK AS A GIRL) Yes, I'm going to bed. (GOES BACK; COMES OUT AGAIN

AS ERIC: COMES DOWNSTAIRS WITH WIG ON AND DRESSING GOWN) Now my sister's in bed and she won't be getting up tonight.

HATTIE: Eric?

ERIC: I'm sorry, she's got a headache, but there's a codicil in my father's will that Hattie mustn't be married till she's 52. She gets £100.

TOM: Oh a codicil, eh?

ERIC: Yes, para three, page seventeen.

TOM: You are identical twins aren't you?

ERIC: Eh?

TOM: (TAKES ERIC'S WIG OFF) Ah, I thought so. (THROWS ERIC OVER SETTEE) I sussed you wasn't you when you first come in here. Doing the double act, eh. Well two can play at that game.

(TAKES JACKET OFF: ERIC PUTS HIS FISTS UP)

Above: A musical interlude with Hattie in The Eric Sykes Show *for Thames TV in 1977.*

HATTIE: What are you going to do?

TOM: Give us a hand with that dress.

ERIC: That's mine – it's my best dress.

TOM: If you don't let go there won't be enough of you to put a dress on. Get out of it or be cut out of it.

HATTIE: Let him have it Eric – you can always buy another one....

ERIC: Oh....he's going to be a riot on his ship in that.

TOM: Ship – the only ship I've ever been on is the ferry over to Parkhurst. I've just ten years been in the bird.

HATTIE: Bird?

ERIC: Bird, Hat, for the last ten years this gentleman – you're a convict!

TOM: Was a convict, I went over the wall, and a nice little hiding place this has been. By the time the fuzz have traced me to here I'll have flown.

HATTIE: Fuzz.

ERIC: Police. Police, Hat.

TOM: Tommy Grando the escaped con walks in and Hattie Sykes – alias me – walks out, ...clever aye? (KNIFE) Using the phone? Just in case you do (HE BREAKS PHONE IN HALF)

(ERIC'S REACTION)

GRAMS: CAR ARRIVING.

TOM: It's the fuzz – now I warn you not a word or (MAKES SLIT WITH THROAT SIGN)

(TOM GOES INTO KITCHEN HATTIE SITS DOWN)

ERIC: I'd better let them in though.

(OPENS DOOR)

PC: COMES IN

ERIC: Come in constable.(TAKES HIM TO THE DOOR – TRIES TO MAKE SIGN WITH

FACE) Lovely day, Constable. (MAKE
FACIAL TOWARDS KITCHEN)
Constable...

    PC: Are you alright sir?

    ERIC: Never felt better – lovely day.
(MAKES ANOTHER SIGN)

    PC: (WRITES) Never felt better
        – lovely day.

(ERIC SIGNALS WITH EYES)

    PC: (WRITES) Then his eyes
        went funny.

    ERIC: Can I help you constable?

    PC: Were you in the war? Sir?

TOM ENTERS FROM KITCHEN

    PC: Constable.

(ERIC MAKES SIGNS ETC.)

    PC: Oh very good sir.

(KITCHEN DOOR OPENS AND TOM
COMES IN DRESSED AS A WOMAN)

MANAGER: There you are constable, this
        is the man.

(POINTS TO TOM)

    TOM: Eh?

*Above: Explaining his grand schemes to Hat and Corky were
never easy for Eric . . .*

Sykes and a Stranger

PC: Excuse me, madam.

MANAGER: Or sir, eh? (TAKES OFF WIG)

TOM: Here, what's the game?

PC: That game's up Jessie, you'd better come along with us. Hello sailor.

TOM: Who gassed?

PC: This gentleman followed you from the shop.

TOM: What shop?

MANAGER: The shop you stole that wig and this dress from.

TOM: I'm not a drag man. I'm a GBH man.

HATTIE: GBH?

ERIC: Grievous bodily harm, Hat.

TOM: One of the best, I've done the lot.

PC: If Mr Jones is on the bench, he'll get seven days for this.

ERIC: If he hadn't put that wig and things on he could have walked out a free man.

HATTIE: Pity, he had some nice points about him though.

ERIC: Like what?

HATTIE: Put one on you.

ERIC: Put what?

(HATTIE THROWS ERIC OVER SETTEE)

CLOSING TAPE

Above: . . . but the penny always dropped eventually.

CHAPTER FIVE

Circumstantial Evidence

I was once held by the police on suspicion of murder. Never again. Take my advice and stick to having no dog licence or road fund tax disc, but don't get arrested on suspicion of murder because it's too much of a hassle. However, if you should be unfortunate enough to have your collar felt, make sure they don't find the body, because without it they're stymied. There must be habeas corpus. So it was with me – they couldn't find the body. But in my case it was because the body was still living, and it's no good the police digging up gardens, testing the ash in the boiler, and taking samples from the bath if the body is alive and well with a large gin and tonic in its hand, all unaware that it's supposed to be the body. However, we'll come to that later; let me tell you how it all began.

I woke up one morning with the feeling that all was not as it should be. I turned my head towards the alarm clock – it hadn't gone off, but then it was a very indifferent alarm; many's the time I've had to wake up and bang it before it would ring. Why I bothered to wind it up every night I don't know – it only had one hand – but it wasn't that. A movement caught my eye. I looked up suddenly and there, perched on the bed rail, was a dove. It was looking at me with its head on one side and doing a little side shuffle along the rail. A dove. Yes, a real live dove, pure white, and there it was on my bed rail; but why had it

come to me? Noah had a dove land on his boat but as far as I can recollect there wasn't much else in the world it could have landed on. I believe in the mysterious ways of the universe and some force greater than us must have sent that dove, but again – why me? Mind you, if I'd known the trouble that bird was to cause me I'd have flattened it with a cricket bat there and then.

I slid out of bed so I wouldn't frighten it, and gently started to take off my pyjamas. Not only was the bird unafraid, but it fluttered on to the bedside table to get a better look. Well, I suppose there are lots of people who don't mind being watched by a bird when they get dressed, but I'm not one of them. In any event I went behind the wardrobe door to put my underpants on – silly, I suppose, but it's the way I've been brought up.

Now for those of you who don't know, I live with my sister Hattie. Well we're twins actually, although we've grown into very different-shaped people, but as I'm slim I make it a rule never to talk about her size – so I won't mention it. Anyhow, I couldn't wait to see the look on her face when I walked downstairs with a real live dove perched on my fin-

Above: Hard at work as usual, Eric and Hattie in 1965.

Opposite: Hattie's audience is all ears, 1975.

ger, and I wasn't disappointed.

She came out of the kitchen with a teapot in her hand, and stopped dead in her tracks as if she'd hit a brick wall. 'What are you doing up so early? It's not ten o'clock yet.' As she spoke tea was pouring out of the spout on to the floor. 'Oh, now look what you've made me do,' she said. 'Go and get a cloth.'

'It's a dove, Hat. Look', I said.

'I can see it's a dove. I'm not blind. What are you doing with it?'

'It was on my bed rail when I woke up.'

'On your bed rail?'

'Yes, just above my head.'

'It must have come through the window.'

'Yes.'

'It's funny, that.'

'It is really, when you come to think of it.'

Above: 'Plagued by a mouse, I was ready to take drastic steps . . . my sister was suggesting I see a doctor.' – E.S.

'Was it raining last night?'

'The weathermen said there was a low coming in from the Azores.'

'I'll put the kettle on.' And with this she swept into the kitchen....

It's surprising really, the amount of time and energy Hat and I spend on useless dialogue, but that's life. If people didn't make stupid remarks all the time there wouldn't be much conversation at all, so I suppose one mustn't grumble – which is precisely the kind of remark I'm talking about. As we ate breakfast the bird perched on the toast rack, having a go at the toast when it thought we weren't looking, and I started to tell Hat in detail how I'd woken up to find the bird on the bed rail. It was four o'clock in the afternoon before Hat finally grasped the events of the morning, which means either that my explanations are getting more lucid or that Hat is becoming more perceptive.

During the next couple of days Hat became reconciled to the fact that the bird was no casual visitor but a regular boarder; indeed she was the one who christened it Muriel, because she's always been good with names – for instance Peter for the cuckoo clock, Jaws for the goldfish. There was a time when she wanted to call the settee Ernest, but I soon quashed that. I mean, there's no end to it once you start that lark – everything has to have a name.

'Where's my socks?'

'I've put 'em in Wilfred and you look in the drawer.'

'Not Nellie, Wilfred's upstairs next to Albert.'

That's the straight road to madness.

However, getting back to Muriel, the dove, she couldn't just do as she pleased if she was determined to stay; she had to be trained, and I haven't watched the Barbara Woodhouse programmes for nothing. I know she's dogs, but it's basically the same. However, I felt there was a rapport between Muriel and me; after all she had perched on my bed. I know whose bed I'd perch on if I had half a chance, but then that's another story. Anyway, I felt she shouldn't be too difficult to train. I tied a little bell on the bed rail, and she watched me, head cocking from side to side, and she cooed, which I wrote down, because it obviously meant 'What's that?' I pointed to it and said 'Bell', and she cooed again, but it sounded exactly like the coo she did for what's that, so I decided to leave verbal communications for later.

Lesson One: first of all I hit the bell with my head, then ate a piece of corn, and then I hit the bell with my head again, and ate another piece of corn, and all the time the bird watched me quizzically. The message was simple – hit the bell and you get some corn . . . even a stupid bird should be able to

Right: Super sleuth Sykes on the track of a pesky rodent in Sykes And A Mouse, *1963.*

understand that. With infinite patience I demonstrated again and again, but it was useless. I can now only surmise that the bird hated corn or else it had a secret stock of food on the side, but either way it refused to ding the bell. After a week of this I gave up; I not only had a lump the size of an egg over one eye, I was constipated as well.

I only wish the same could be said for Muriel, because this was the start of the trouble – for a little dove she made a terrible mess all over everything. She not only had bowels, but her feathers wouldn't stay in. Hat of course spent hours scrubbing and polishing and chipping, but no sooner had she got the house reasonably clean than whoosh . . Muriel was flying about dropping stuff all over again. But you can't put a bird out every night like a cat, or take it for a walk round the block like a dog. Muriel wasn't dim, though – in fact she was very good at one trick. I had her on my finger, then with a hup I flipped her in the air, and she'd stand on my head. This was dangerous for obvious reasons, but the crunch came when she got her feet entangled

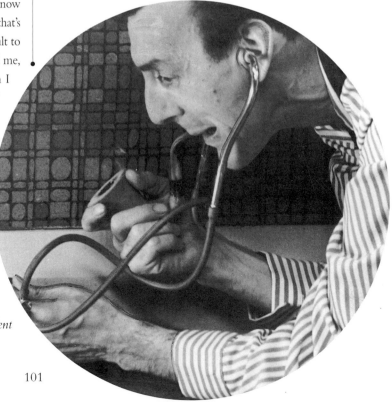

in my hair, panicked and nearly lifted me upstairs, so I never did that again.

By now you are wondering what this dove has to do with me being on a suspected murder charge. Well, I'm coming to that.

By this time Hat's patience was running out; she was barely civil to the bird, and one day it happened – one of those tiny links in the chain of inevitable disaster. It was twenty past three in the afternoon when Peter the cuckoo clock decided to cuckoo. I was just checking my watch, and as Peter came out for the fifth time the dove, supposed to be a symbol of peace mind you, attacked it. Well Hat went mad, and as she lunged at the dove with a rolled-up newspaper Muriel did what one might expect her to do when afraid, and Hat, having just spent three hours at the hairdresser's, was underneath. That was the straw that broke the camel's back, and in tears she delivered her ultimatum.

'Either that bird goes or I do.' Then she stormed upstairs to wash her hair. At least that's what I thought, but when she came down again she had her overcoat on and a suitcase in

her hand.

'Where are you going?' I said.

'Never you mind, and don't come crawling to me when this house is filthy.'

'Suppose you get a letter, where will I send it?'

'I don't get letters,' she said, full of self-pity.

'Ah yes, but when people know you've gone they'll write to you to find out why.'

'In that case get that filthy bird to deliver it.' With that she bundled out of the door.

I wasn't unduly worried. I knew Hat better than she knew herself – she'd be back in a couple of hours saying she'd forgotten her nightie, or don't forget the gasman's coming tomorrow, or some pretext that would have me pleading with her to stay, then she'd gradually weaken and agree, but not before I'd gone and got rid of that bird, given up my club night, seen to the guttering, and she might even have a go at my smoking. No, I knew her only too well . . . so it was a matter of no little surprise to me that she was still absent three days later, and no word from her.

In those three days the house got into a shocking state, but I couldn't bring myself to get rid of the bird – well, not completely. I came to a compromise. I decided to plant a tree in the front garden so that the bird could live out, as it were, but come in for meals etc., and if the tree was high enough I'd be able to lie in bed and keep an eye on her through the bedroom window. Having come to this decision I forged another link in the chain of circumstances. I should have gone out and bought a tree, but no, I had to be clever. I decided to take a tree from Hyde Park – I reasoned that I could select one just about the right height and transplant it in my garden; even if it died it would still have branches, and Muriel wouldn't really mind if it was a dead

Left: Eric in a BBC Comedy Playhouse production, Clicquot Et Fils, *1961 . . .*

Opposite: . . . and in the same year, as a German officer in the MGM movie, Invasion Quartet.

tree, as long as it had good footholds.

Not many people would think of taking a fairly large tree from Hyde Park and getting away with it, but then you're not me. Oh yes – there's more to me than meets the eye. I often think that, had I been a POW in Colditz during the war, I would have escaped not once but several times. However, that's as may be; the problem now was how to take a tree from Hyde Park, and I must confess that my scheme almost amazed me. It was so simple it took my breath away. First I hired a black jacket, striped trousers and a bowler hat, then with a clipboard under my arm I just strode into the park and started to cut small slivers from trees and make notes. Naturally it wasn't long before this attracted the attention of one of the park keepers. He was an elderly man, and while pretending to pick up litter he followed me at a respectable distance. I had by now found my tree and I walked round it several times with a magnifying glass. Eventually he came up behind me and coughed discreetly. I ignored this approach, pretending to be engrossed in the

tree. I even picked up a leaf and put it in an envelope, this turned out to be a master stroke, because he touched his cap, and said:

'Can I be of any assistance Sir?'

I looked him up and down and said: 'In six months' time it could be all over the park.'

He looked around and said, 'Yes Sir, I suppose it could.' He hadn't the foggiest idea what I was on about, but he hadn't long to go before his pension, and he was keeping his nose clean. I beckoned him to me, and looked furtively around to make sure we wouldn't be overheard.

Then I dropped the bombshell: 'Dutch Elm Disease.' He paled and stepped back in case he should catch some of it, and repeated: 'Dutch Elm Disease.' He obviously wasn't au fait with Dutch or Elm but he understood the word Disease.

Before he could recover I said: 'I want this tree up, roots

Below: Things go badly wrong for Eric and Hattie, as you might expect. in Sykes And A Pancy Dress, *1960.*

and all, and placed on one side.'

'Right away,' he said.

I held him back. 'Not now, this must be done after dark – if it gets out we'd have panic. Dutch Elm moves like the clappers – don't even tell your fellow keepers.' He nodded wisely.

'I'll be back tonight,' I said, 'with a ministry hand cart, and with a bit of luck nobody will be any the wiser.'

He looked at the tree, and I could see that the idea of all that digging was beginning to dawn, and his devotion to Hyde Park was wavering. I was in like a shot – I pointed to a giant beech tree and said: 'If that one catches it, you'll have a job – but with this one out of the way we can stop the rot.' He spat on his hands and I knew I had him. Well, that's how I came by the tree, and it was a mistake.

A week went by and still no news from Hat. Where she was I had no idea, unless she had a chap somewhere that I didn't know about, but that was highly unlikely because Hat hasn't had a lot of romance in her life. There was that GI during the war, but he turned out to be a British Army deserter from Bolton. Hat had a bit of money put by for a rainy day, and he turned out to be the rainy day. He pinched her bike as well. So she's always been a little bit wary of men ever since. However, I had other problems to occupy my mind.

The tree was now planted in my front garden, and although it was heavily braced by ropes and stakes it didn't look too bad. The only fly in the ointment was that, after slogging away digging a six-foot hole for it, nearly causing myself permanent internal damage, Muriel had vanished. Can you imagine that – she'd just gone as mysteriously as she had arrived. I couldn't believe it at first. I walked around the house calling her name, whistling, and rattling a biscuit

Above: Eric on stage with Hattie and Jack Parnell, 1954.

tin, but nothing. Examining some of the white splotches, I realized she hadn't been gone long, but nevertheless she'd gone. So there I was – no Hat, no Muriel, and a very weary-looking tree blocking out the light from the lounge window. To be truthful I wasn't really heartbroken at the loss of Muriel, but I was beginning to miss Hat; I was down to my last two clean plates and the house had a very nasty smell about it. So I was in the middle of writing an advert for a daily woman when the doorbell rang. My first thought was that Muriel was back, which will give you some idea of how besotted I'd become with that bird; but it wasn't Muriel, it was the police. When I say the police I mean Constable Turnbull, and he's about as likely a policeman as me being

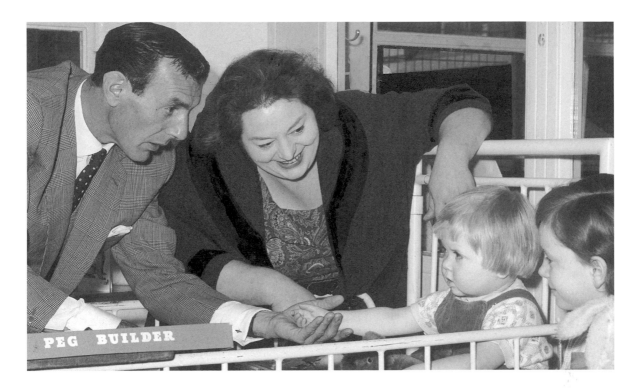

PEG BUILDER

opening bat for the West Indies. Constable Turnbull was known to all and sundry as Corky, and was well past retiring age, but as he didn't harm anybody and kept his boots shiny it didn't seem christian to discharge him.

'Hello, Corky,' I said.

He didn't reply for a moment, and he didn't take his helmet off, which is always a bad sign. Then he said:

'Constable, if you don't mind.' He teetered to and fro on his heels, and the light flashed on his row of medal ribbons.

He had six of these that looked impressive, but they only meant he'd been at the back in a lot of places. His eyes wandered round the room, but he never turned his back on me. 'The RSPCA wouldn't let you keep a pig in here,' he said, his eyes boring into mine. I edged away. After all, it was no concern of his if I wanted old newspapers all over the place, and empty bean cans, beer bottles and a bucket on the floor.

Opposite: Eric receiving a comedy scriptwriting award for the radio show Educating Archie *in 1952.*

Above: Eric and Hattie at Great Ormond Street Children's Hospital, having handed over a cheque from the Leukaemia Research Fund, 1962.

I was entitled to live like this if I so wished and he couldn't touch me for it. I decided to make the point, though, in case a new law had come out that I hadn't noticed.

'This is my home,' I said.

Again he teetered back and forwards. 'Would you say it lacks a woman's touch?' he said.

'Yes, I suppose it does.'

In a flash he thrust his face into mine and said: 'Where's your sister?'

By this time I was getting fed up with people asking after Hat. I mean what about me – I was the one who was the innocent victim. I didn't own a clean shirt and was down to wearing one of Hat's blouses, which made me look like the soloist in St Paul's choir. 'I don't know where she is, she just went, gone, folded her tents and crept off – *arrivederci*.

What's it got to do with you anyway?'

He smiled knowingly. 'A minute ago you said it's your home – not our home, why?'

'You don't live here,' I replied. That floored him.

I had it figured out now. All he was interested in was the fact that Hat wasn't here, and when she wasn't here bang went his free breakfasts, his cheese and pickle sandwiches, and pots of tea at all hours of the day and night. Our house was only one of his watering places, but it was a good one.

Then he really shattered my complacency. Very quietly he spoke, not even looking at me: 'I must tell you that I've applied for a warrant to dig up that tree of yours.' That really shook me – the park keeper must have reported it, or else Corky must have seen me trundling it on the hand cart. Well, it could only be a fine or even seven days, and seven days in the nick would be better than this rat hole; at least I'd get my meals regularly.

'How did you find that out?' I asked.

'Just put two and two together,' he said. He was shaking with excitement as he took out his notebook. 'Oh yes,' he said. 'I'm not just the bumbling bobby that people make out – this could be the climax of a long and distinguished career.' His eyes were gleaming and he was in such ecstasy he could hardly find enough spit to lick his pencil. All because of a measly tree which for all I know had Dutch Elm Disease.

'The climax of a long and distinguished career,' I said. 'It's not the great train robbery you know – and I've only done it once.'

He jumped up, shocked 'Gordon Bennett' – he exploded, his glasses beginning to steam over. 'You'll be lucky to get off with twenty years.

I was staggered . . . everybody knew Corky's views on the leniency of present-day courts. He was all for the return of capital punishment, flogging, and even bringing back the gibbet for football hooligans, but twenty years for stealing a tree . . . . 'Come off it,' I said, 'twenty years . . it's my first offence.'

He stared at me in amazement: 'Yes,' he said. 'It's your first offence. God knows what you'll do when you get the hang of it. First offence . . . that's typical of you that is. When you

go to Blackpool you don't just paddle out to sea, you have to jump off the tower. Well, you've jumped this time my lad.'

I still couldn't take it in.

'Yes, but twenty years, Corky.'

'Yes,' he said, 'and you'll be lucky to get that, and only then if you plead insanity . . . incidentally,' he said, and his voice dropped to a conspiratorial whisper, 'that's your best bet. There's a lot of people around here who'll vouch for it . . . Now come on lad', he said, all brisk again 'chop chop . . . let's get weaving . . . the canteen'll be open in ten minutes.'

I was now more than a little worried. I mean a joke's a joke, but here I was putting a few personal belongings in a bag, closely watched by Police Constable Turnbull. He allowed me to take my shaving gear but refused to let me take a razor, which was stupid – like buying a car with no wheels. I tried to reason with him: 'Listen, Corky,' I said.

He held up his hand and I stopped dead. It was such a definite gesture that I looked round; I thought he was about to wave somebody through. 'I feel it my duty to warn you, sir, that anything you say may be taken down and used in er . . . in er . . . .' he faltered, and moved to the table from which he picked up a pork pie. He sniffed it; 'How long have you had this?' he said.

'I bought it this morning from Madge's bread shop.'

'Oh, yes?' he said. Then he pulled himself together: 'As I was saying, I must warn you that everything you say will be taken down and may be used in evidence against you. And all the time he was talking, he was munching away at my pork pie. I swear that if he had a choice between promotion and a hot dinner, he'd be hard pushed to make up his mind.

Anyway, that's enough about him. It was me that was in trouble right up to my neck – I only realized how deep when I was being questioned at the local police station. They hadn't charged me for anything; I was merely helping with their enquiries. And do you know what those enquiries were? Murder . . . yes, murder. Well that's ridiculous; you can't murder a tree, and in any case, to my knowledge when I left home it was still living. Strangely enough the detective who was asking all the questions never

mentioned the tree at all but kept asking about Hat. Was she insured? Was the house in her name? Was I her only relative? I played it cool. Answering only yes and no etc. I'm not a Bogart fan for nothing. All this time Corky stood by the door with his arms folded. Well, he did disappear once, and when he came back there was a bit of egg on his chin. I could see that the detective was uneasy and didn't seem to be getting anywhere; it was Constable Turnbull who had instigated the proceedings, and he had the niggling feeling at the back of his mind that when Constable Turnbull had anything to do with anything the chances of it ending in disaster were infinite.

For my own part I couldn't see where his line of questioning was leading, but on the second day the penny dropped. The detective had obviously been up most of the night, whereas I'd had a fairly good sleep and the best break-fast since Hat had left. Straightaway he started at me.

Above: 'Hat and me in a repertory sketch – some people maintain that after this showing, many theatres closed down.' – E.S.

'Let's stop playing games, shall we?' He put his jacket over the chair back and loosened his tie. He tilted the lamp so that it shone in my face, then he started the questioning. He kept walking round the back of my chair, and to emphasize the point he hit the desk with a heavy ebony ruler. 'So you have no idea at all where she is.' THWACK with the ruler. 'You expect me to believe that?' THWACK. 'I can be a hard man, a very hard man.' THWACK.

I kept my hand off the desk. If that ruler caught me that would be it – I'd never be able to play the violin. I didn't even own a violin and up to now had never had a go on one, but the same night that Hat left home I watched Stephane Grappelli on the television, and to play like that was my next

challenge. After all he's 70 years old, and I'm comparatively young. I was just about to walk on stage in a crowded Albert Hall when THWACK – the ruler hit the desk again.

I jerked up: 'Yes father,' I said.

He could see that my thoughts were all over the place, so he took on a softer tone. 'Listen carefully,' he said, 'because I'm going to read to you . . . .' Then he started to read a statement from the milkman.

As I listened the picture fell into place. For two days running the milkman had seen me digging in the garden; I remembered him putting a bottle on the doorstep, then sauntering casually over towards the hole.

'Sister gone away, then?' he said.

'Yes.' He dodged back as I slung a shovelful of earth over his boot.

He edged forward again: 'Funny that, she doesn't usually go away on her own, does she?'

I didn't reply. I was so far down in the hole that I was looking up his trouser leg, and I noticed that, although the weather was quite mild, he still wore long johns.

He jiggled his milk carrier. 'Did you have a row then?' he said.

I leaned on my shovel. I knew he wouldn't go until he had all the facts – he has a big milk round and people rely on him to find out what's going on in the neighbourhood. 'Yes we had a row. Well, a few words,' I said. 'I had this bird, you see.'

'You had a bird living here?' he said.

'She's still here,' I said. 'You see Hat and I . . . .'

But he wasn't listening. He looked round at me: 'That's a big hole you're digging,' he said.

'Yes.'

But before I could finish he had backed away, falling over one of the gnomes in his haste to spread the news. Well, I should have tumbled to what he was thinking, and by the time the story had passed around the variations would be

Opposite: Eric and Hattie managed to 'lose' the world's biggest land mammal in Sykes And An Elephant, *1962.*

enormous . . . Muriel would be a dolly bird, 38 bust, high heels and a split skirt, and poor old Hat was stuck in the fridge till the hole was ready. I wasn't too wide off the mark . . . the detective then read me a statement from a woman across the street who said she'd heard screams, and two women arguing.

It was ludicrous. 'It couldn't have been two women,' I laughed. 'Muriel was a bird, a dove, a white muck-spreading variety with feathers, and that's why Hat left home. She just left because she couldn't stand cleaning up after it. Unfortunately, the bird's gone too now, so she can't corroborate my statement either.' The detective was unmoved, so I tried again: 'The bird's gone but there's enough evidence spotted around the house to show you where she's been . . . .' I tailed off lamely.

How could I convince him that Hat and me were great pals? As far as I can recollect, we'd only had one serious row in all our lives and that was during the war when they were taking down the railings everywhere in order to make guns and tanks, and Hat sent off my Meccano set. I've often thought that if the rest of the world got on as well as me and Hat, there'd be peace all over . . . no need of passports, and everybody would have a full belly. Me murder her? Kill off the best cook in Sebastopol Terrace? I'm not that thick. Mind you, there's a lot of people I wouldn't mind doing away with, but Hat is the last person in the world . . . with her gone it would be a life of cold beans out of a tin, no buttons on my shirts, holes in my socks. I might even be forced to marry and you can keep that for a lark. Where've you been? Who with? Are you coming to bed? Isn't it time you got up? Yackety yackety yack. Even buttoned up shirts and a good hotpot aren't worth that.

Time went by . . . questions by day and down to my cell for the evenings. It wasn't so bad in there – the food was substantial and there was plenty to read, although some of the stuff on the ceiling was a bit obscure – but the circumstantial evidence was piling up against me. Where was Hat? Scores of detectives were going round interviewing people, showing photos of Hat and asking had they seen her, but nothing turned up. They even showed a picture of her on television, and of course letters came in. She'd been seen on the Holyhead Ferry, in Polperro, in Swansea, all over - in fact somebody even wrote in to say she was a clippie in Wolverhampton. Hat must have read about it in the newspapers or the telly and she'd be round like a shot to have me out . . . but she didn't come. So where was she? Perhaps she was dead? Suppose she'd fallen off Beachy Head and even now was floating around the Channel, not only unable to help me out of this mess but a danger to shipping as well. It was now eight days since the disappearance and it was beginning to show. Gone was the Bogart image – I was now more like Woody Allen in the middle of a breakdown; my nerves were shot to pieces and I was smoking so much that the constable would open my cell door in the morning and say 'Are you there?' Strangely enough I wasn't pale due to being under the hard light so long for questioning. Perhaps if I'd had my shirt off during the interrogation you would have thought I was just back from the South of France.

It was on that morning that they decided to take me back to my house to reenact what had happened on the day Hat left. Well, it made a change, and it would be good to see the outside world again, but I didn't even get that pleasure. They bundled me into a car with a blanket over my head, although it wasn't raining, and I sat like that in the back of the car between two policemen. I suppose they kept the blanket over me so I wouldn't know which police station I'd been at. Anyway the car stopped and I was rushed up the path and into my front door. Then they whipped off the blanket. I couldn't take it in at first -what a shambles, everything had been shifted . . . walls were taken away, and some of the floorboards were gone; there'd been nothing like it since I tried my hand at decorating. Police were all over the place. They were digging out the back and in the front, and I could hear the sound of pickaxes coming from the boiler-room. A big fellow came towards me, then perched on a corner of the table and took out a notebook.

'Right, lad,' he said. 'What were your sister's five last words before she . . .' he paused and cleared his throat, . . . before she went?'

I tried to think – what did she say? It's very difficult to remember anything that Hat says since its mostly useless trivia anyway. Then I noticed that the noise of digging had stopped and the pickaxes were silent. The big fellow slowly rose and looked over my shoulder. I turned, and my legs nearly gave way. There was Hat standing in the doorway . . . what a moment. It would have made a marvellous tableau like When Did You Last See Your Father? It could only have been a few seconds, but it seemed hours before anybody moved. Then Hat spoke.

'Typical! I turn my back for five minutes and come back to find this.'

I still couldn't believe it. 'It's great seeing you, Hat. We thought you were dead.'

'Did you,' she said. 'And the first thing you do is have a party.'

By this time Constable Turnbull, who had been standing in the corner with a beef sandwich, was unobtrusively backing into the kitchen. Some of the diggers were putting their jackets on, and the big fellow looked as if he'd just eaten a 500-year-old oyster. He had a horrific vision of himself directing traffic at Marble Arch. 'Just a moment, madam. I'm Detective-Superintendent Bullshaw.' He wondered fleetingly how much longer he would be able to use that title. 'I take it you are this man's sister?'

'Police,' said Hat. 'What are you doing here? What's happening? I knew I shouldn't have gone away.'

The Superintendent was still trying desperately to salvage something: 'May I ask, madam, why you didn't come forward to our call for information before now?'

'Because,' said Hat, 'the first I knew that anything was wrong was when I turned the corner of the street and saw the crowd.'

I stared at her in amazement. 'You mean you didn't know that the police were looking for you?'

'Looking for me?' said Hat. 'I didn't know they were looking for me. I've done nothing wrong.'

'Yes, but they even showed your picture on television asking for your whereabouts.'

'My picture . . .' Hat's face lit up. 'Where did you get the picture from? I hope it wasn't the one you took of me at Gravesend.'

'Never mind what picture it was.' I was beginning to feel the frustration of the last few days.

Hat was still thinking of that magic moment when the whole nation had been looking at her picture on the television. Then she continued: 'I never saw it because I've been staying with Jessie Crutcher. You know, Eric, Jessie Crutcher; she used to sit in front of you at school . . . tall, thin girl with bad eyes, and she had a lot of trouble with boils.'

I still couldn't remember. As a matter of fact I was hard pushed to remember the name of the school.

Hat went on: 'Jessie Crutcher . . . you fancied her at one time.

Fancied her? It must have been me who had bad eyes. 'OK, OK,' I said. 'What's that got to do with you not coming forward to help the police?'

Hat looked at the policeman as if to say, that's the kind of idiot I have to put up with. 'Because Jessie lives by herself on a farm in Wiltshire and she doesn't have television, nor a radio.'

I couldn't believe it – no television. It's incredible that people in this exciting technological age still prefer to put their head in the sand . . . How can you live without a television set? How can you join in a conversation if you haven't seen *Coronation Street*, or *Crossroads*? How can one appreciate the history of our island heritage if you haven't watched *Poldark*, not to mention that I now have a smattering of several languages, and possibly if the occasion arose could assist in open heart surgery . . . . And not even a radio for goodness sake – what do they do for the time without the six . . . look at the sun?

'And I don't suppose you ever noticed it in the newspapers either,' asked the superintendent.

'Jessie doesn't get the newspapers.' Hat took her headscarf off and wondered if she put her suitcase down whether it might go through the floor never to be seen again.

I couldn't get over it. Not even newspapers – good grief,

Above: Hattie fires Eric! Sykes With The Lid Off, *Thames TV, 1977.*

what does she light the fire with? And does she know the war's over? Hat said she did but not the last one . .

Anyway that was how I beat the rap of suspected murder and it wasn't all black news. We got a tidy sum from the police in compensation, and they even offered to plant a new tree, but I wasn't having that. I've had my fill of country so I told them to put concrete down – it looks just as good painted green and you don't have to mow it. Corky was suspended for a while, but he still walked his beat everyday; now they've let him wear his uniform again and he's being well fed. As far as the superintendent in charge of the case is concerned he seems to have disappeared off the face of the earth, but my bet is he's odd job man on a lonely farm in Wiltshire.

CHAPTER SIX
Burglary

We have a fellow living next door to us who's fifty odd years old and a bachelor. Everybody calls him Mr Brown – everybody, that is, unless you happen to be the mayor, or the captain of the golf club, or even if you have a title; then you can call him Charles. We call him Mr Brown. I did suggest to him once that Brown was a common name, but he put up one of his eyebrows, looked at me coldly and said he was one of the Shropshire Browns, so I mentioned casually that I was one of the Lancashire Sykeses, and before he could get back at me Hat was in with a cup of tea, and that quelled another peasant uprising. He's always on about 'us' against 'them'; he's 'us' but Hat and me are definitely third-rate 'thems' so why he's always popping into our house trying to impress us beats me. Hat really thinks he's something special, and if I wasn't there she'd be in his house every morning first thing in a black frock, white apron and a little frilly cap, bobbing and curtseying all over the place . . .

Anyway another day dawned – well, it had dawned four or five hours ago – and I was sitting up in bed writing to Sophia Loren. I write every week, but she doesn't reply, so a lot of the passion's gone out of it now and it's more or less a duty letter. I was just telling her how my rash had cleared up nicely when Hat burst in.

'Mr Brown's been burgled,' she gasped. 'They did him last night . . . the postman just told me.'

'How much did they get away with?' I asked.

'Well, I dunno,' she said, 'but it must be thousands and thousands.'

I looked at her. She's so impressionable – she reckons Mr Brown's furniture is all Wedgwood and he eats all his meals off genuine Chippendale, but as I keep pointing out to her, if he's landed gentry what's he doing living in Sebastopol Terrace next to a dump like ours? She says there's no disgrace in being impoverished. I'm still trying to figure that one out.

However, Hat was upset, and all for dashing round to Mr Brown's with a bowl of hot soup; I was worried too – in the past three weeks there had been two other burglaries: next door lower down, and the one next to it. Now, with Mr Brown's, the thought ran through my mind that if they'd really cleaned him out there might have to be a whipround, or worse still Hat might take him in till he got on his feet again. I decided that whatever happened Hat mustn't go and call on him. I know Hat. 'Can we be of any help? And wallop! He'd have his feet under our table so quick she'd still be in his house. He'd get all the treatment. Oh yes. He'd have my bedroom while I would have to make

Above: '"I'm one of the Gloucester Fulbright Browns, on my mother's side. She was a Lady In Waiting." Hat is suitably impressed but I think it's a load of horse feathers. If he's so well connected, why is he living next door to us in Sebastopol Terrace?' – E.S.

Opposite: 'Segovia and John Williams had to start somewhere . . .' – E.S.

114

Burglary

do with the settee, and I'd have to eat with my jacket on. Oh yes, we've had him here before, so I know the score. I dressed in a flash and got downstairs just in time.

Hat was about to slip next door to see if she could do anything – couldn't we take him in till he got sorted out? I soon put a stop to that, and I was in the middle of explaining how they had some very nice institutions for elderly gentlefolk when the doorbell rang. I knew that only Mr Brown could ring our doorbell like that. It didn't make its usual pleasant chime, it was more of a command. In he walked – well he never seems to walk in, it's more of an entrance – and I was amazed. I'd expected a broken old man with a blanket round his shoulders, but not a bit of it. He was dressed impeccably as always, handkerchief sticking out of his cuff, and he was beaming all over his face.

'Heard the news, Sykes?' he gushed. 'I've been burgled.'

I was dumbfounded. Here was a man who'd just been pillaged, and he was grinning all over his face as if he'd just got the OBE.

'I would have been in earlier,' he said, 'but what with the press and everything . . . oh, and the TV people are coming this afternoon.'

Now I began to see the picture. He was actually glad he'd been done because now he'd be a celebrity . . . but I only knew the half of it.

He put a cigarette in a long holder and sat back in the armchair. 'You know Sykes,' he said, 'the more I think about this burglary, the more I realize how carefully planned it was.'

I looked at Hat and winked, but she was so busy trying to look desirable that she missed it.

'Yes,' he went on. 'Three homes have been robbed in the street, and all of us top people . . . .' He looked round for an ashtray and Hat jumped up and came towards him with cupped hands. He ignored her, and the ash fell on the floor. Hat went sheepishly back to her chair but I stared pointedly at the carpet. If it was me that had done that I wouldn't have heard the end of it . . . but then I'm not Mr Brown. If he came in with a dustbin and emptied it on the table Hat would say, 'Oh, thank you.'

Anyway, Mr Brown went on: 'Oh, yes. These burglaries aren't haphazard you know. There's thought behind them.'

'Thought?' I said.

He stared at the ceiling. 'Examine the facts. Three weeks ago they burgled two doors lower down. Then they go in next door. They miss you, of course . . . and last night they come into me. Do you see the point?'

Oh, I got the drift now all right. According to Mr Brown being burgled was a status symbol. He wasn't getting away with that. I looked at him steadily: 'They'll probably come into us later on when they get the hang of it; they're probably working up to ours.'

His eyebrow lifted again. 'I hardly think they'll bother you, Sykes. This gang know where the good stuff is.'

Hat was hanging on his every word. . . . If she was invited to Buckingham Palace she'd tell the Queen she lived next door to Charles Brown. And that's another thing – he calls it Buck House and he refers to the Queen as Betty Windsor. Well, I mean, I run my household with a firm though benevolent hand, but Hat would never let me get away with that kind of irreverence . .

All the time I've been thinking this he was still going on: 'Oh yes, I'm well insured of course, so I shan't be out of pocket financially. It's the family heirlooms that can't be replaced.'

I got up and walked to the window. 'We've got property too, you know,' I said.

'Oh yes,' he replied, 'you've got a nice little cosy place here, a few sturdy bits of furniture. But really, Sykes, there's nothing here that would attract a top-class burglar.' He glanced round the room, then sauntered over to the wall: '. . . Unless of course your burglar is a pot-duck fancier.' And he chortled.

Hat simpered happily. 'We bought those in Wimbledon,' she said.

He smirked. 'Very nice, too. I suppose they'll fetch about

Opposite: A sit-in on a building site in Protest, 1973.

116

Above: Drumming up huge audience figures with Sykes And A Band, *1964.*

fifty pence in Shepherds Bush market.'

Hat straightened the little duck at the end. 'Oh, we weren't thinking of selling them,' she said.

Poor old Hat. She couldn't see that he was taking the micky, but I wasn't going to let him get away with it. 'They're not brilliant,' I said, 'but for your information they cost over a pound in 1947.' He looked at me pityingly, and I could feel myself getting uptight. I gestured towards the room in general: 'Oh yes, I agree it doesn't look much. As you say, a few sturdy bits of furniture – but that's deliberate.'

Mr Brown's eyes narrowed. 'What do you mean, deliberate?' he said.

'Ah! You 're curious now, aren't you?'

'Not at all,' he said loftily. 'Just wondering what feeble excuse you're concocting for having to live here.'

I looked at him steadily. 'I'm not concocting excuses,' I said. 'I agree with you it does look cheap, ordinary, in fact downright suburban.' Hat was about to protest but I stopped her. 'Oh yes,' I said, 'but we don't have to live like this. We could have a big leather settee if we wanted, Persian rugs, a chandelier – we could have four ducks if we wanted – but we decided this was the clever way.' I tapped the side of my nose knowingly and winked.

'I'll go and put the kettle on for some tea,' said Hat, and went into the kitchen flashing me the 'why don't I shut up' look. And I would willingly have left it like that, with an air of mystery hanging about, but Mr Brown's a niggler.

'I fail to see how living in a slum condition can be deemed clever.'

I lit a cigarette with studied nonchalance. 'Let's put it this way,' I said. 'You wouldn't walk through the dock area at night carrying a jewel case, with a big gold chain round your neck.'

'What are you talking about?' he said.

I smiled at the end of my cigarette and said nothing. Hat came in with the tea things. 'Have the police any idea who did it?' she said. Mr Brown ignored her.

'What has walking round the docks in a gold chain got to do with my being robbed?' he said.

I took my tea from Hat, and said: 'Think about it.'

'Would you like a biscuit, Mr Brown?' gushed Hat.

'No, thank you,' he snapped, eyes never leaving me. His composure was slipping and I was beginning to enjoy myself. 'Are you trying to tell me Sykes, that you deliberately live like this, so burglars will give you a miss?'

'Got it.' I said. 'Oh yes, a lot of people have access to houses – postmen, milkmen, gas meter men – and when they see your place, they go: "Hello, he's worth a bob or two. Mr Brown sniffed in derision, but I pressed on. 'I'm not saying they've got anything to do with the burglaries, but people do talk, and there's a lot of big ears about. Now the gas meter man, the coalman, they come in here and the first thing they do is go "Pooh!"'

Hat slammed her cup down in her saucer. Mr Brown snorted derisively: 'I see now all this is just a blind. Your heirlooms are tucked away somewhere safe – silver plate, jewellery, priceless antiques.' He chortled again.

I put down my cup and saucer deliberately and stared at Hat. 'Have you been talking?' I said. She looked back at me in astonishment.

Mr Brown downed his tea and stood up. 'You know, Sykes, you really are pathetic. "Priceless family heirlooms".'

I stubbed out my cigarette. 'I'd rather we didn't say any more about it.'

'I'm sure you wouldn't,' he crowed, 'because you haven't got any.'

Now if there's one thing that gets me going it's being crowed at, especially by Mr Brown. Caution went out of the window. 'Oh, haven't we?' I said. 'You're not the only one who's been bequeathed, you know. We have more family heirlooms in that strong box than you've had hot dinners.'

'What strong box?' he said.

'In the cellar.'

Hat looked at the ceiling in exasperation and I knew I'd gone too far, but Mr Brown affects me like a match in a fireworks factory. He straightened his tie and his eyes were crafty. 'I'd like to see these fabulous heirlooms,' he purred.

'Well you can't,' I snapped, 'because we keep the keys at the bank.' Hat was now behind Mr Brown, giving me 'I'll murder you' over his shoulder, but that sort of threat only makes me more reckless. 'And what's more,' I said, 'the box is not allowed to be opened except in the presence of two solicitors.' A nice authentic touch, I thought.

Mr Brown's composure was slipping. He'd strolled in here full of condescension to remind the peasants why they were peasants and why he was the squire, and here he was with all the bounce knocked out of him. He really is no match for me. He tried to pull himself together. 'Well, if you've got all these things, Sykes, it seems rather strange that you haven't been burgled yet.'

'It's not strange at all,' I said. 'They'd like to. . . . Oh yes, this is the big one all right. They'd *like* to very much, but

Above: Racing driver James Hunt flew in from Monte Carlo for a ten second cameo appearance with Eric in The Plank *in 1979.*

they wouldn't dare.'

'Why wouldn't they dare?' he said, suspiciously.

By now my imagination was way ahead of my tongue, and I was almost believing it all myself. Indeed I'd made a mental note to have the box moved to the vaults of the bank

. . . and then I realized there wasn't a box. 'I'll tell you why they wouldn't dare – because of Nero.'

. . . and then I realized there wasn't a box. 'I'll tell you why they wouldn't dare – because of Nero.'

'Nero,' he said, and looked quickly at Hat. She wasn't any help. She was pretending to wind up the cuckoo clock, but I could tell by the expression on her back that as soon as Mr Brown had gone I was in for a real ding-dong.

'Yes, Nero.' I repeated. 'My dog, specially trained for us by the police. That's the reason we haven't been burgled.'

'Really, Sykes,' he said, all silky, 'I'd very much like to see this dog of yours, or are you only allowed to show him in the presence of two solicitors?' He chuckled at Hat and she smiled a sickly smile back.

I realized that he was gaining the ascendancy again, so I

Above, Bernard Breslaw, Bruce Forsythe, Arthur Haynes, Harry Secombe and Eric at a Variety Club lunch, 1965.

played it cool: 'You can't see him today because he's down at the police dog school; and when he comes back he gets his food, then he's on guard again.'

'But don't you ever let him out?' he said.

'I daren't. I had to promise the police that I wouldn't. He's too ferocious.'

Mr Brown looked at me suspiciously. 'But surely, Sykes, I'd have heard him bark?'

'Bark?' I said. 'I won't let him. That's why he's such a good guard dog. You should see him every night checking all the doors – it's uncanny. I tell you I wouldn't like to be the one to break into here at night.'

He looked at me steadily. 'Quite frankly,' he said, making his way to the door, 'I don't believe a word of it, but I'll be round tomorrow to see this wonder dog of yours.' And with that he went.

As the door closed Hat exploded. 'Well, you've done it now, haven't you? You've really gone over the top this time.'

'For goodness sake don't you start,' I said, and turned away.

She was round the front of me like a shot. 'Go on. Tell me why you always have to tell such lies all the time. Go on. Why?'

'Why?' I said. 'I'll tell you why. I did it for you, that's why.' She was amazed.

'Oh yes,' I went on. 'I deliberately try to shield you and this is all the thanks I get.'

Her mouth kept opening but her brain couldn't find the words.

'Listen, Hat,' I said, getting her to sit down. 'Do you want to walk down the street and have everybody pointing at you, and looking at you with pity, because you're too poor to be burgled? Is that what you want? You know what will happen. Letters will start coming in with the odd pound note. Food parcels will be left on the doorstep.

People will stop you at the market and slip an odd frock or two in your basket. Do you want the welfare people round twice a week?' She was calmer now, feeling a bit sorry for herself, and I could almost hear the violins in the background . . . 'You heard what Mr Brown said, "There's nothing here worth pinching" . . . I don't want people thinking we're not as good as he is because we haven't been burgled.'

She pulled herself out of her reverie. You're right, Eric,' she said. 'The only thing is you'll have to get a dog.'

That floored me. Come what might there wasn't going to be a dog in this house. Dogs and me are natural enemies. They all go for me – even one that was tranquillized and had no teeth would try and bowl me over. 'No fear, Hat. We're not getting a dog.'

'But you'll have to now, after what you told Mr Brown . . .

Above: Erich Von Sykes and the Frankfurt Nightingale in a scene from Sykes And A Big, Big Show, 1970.

and it'll have to be a big one.'

'No dog,' I said.

'All right,' she said. 'If you don't mind losing face.' I came back fast. 'It's not a question of losing face,' I said. 'It's limbs – arms, legs . . . bits.'

She went off into the kitchen and I sat there and pondered what to do. I could put a black armband on and say that the dog had been killed crossing the road, but that's no good – knowing Mr Brown he'd insist on seeing the remains. Or I could go round the streets whistling for a day or two, saying

Burglary

Above: Keeping the orchestra on their toes, Sykes And A Big Big Show, *1970.*

it was lost. Anyway I decided to sleep on it. I often to go bed when I have a problem. Once I didn't get up for a week and I still hadn't solved the problem. As a matter of fact I'd forgotten what it was – which is the next best thing.

It was the middle of the following morning. I was propped up in bed, wondering whether I should ring down for another egg, when the idea hit me like an exploding star-shell. In two shakes of a duck's tail I was dressed. I must have knocked seconds off my other quick dressing time, only on this occasion I ran down my own stairs instead of having to drop out of a first-floor window. That's the worst of the night shifts these days; you never know when they're going to come out on strike.

Anyway, when I got downstairs Hat shouted from the kitchen: 'Oh, you're up then?'

'Yes,' I said. Then I put on my coat and let myself out. All the time Hat was talking to me from the kitchen. I could still hear her when I turned the corner of the street.

In an hour I was back, and as I hung up my coat Hat came out of the kitchen, still talking. 'Well,' she said. 'What d'you think, then?'

'It's a marvellous idea,' I said, and she went back into the kitchen quite happy. I wondered what I'd agreed to. I don't suppose I'll ever know now. Anyway I had a big surprise for her, which I set up, then I slipped into the kitchen. 'Listen to this, Hat,' I said.

She cocked her head on one side. 'What?' she said.

'Shhh. . . . Listen!' And we waited for a few seconds. Then *woof woof* a colossal great dog bark . . .

Hat's face lit up. 'Oh, let me see him,' and she rushed into the living-room. She looked behind the settee and up the staircase, and the dog still barked away. 'Come on, Eric,' she said, 'where is he?'

'You're leaning on him,' I said, and she sprang back. I lifted the lid of the gramophone.

'It's a record,' she said.

'Yes.' How's that for quick thinking? 'Now Mr Brown can hear Nero barking, and we don't have any hassles. No licence necessary, we don't have to feed him, and he's house-trained.'

'You'll never get away with it,' she said.

'Oh, no? It fooled you, didn't it?' which she grudgingly admitted.

A prophet is without honour in his own country . . . I mean why can't she come straight out and say I'm a genius?

If Mr Brown had thought of a trick like that she'd be writing off about it to the newspapers . . . Never mind about that, though, there was plenty to do yet before I was finished. I got one of my old leather belts and put studs in it. Hat was mystified.

'It's his collar,' I said.

She laughed, but I could see she was entering into the conspiracy. When she came back from shopping she had something wrapped in a newspaper.

'What you got there?' I said.

She unwrapped it. 'It's Nero's dinner. It's a hambone,' she said. And what a size – it looked to me more like the thigh of a Suffolk Punch.

And then again, another of those flashes of brilliance. I found an old tin bath in the cellar, put a bit of water in it and wrote 'Nero' on the side.

The scene was set. All I had to do now was bring on the sucker. I couldn't wait to see Mr Brown's face when he saw all the paraphernalia. The gramophone would be going full blast in the kitchen, with me keeping guard with a chair in one hand and a bull whip in the other. The minute I rang the doorbell that evening I briefed Hat on what she had to do. Having done so, I put a fresh needle in the gramophone, wound it up, and showed her the exact spot on the record to get the maximum effect. Then I set off for the station to meet Mr Brown – accidentally, of course – on his way home. Bang on time there he was, showing his season ticket at the barrier, smiling all over his face and turning from side to side so they could all get a good look at him – and he'd only been on television for two minutes. I fell into step beside him.

'I thought it was you,' I said.

'Ah, Sykes,' he beamed. 'How's that dog of yours getting on?'

'All right,' I said, non-committally. 'It looks like we'll be having some rain.

'I must say, Sykes, you keep him awfully quiet. I strolled round the back of your house last night and didn't hear a sound.'

'Oh, never mind about Nero,' I said. I was stringing him along beautifully. 'That's a nice briefcase you've got there', I said, as if trying to change the subject.

'Is he at home yet, or is he still at the police school?'

'Oh, he's at home. He only goes to the school twice a week.'

Right: A shot taken as the BBC launched the first of his BBC TV series, Sykes And A Telephone, *1960.*

'Not studying for his 0-levels then, is he?' And he chuckled. He never laughs really, he always chuckles. Hat thinks it's infectious, but I think he's wary about his teeth coming out. Do you know what, Sykes?' he said. 'I think I'll pop in as I go by and say hello to your Nero.'

I pretended to be flustered. 'Oh no, I wouldn't do that,' I said. 'He's been in a bad temper today. I don't think that horse's head agreed with him.'

By this time we were at our gate, and I acted as if I didn't want him to get by. I only hoped Hat wouldn't panic and put the wrong record on. It'd be just like her to do that, so that when I shouted through the letter box 'Down, Nero' we'd hear 'A Sleepy Lagoon' by Mantovani. Mr Brown brushed by me and rang the doorbell. Straightaway there was a great bark. Well, he sprang back from that doorbell as if it had ten thousand volts coming through it.

I looked at him ruefully. 'I told you, didn't I?' Then I shouted: 'Down, Nero. Down, boy . . . the master's home.' I

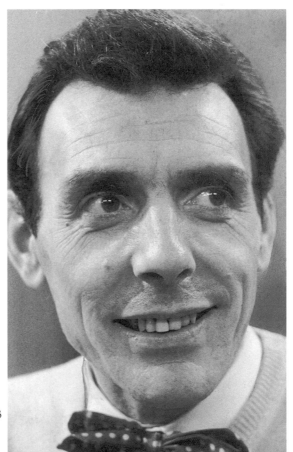

Above: Eric with his long-time friend Spike Milligan at Spike's 75th birthday party in 1993.

must say Hat was doing a great job. She was obviously moving about the room with the gramophone in her arms and every so often she'd lurch against the door as if Nero was trying to get but. 'We're going in now,' I said to Mr Brown.

'Don't show fear. Give me your bowler hat so he can get a sniff of it, but don't show fear. They can smell when – ' But I never finished what I was going to say because when I looked round he'd vanished; his briefcase was on the path and there was still a faint whiff of brilliantine in the air. I mean, he really shouldn't tangle with me; he's out of his depth, I thought, as I let myself in. 'I'm home, Hat,' I said automatically. 'It sounded great, Hat. I . . .' And as I turned from the coat rack an enormous black dog leapt at me and bashed me against the staircase. 'Hat!' I shouted. 'Hat!'

By this time the dog had hold of the back of my jacket and was dragging me into the kitchen, with me like a fool saying, 'Good dog, good dog.' I grabbed hold of a chair to save myself, but all that happened was that me and the chair ended up by the fridge. Then the dog backed off, no doubt to select which piece he'd have first. What a monster! I'd never seen anything like it – he must have been a cross between a Dobermann and a mastiff, but part panther. He was crouched ready to spring and I edged slowly along the floor toward the kitchen door . . . then, all slavering jaws and teeth, he sprang, and with a tremendous yelp I rolled to one side. Bang! He hit the fridge with such a crash that I heard the milk bottle breaking inside, and the door flew open. That was the only thing that saved me. Sunday's joint fell out and the dog spotted it – that dog was no fool; he knew the meat might go off, but I'd keep for another day, so he got stuck into the joint. Gradually I eased towards the back door and opened it gently. Now I had to do the tricky part . . . while he was crunching on a piece I kicked the rest of it outside. In a flash he was after it and I slammed the door, shot the bolts and slumped back against it in a trembling mass of humanity. After a time I took stock of myself and found I was all there, but the back of my jacket had gone. I was still standing by the door, white-faced, when Hat poked her head in.

'What's all the noise about?' she said, as if nothing had happened. 'I must have been upstairs when you came in.

I tried to speak, but my throat had dried up.

'Did you say hello to Rex?' she said.

I wiped the sweat off me. 'Rex', I croaked. 'Where did you get that thing from?'

She said: 'It's really funny. Just after you'd gone this man came to the door. He was a detective or something, and asked me a lot of questions about the burglaries, and did I live alone, you know, all that sort of thing . . . and did we have anything of value . . . he knows Madge – and Oooh,' she said, 'and you know Madge went to the doctor's with her leg' – I stopped her quickly.

'I don't care if Madge went to the doctor's with both her legs. I want to know about that dog.' Hat was a bit put out, but she does go on once she gets started, and to tell you the truth I'm up to here with Madge and her surgical stocking. 'The dog,' I said. 'How did you come across that werewolf?'

She said, 'Oh, Rex. Well this man had Rex with him, he is a police dog by the way, and apparently he's been with the drug squad, and he's got four sons.' . . . I realized it was the detective who had the family, not the dog, but I'd had all the fight knocked out of me so I just had to let her go on . . . eventually after the eldest boy was twelve and was going to

be a jockey and you wouldn't think he had a wig on . . . the detective, not the aspiring jockey . . . it was ten minutes later before she got round to the information I was after. Apparently the detective was going to be in the district making enquiries, and Hat had agreed to look after the dog for a few days. 'By the way,' she said, 'where is he?'

'Where is he? I'll tell you where. He's out there terrorizing the countryside. There'll be panic in the streets, dead cattle all over the place. They'll have to call the army in.'

'He was only playing with you,' said Hat.

'Playing! Yes, I've seen a lion playing with a gazelle, but only when it's had enough to eat. By the way,' I went on, 'we'll be having egg and chips for Sunday lunch.'

Hat stopped and listened. . . . 'What's that?' she said.

Then she went through to the living-room and I heard her open the front door. A stab of panic gripped me. I heard her say: 'Ooo's a naughty boy then,' and I knew it wasn't

Below: Eric with Hattie and Tommy Cooper in Sykes Versus ITV*, 1967.*

Burglary

Mr Brown at the door. I was struggling to pull the fridge in front of the kitchen door when Hat popped her head in 'Come and say hello to Rex,' she said. 'He's come back.'

'I'm not saying hello to that thing,' I said. My voice didn't sound like mine but I wasn't going to introduce myself again. I know they do marvellous things with artificial limbs, but I'm too old now to start that game. No. I was resolved to sleep in the kitchen, or better still sneak out the back way and get a hotel room somewhere.

Half an hour later, Hat popped her head through the serving hatch. 'It's all right,' she said, 'he's asleep.'

Suppose he's pretending.' I said.

'No, look. He's stretched out on the settee.'

I poked my head round the door, and sure enough there he was on the settee, and stretched out was the right expression. It's a big settee but his head was flopping over one arm, and his back legs were on the table by the window. I knew now that my bedroom was the safest place. I could barricade the door and even the incredible hulk wouldn't be able to leap up through the window. So gradually, moving sideways and using Hat for a shield, I made my way upstairs. In the last couple of yards to sanctuary I panicked, and rushed in pulling Hat with me. I was only just in time, for as I slammed the door that dog was off the settee and up the stairs in two strides, and the door shuddered as he flung himself at it. Me and Hat were struggling to get a chest of drawers in front of it. He had another leap at the door and a panel splintered, but by the time he'd gathered himself for another go, the drawers were firmly in place, with my bed wedged in front of them, and me and Hat sitting on it for extra protection.

Hat looked at me, frightened. 'He's been quiet all the afternoon,' she said. She tried to talk to it through the crack in the door, but it snarled and had another go, and so it went on. That was the longest night I've ever spent. I only managed a few hours' sleep while Hat kept watch. Well, after all, it was Hat who brought the dog in the first place, and it was my bedroom.

When I opened my eyes it was light, and Hat was dozing in a chair with a blanket round her shoulders. It was my

Above: Eric played a privte eye in the movie Rotten To The Core, *1965.*

thick blanket, too – no wonder I never got warm. I knelt quietly up in bed, and put my eye to the crack, but I couldn't see the dog. Then I whispered, 'Rex . . . Rex, here boy,' but there was nothing.

Hat came up beside me. 'He's not there,' she said, and after ten minutes we decided that he must have gone, because no dog would have put up with some of the things I called him through that door. Very carefully we took down the barricades and Hat went out on the landing. Then she cautiously went downstairs. At the bottom she stopped abruptly.

I looked around my bedroom door: 'What's happening?' I whispered.

Hat looked back. 'Come down here and see for yourself,' she said.

When I looked round the room I couldn't take it in at first . . . the settee had gone, there was no carpet . . . no telly . . . it seems the only thing that was left was the goldfish bowl and the three pot ducks. Then the penny dropped. We turned to each other and both together we said: 'We've been burgled?' More importantly, they'd taken the dog as well. I know it seems funny now, but we were like a couple of kids on Christmas morning, dancing round as if Mafeking had been relieved again. Then the doorbell rang.

It was a police constable. 'Good morning, madam,' he said, and cleared his throat. 'As you know, there have been a series of burglaries in this area, and it is my duty to warn you of the method they may adopt.' We just stood and grinned at him – he must have thought we were mentally retarded so he hurried up with his duty. 'One of the gang may visit you posing as a detective. He arrives with a large black dog. He arranges to leave the aforesaid animal in order to lull the householder into a false sense of security, but later that evening the gang will arrive and ransack the house while the dog takes care of the occupants. We were still grinning. 'I know, sir, that you may find this very hard to believe, but I can assure you. . . .' He stopped as I gestured grandly at the empty room. He pushed back his helmet: 'It's happened, hasn't it sir?'

I nodded and he took out his notebook.

At that moment Mr Brown strode in: 'Sykes,' he started, 'I really must complain about the noise last night and I . . . He looked at the policeman, then at me and Hat; then he took in the room.

Hat said: 'Look, Mr Brown. We've been burgled.' She was beaming like an African sunrise.

He was astounded. 'You?' he said.

'Yes, us, Mr Brown,' I said triumphantly. 'Cleaned out . . . right out. Oh yes, they know where the stuff is all right. That makes four of us in this district. All top people. But they had to use a dog in ours.

Mr Brown's shoulders sagged. He accepted defeat gracefully I'll say that for him. 'Ah well,' he said, 'let me give you a piece of advice from personal experience. Get on to your insurance people immediately.'

I looked at him blankly. 'Pardon.' I said in a small voice. He looked at me. 'The people you insured the stuff with.'

All the bubble went out of the day. Hat looked at me and I looked at Hat, and Mr Brown saw the look on our faces and started to laugh. And this time it wasn't a chuckle. We heard him laughing all the way to his house, supercilious old fool.

Below: Hattie tries out 'the quail' a whistle blown by using a puff ball.

CHAPTER SEVEN
The Marriage

I came home the other night and I was choked. It has been one of those days that started with the dawn, then got darker. From the minute I clocked on at the factory there had been nothing but hassles, and all because of a toolbox that had gone missing. Last year the firm had a turnover of £15 million, and here they were coming the Gestapo because of a miserable toolbox. We'd all been questioned and even forced to turn out our lockers. We accepted the situation stoically, although time was going by and we were eager to get to work; in fact one man actually started his machine, but such a howl went up he quickly switched it off again.

However, the mood of calm resignation suddenly changed when word went round that they would be docking our pay unless the missing toolbox was returned. That put the cat among the pigeons. The lads had a meeting and it was unanimously decided that if they docked us one penny we were out; there could be no other course open to us except industrial action. We even approached the transport section with regard to their coming out in sympathy, but unfortunately they were already out in sympathy with the packers. That shattered us completely – the transport section's first sympathy should have been with us, because only a month ago we'd been out in sympathy with them over their right to pick up hitch-hikers, and after that dispute had been settled it was tacitly agreed that they would back us in any of our grievances. Now, when we needed them, they were out with the packers of all people – half of them could

hardly speak English, and six months ago their shop steward ran a bicycle shop in Bangladesh. On top of all this they were out because they claimed the stuff used in packing made them cough. Well, that's a laugh. I mean for a start they're bound to cough coming over here to our cold climate, and secondly you can't see two yards in front of you in the packing department for cigarette smoke. And the pathetic thing is the management daren't come the heavy with them or they'd be up before the race relations board.

Anyway the news that we were on our own cast a gloom over the meeting. I'd hoped we'd be back at work by this time because it was my turn to buy a round. Luckily before I could say 'Same again' the foreman walked in and told us the missing toolbox had turned up, just like that. Then he stood there looking round at us, and we just looked back at him. He repeated the news as if he expected a round of applause, or perhaps we'd sing 'For He's a Jolly Good Fellow' and there'd be a mad stampede to the factory to get our machines started up, but we'd already been through too much. He was asked politely to withdraw. Well, he was asked to withdraw. Or rather, told to withdraw – to be quite truthful Jack Cronkle told him to. Anyway he went.

Above: Madge's doughnuts have always been the talk of the neighbourhood and irresistible for Hattie . . .

Opposite: Dressed for a hard day's work on the original version of The Plank, *1967.*

128

The Marriage

Above: 'Many times I've looked down from beachy head to the jagged rocks below, but this it the closest I've ever been to jumping. Madge from the bread shop played by the lovely Joan Sims.' – E.S.

There and then we convened another meeting with regard to compensation re: casting aspersions on our integrity, and by the time the pub closed we had agreed to return to work on receipt of a written apology from the management, and a shorter working week. With this motion in hand we trooped back to the factory canteen for lunch, only to find that being after two o'clock it was officially closed. Straightaway 1 was on a deputation to the management, because although our meeting had taken longer than anticipated we were still entitled under the Factories Act to a lunch break.

The management agreed to approach the canteen staff, so we had to hang about while negotiations went on. This was another disaster because I lost £15 in a poker game, and just when I was hitting a lucky streak a spokesman came in to tell us the canteen had agreed to open for half an hour. We later found out that in return the canteen staff got concessions of double time and an extra holiday; and also just as we walked into the canteen the whistle went for knocking off, so we went out again – nobody in his right mind eats canteen food in his own time.

That's the sort of day it was, and all because of a toolbox – there were still a couple of spanners missing but the management weren't going to make an issue out of that, and you can bet your life I wasn't going to return them. As I walked home I came to the conclusion that I was up to here with the industrial scene. I was so deep in depression I walked into Madge's bread shop. Why I walked in there I'll never really know, because normally I try to avoid her. I mean she's all right, and she makes doughnuts like you dream about, but she fancies me, and deep down in my heart I think there's something wrong with anybody who fancies me. For instance if she sees me pass the shop she'll dash out and thrust a bag of doughnuts in my hand and say: 'For my inner Ricky.' This has been going on for years, and although I'm fond of doughnuts I'd rather she delivered them to the house when I'm out. So why I walked into her shop of my own volition is beyond me.

'Ricky,' she gasped, her eyes lighting up like two currants in a suet pudding.

I smiled weakly. 'A small brown loaf please, Madge.'

'What you on about, you naughty boy? Your sister picked up the bread this morning.'

I glanced through the window across to our house, and I saw the curtain fall back into place. Hat was watching, and she'd seen me in Madge's. So what, and what was I doing here? What prompted me to walk in? I suddenly realized that Madge was leaning across the counter towards me with her eyes closed and a doughnut in her mouth, and I knew what was expected of me, but I wasn't going

Below: Eric with Fanny Carby in Johnny Speight's Curry and Chips.

The Marriage

to bite the other half.

She opened her eyes and looked at me like a fat labrador you've just hit over the head with a shovel: 'Ont oo ike dowuts anino?', which roughly translated without a mouthful of doughnut I took to mean 'Don't you like doughnuts any more?'

'Of course I do, Madge,' and as I said it I had a blinding flash of inspiration. Most of my disasters in life have been triggered by a blinding flash of inspiration, but I never lose faith, and it occurred to me in that split second that doughnuts were the answer. After all I must be one of the greatest living experts on doughnuts, and I knew without a doubt that Madge was a genius when it came to creating them.

'What's the matter, Ricky?' she pleaded.

I ignored her and paced up and down while my imagination took hold. Brie cheese was known worldwide; Chateauneuf du Pape, Aylesbury duck – why should not Madge's doughnuts be prized worldwide? She could be another Colonel Sanders' Kentucky Fried Chicken. It only needed a man who was intelligent and willing to work at it, a man with drive and imagination, and here I was. Fate had turned my footsteps into Madge's shop. I'd be free of the factory and its disputes, labour relations and petty squabbling. Already I was planning. First I'd get Madge's doughnuts known around the district, then the country, leading into the EEC; but America was the big one – they practically lived on doughnuts out there. I stopped pacing and faced Madge.

'Oh, Ricky,' she gushed, and wobbled all over.

I looked at the sugar round her mouth and the bit of jam on her nose, and I shuddered. Was it worth it? But I dismissed the thought quickly. 'Madge,' I said. 'Your doughnuts.'

Straightaway she was on the defensive. 'What's the matter with 'em?'

'There's nothing the matter with them, Madge. They're delicious, brilliant works of art.'

She looked at me sideways, wondering if I was pulling her leg.

'Your doughnuts, Madge, are marvellous, but who buys them?'

She shrugged.

'I'll tell you who buys them – a few scruffs, just yobboes in this area, and they don't really appreciate them.'

She looked sharply at me.

'They don't Madge. I've seen them giving 'em to kids.'

I paused to give her a chance to say 'So what?', and she did.

'Listen, Madge, your doughnuts are not being exploited. You should be getting orders from all over England, you should be inundated, then there's the EEC, all the Benelux countries; now there's a market for you. Do you know they can't get doughnuts in France? They have to eat patisserie, and what's more they eat it for breakfast. They're not like us with bacon and eggs – they like patisserie. So can you imagine what they'd do with a good doughnut?'

Above: Hattie joined the ITMA team at the BBC in 1947.

Opposite: Eric the athlete in Sykes And A Walk*, 1963.*

132

The Marriage

'That's all very well,' she said, 'but I've only got one pair of hands.'

'Ah, yes. Now you have; but Hat's doing nothing.'

She looked at me blankly. 'I don't know what you're on about,' she said.

I leaned over the counter. 'What I'm trying to say, Madge, is this: you need someone behind you, someone to push you.'

She sniggered coyly and touched me playfully on the nose. 'Cheeky,' she said.

'I'm serious, Madge.'

She stared at me for a moment, then she placed her hands flatly on the counter and her eyes went dull. 'You're playing a game with me aren't you? You're having a bit of fun.'

I shook my head. 'I'm not, Madge, honestly. If I wanted a bit of fun I wouldn't be here, would I?'

She jerked upright.

'What I mean is, well you probably think I'm a bit pushy, but – er – well, I'm not going to beat about the bush. What it boils down to is, why don't you and me go into partnership?'

Her mouth fell open, and a split second later her top dentures sagged, but being a gentleman I turned away. 'Fartnershiff', she croaked, too stunned to realize that her top set was still out of kilter.

I picked up a loaf and pretended to examine it so she could adjust herself.

'You and me in partnership?' she said, and I knew it was safe to look at her.

'Why not? The way you make doughnuts, and my brains, it's a natural combination.'

Her eyes glistened and I knew I had her.

I went on: 'It's funny, isn't it,' I said. 'You look for something all your life, and here it is on your own doorstep.'

A tear rolled down her cheek, and she brushed it away leaving a black smear. 'Oh, Ricky! I'll have to think it over,' she blubbed, and wiped mascara down her other cheek.'

'That's it, Madge,' I said, and patted her hand. 'Think it over.' Then I hurried out of the shop – I didn't want any-body catching me in there. What with the jam on her nose, the sugar and the black cheeks, she was beginning to look like a Picasso.

Hat wasn't too excited when I told her the news; in fact she was decidedly lukewarm. 'How can you buy half of Madge's shop?' she said. 'You need bread for that.' Then, realizing what she'd said, she fell back laughing. 'You need bread for that,' she spluttered.

I looked at her coldly.

'Don't you get it Eric? Bread.'

I turned away and I knew how Michelangelo must have felt dashing home excited to tell his mother: 'Mamma mia, they want me – Michelangelo – to paint the Sistine Chapel.'

And his mother calmly doing her tapestry, saying: 'Well, before you start that, the back bedroom wants doing.'

Hat had finished laughing now, but I could see she was wondering who she could tell it to.

'I'm not buying the shop,' I said. 'I'm merely going into partnership with her.'

She was scornful. 'You in a bread shop?' You can't even make toast.'

'I won't be actually in the bread shop as such, will I? I'll be Head of Sales.'

'Oh,' she said. 'A delivery boy.'

'Listen, Hat. I know it's only a small bread shop now, but it's a goldmine. Madge's doughnuts, I mean you can't beat 'em. You know how good they are – I bought you one for your birthday. Remember? With a candle in the middle. And you said then, if they weren't so fattening you could eat them morning, noon and night.'

'It wasn't much of a birthday present, was it? After all, I bought you a thermal vest.'

'Never mind the birthdays,' I snapped. 'Madge is a genius, but no business sense. Well, that's where I come in. I intend to put her doughnuts on the map.' And with that I made to go upstairs.

Opposite: Eric and Hattie help to free a crane which stuck in the mud during filming by the Thames in 1974.

Above: Sykes And A Bandage, *in black and white, 1961.*

'Has Madge agreed to this?'

I leaned over the banister. 'How can she refuse? She won't turn her nose up at a fur coat and a few million in the bank, not to mention the Queen's Award.'

As I ran the bath I felt good about that Queen's Award bit. If there was any hesitation on Madge's part that would swing it. She was very pro-royal, as we all were – she'd even taken a bag of doughnuts to the palace on the Queen's Jubilee, but she'd had to leave them with the policeman on the gate. And here I take my hat off to our police: he said he would deliver them personally as soon as he'd walked the

Corgis. I lay back happily in the warm, sudsy water, oblivious to the dark storm clouds gathering. Half an hour later I was still in a semi-comatose state in the bath while downstairs Hat was opening the door to a freshly made-up and breathless Madge.

'Oh hello, Madge. Come in. Would you like some tea? I'm just having a cup.'

Madge smiled and sat down on the edge of the chair, as if she was waiting to see the doctor.

Hat pointed to the ceiling. 'Eric's in the bath.'

Madge blushed at the thought. Hat handed her a cup of tea, and settled down on the settee. They smiled at each other, then looked down at their cups, then they looked at each other and smiled again. Hat decided to jump in at the deep end.

'Eric's told me all about it.'

Madge spluttered on a mouthful of tea. Here was Hattie coming straight to the nub of the matter, and they hadn't even discussed the weather. She put her cup on the table and joined Hat on the settee. 'Hattie,' she started. 'You may not believe this, but I never said a word. The first I knew of it was this evening.'

'That's all right, Madge. But are you sure – I mean really sure – you're doing the right thing? After all, Eric hasn't had a lot of experience.'

'I know that, Hattie. But that's what makes it right because . . .' and here she looked away, '. . . well, to tell you the truth I haven't had many chances either.'

Hat put her arm round her. 'But don't you see, Madge? That shop is your whole life.'

'I know, and I want to share it with Eric.' She looked earnestly at Hat. 'You don't mind, do you? What I mean is, he always led me to believe that you were against him getting married.'

It was Hat's turn to splutter – well, splutter is hardly the word; a jet of tea shot across the room that would have done credit to a fully grown whale. Madge pumped her vigorously on the back. Hat struggled to her feet, fighting for breath. 'Sorry, Madge,' she gasped. 'I thought you said "married".'

Madge blushed. 'Isn't it marvellous? I've always felt that doughnuts were half an excuse to see me, but I never thought he'd ever get serious.'

Hat flopped back on the settee. 'Married? He actually asked you?'

'Yes. Typical Eric, he didn't come straight out with it, he said a partnership for life – well, you know what he's like.'

Hat blew her nose.

'Don't worry, Hattie. I'll take care of him, I promise.'

Hat turned to her and took her hands. 'Madge, are you sure that that's what he meant – I mean to get married?'

Madge smiled. 'It's not what he said, it was in his eyes . . he's never looked at me like that before.'

Hat tried again. 'Yes I know, Madge – .'

But Madge wasn't listening. She broke in: 'Hattie, you know what people round here are like. Let's keep it dark for the time being. Let's not mention it to anybody.'

Hat shook her head sadly. 'I think we should tell Eric.' And at that moment I made an appearance down the stairs.

'Hello, Madge,' I said. 'Thought it over yet?'

Madge bounced off the settee and flung herself at me. 'Ricky, oh Ricky,' and she gave me a kiss on the cheek. Well, I say a kiss, but it wasn't human. I made a mental note that next time our sink was blocked to hell with the plumber, I'd send for Madge. I looked up into her face, and that was odd because I'm taller than she is; then I realized she was

Below: The colour version of Bandage, *1974.*

wearing her corsets, and they tend to take her in at the middle and add nine inches to her height.

'For goodness sake, Madge,' I gasped. 'I haven't had my tea yet.'

She let me go then, and minced to a chair. 'Tell me again what you said in the shop.'

'Yes, go on, Eric. Tell her again,' said Hat, and handed me a tumbler half-full of whisky.

I stared at her in amazement. Hat doesn't mind me having the odd night out with the lads or even pouring myself a snifter at home providing I'm not well, but she has never ever poured me a drink of her own free will, except for that time when I fell off my bike, and then she rubbed it on my leg. I raised the glass to Madge and said:

'Here's to us.'

'Oh, Ricky,' she said, and sniffed into a minute hankie. That took some of the powder off, and there she was with a red nose again. She reminded me of an overdressed snowman with a cherry in the middle of its face. I knew then that I was going to have to earn my first million, and resolved to spend most of my time on sales trips abroad.

I took a sip of whisky, and it caught me in the back of the throat. Hat hadn't even put water in it. She led me to a chair. 'I think you'd better sit,' she said. 'I don't want you hurting yourself when you fall down.'

I looked at her quizzically. 'On one drink?'

'It's not the drink I'm worried about,' she said, and inclined her head meaningfully towards Madge.

Something stirred in my bowels, and it wasn't just the whisky. I looked across at Madge and she was sitting on the edge of the chair leaning forwards eagerly bright button eyes watching my every move. I swear if I'd thrown a stick she would have fetched it.

Hat jogged my elbow. 'Go on,' she said. 'Tell us again what you said in the shop.'

I pulled myself together. 'The first thing we've got to do, Madge, is put your doughnuts on the map.' I wasn't sure, but I thought I saw some of the eagerness go out of her eyes. I pressed on. 'While I was having a bath just now it came to me. We have to use the media: TV commercials, that's the hammer.' I started to pace up and down. 'You've seen chocolate ads on the telly, haven't you? Adverts for nuts, cream, pork sausages. But when have you ever seen one for doughnuts?' I looked at them both triumphantly.

Madge looked at me earnestly. 'I'm going to try to make you happy, Ricky.'

I leaned forward, hands on the table. 'And I'm going to make you happy too, Madge.'

I could see she was about to get up and probably leap at me again, so I quickly resumed my pacing. 'A doughnut commercial,' I said, 'and it has to hit 'em.' Out of the corner of my eye I noticed with relief that she'd settled again. 'And what sells a commercial? Come on, what sells a commercial?' I didn't expect an answer, so I carried on:

'Sex.'

They both blushed.

'No. Face up to it,' I said, 'It's sex. There's always a pretty girl in it; a fellow smoking a pipe, and there's always a girl next to him going "Ooooh"; then there's the "Oh mummy, what makes your hands so soft?" That's not her mother, it's a dolly bird, and they're only selling detergent.'

Hat nodded in agreement. 'It they're advertising cars, it's always a pretty girl that gets in and drives off.'

'Right,' I said. 'And I bet if it was a surgical truss some Lulu would hold it against her cheek and say, "He never wears anything else." '

'I've never seen that one,' said Hat.

I shook my head impatiently. 'I'm speaking hypothetically, but I'll tell you something – if it was advertised there'd be many a fit young man walking around in a surgical truss, so they could impress their girlfriends.'

'It costs money to put on a commercial,' said Madge.

'Ah yes, but all depending on how expensive you want to go. I mean if you want Sophia Loren lying on a beach in the Bahamas eating a doughnut it'll set you back a bit, but this is what I had in mind....' I was so wrapped up in my thoughts I pulled my chair closer to Madge and I didn't even notice her put her hand on my knee. 'We can get a

•

camera anywhere – that's no problem – then we can shoot the commercial right here in this house.'

Hat looked round the room sceptically.

'Listen. We shoot it close, a young couple sitting at a table – 'I made a square with my finger as if I was looking through a television set. 'We zoom in – chequered cloth, mandolins playing in the background, a bottle of Chianti and we could be in the south of France.'

Madge cleared her throat. 'Ricky, you are Church of England, aren't you?'

I looked at her puzzled. I couldn't see how two people sitting at a table smiling at a doughnut could possibly be blasphemous.

Hat answered the question. 'Oh yes, we're Church of England and always have been.'

Above: 'This was one of our giggle sesions. It was a dress rehearsal before the show. I can assure you that by the time the curtain went up they'd found a hat that fitted me.

Madge nodded. 'That's all right, then. I knew you weren't Catholic, because they're usually ardent and I've never seen you go to church. I mean, you don't have to go to church if you're C of E, but Catholics are very strict on that sort of thing.'

Hat was quick to agree. 'Too strict, if you ask me. I mean Eric and I used to go to church before they had *Stars on Sunday*, and then we lapsed, but even so the vicar will always give you a "Good morning" or raise his hat. Whatsis-name, Eric? Er – Reverend something.'

Madge shook her head. 'I've never met him. I'm chapel

myself, on the corner of Balaclava Road.'

'Oh yes, I know it,' said Hat. 'It's a bingo hall now.'

Madge's mouth fell open. 'Fancy! I never knew that.'

Hat leaned forward to Madge. 'Have you noticed the young Catholic priest who calls on the McNamaras?'

Madge's lips pursed. 'I know the one, red-faced and always has a boil going on the back of his neck.'

'That's the one,' said Hat. 'He always has a sort of musty smell – religious. Know what I mean?'

Madge nodded sagely. 'It's unction water.'

I coughed for attention. 'Can we shelve the theological discussion till later. After all, I can't see what its got to do with me and Madge.'

They both looked at each other conspiratorially, then Hat

Opposite: Those Darling Young Men In Their Jaunty Jalopies, *also known as* Monte Carlo Or Bust, *1969.*

Above: Eric with Scilla Gabel in Village Of Daughters, *MGM, 1962.*

turned to me. 'Go on, Eric. There's this young couple sitting at a table in the south of France?'

I spoke uncertainly. 'Thats it, with a bottle of Chianti.' I stopped. Surely it couldn't be unction water; unction had something to do with ointment.

Hat brought me out of my reverie. 'Go on, Eric.' She was looking at me in a strange way, as if I was her eight-year-old son doing well in a talent contest.

I pressed on. 'Well, there's this couple, you see, soft candlelight, the man leans across the table, takes a box out of his pocket like an engagement ring. She opens it, and instead of a ring it's a doughnut.'

I stood back waiting for a reaction, it wasn't exactly encouraging. Hat said: 'Would you like some more tea?' and

Madge said: 'No, thank you.'

'What d'you think?' I said. 'A great little commercial, and so far it's cost us nothing.'

'Actors aren't cheap, you know,' said Hat. 'David Niven got £50,000 for coffee beans.'

I sauntered to the window and looked out. 'I wasn't thinking of David Niven. What's wrong with me doing it?'

There was a snigger and I whipped round, but they were both looking at the floor. 'I won't cost anything. Well, a token fee – and we can soon find a young dolly bird who'll give her eye teeth to be on the telly.'

'In that case you're not playing the man,' snapped Madge.

Hat was examining her fingernails. The silence was so dense I wondered why the clock hadn't driven me mad before now. Then somewhere close by I heard the plaintive cry of a lonely cat, but then Madge went beetroot red and I realized it was her stomach acting up.

Hat broke the silence. 'It's all very well, Eric, but you can't just go on telly like that. You have to be an actor.'

'Wrong,' I said, and played my ace. 'Not when you're advertising your own product. Look at Freddie Laker -he does his own commercial, and I've never seen him top the bill at the National Theatre.'

Hat jumped in eagerly. 'Well then, Madge can play the girl.'

Below: Eric lends a helping hand to Valerie Bell and Derek Nimmo, 1965.

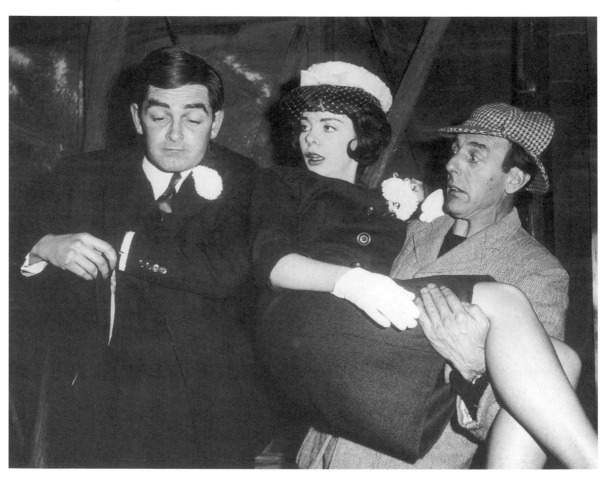

Madge brightened.

I tried to make light of it. 'Well, not really. The doughnut is supposed to be an engagement between two people having dinner, it's not a plug for meals on wheels.'

'Thank you very much,' said Madge. 'I'll remember that remark.'

I tried to mollify her. 'I'm not getting at you, Madge, but you haven't really done anything in the acting line, have you? And I mean, with all due respect, I was in *The Pirates of Penzance*.'

Hat looked sharply at me, but I flashed her a warning glance. I hadn't actually told a lie, but being with the local amateur operatic society as a scene shifter doesn't carry the same ring of authority.

'What I'm trying to say, Madge, is this. The doughnut commercial isn't finalized. It's just off the top of my head and –'

She broke in impatiently: 'Yes, yes. I know all that, Ricky. I appreciate the way you think, I've always admired you for your mind – there isn't a week goes by without Hattie telling me how you're thinking about things and that. But what I'm saying is, first things first.'

'I agree, Madge,' I said. 'I'm sorry I was so far ahead of you, but as you say, I have a brain like quicksilver. I mean, in my mind I've already got a chain of doughnut stands all over the Middle West, while you're still wondering if you've left the gas on.'

'Oh Ricky, what I mean is – ', but I silenced her.

'As you say, Madge, first things first. We put the doughnuts in coloured bags –'

Madge sprang to her feet. 'Bugger the doughnuts, Ricky. What about us?'

There was a stunned silence. Hat quickly glanced out of the window to see if anyone was passing. Madge looked wildly at me, then dissolved in a flood of tears. I didn't know what to do. I floundered helplessly. I mean, I can go a bit when I'm with the lads, but I never swear at home.

'I'm sorry,' she blubbed. 'I didn't mean to say that, but you will keep on about my doughnuts.' Her voice rose. 'But

what about us, you and me?'

'I'm coming to that, Madge', I said coldly, desperately trying to regain control, but also to let her know that as master in my own house I didn't condone bad language. 'Now,' I continued. 'We put the doughnuts in coloured bags, and on every bag in big letters we have the name Sykes and Kettlewell Ltd.'

She stared at me blankly.

'Well, I mean, Madge – it sounds better than Kettlewell and Sykes Ltd, and you have to think of these things.'

She looked at me coyly, finger going round the top of her teacup. 'What about Sykes and Son Ltd?' She sniffed.

It was my turn to stand open-mouthed, I looked at Hat, but she was no help. She just raised her eyebrows at me as if to say 'Follow that', and strolled to the window, whistling tunelessly to herself. I knew that affected nonchalance of Hat's; it usually presages me going into the cart head-first.

I probed gently: 'Sykes and Son Ltd?'

Madge sat upright. 'I'm not too old, you know.' She blushed again.

I shrugged at Hat for enlightenment, but she was still pretending to gaze idly out of the window. Her hands were going pat-pat-pat behind her back, another tell-tale sign meaning 'Get out of that'. The warning bells which had been going in my head for some time were louder now – not only warning bells but flashing lights, sirens and foghorns. Madge broke the spell.

'You do like children, don't you, Ricky?'

'Of course I like children, Madge,' I said fervently, and I believed it. I do like children as long as they don't get too close.

Madge took hold of my hand and looked directly into my eyes. 'And if for some reason or other we're not blessed, we can always adopt one.'

A trickle of perspiration ran from my armpit – adopt a child? That's a bit like having a hangover without the pleasure of getting stoned. She squeezed my fingers and I winced. The thought flashed across my mind that had I been a violinist there'd be no performance that night. 'You can't

Above: Eric with his old sparring partner Jimmy Edwards in TV's television adaptation of Charley's Aunt.

adopt a child just like that, Madge. You have to be married.'

'Isn't that what you want, Ricky?' she said softly.

I snatched my hand away. 'Married?' I gulped.

'It wasn't my idea, you naughty boy. It was you who came into my shop and proposed.'

The whole jigsaw fell into place in one horrific moment. I reached automatically for the bottle, but Hat was already pouring me one. 'Married,' I said, as if it was a new word in the dictionary. 'Listen, Madge. I'm offering you a chance to make millions, shops all over the world, cars, mink coats, but I'll have to concentrate. Good grief, you should know it doesn't pay to mix business with – 'I stopped short and looked at her, and I couldn't bring myself to say 'pleasure'. I tried a reasonable approach. 'You know, Madge, much as I'd like it, let's shelve the marriage.' She half rose, so I rushed on: '. . . for the time being.' She settled down again. 'First of all let me make you internationally famous, Madge, and when I've made you a millionaire then we'll talk about marriage. After all, Madge, I have my pride. I don't want to come to you with nothing.' I looked at her earnestly.

'Ricky, oh Ricky. I have a little bit put by – it'll be

enough to see things through.'

I turned away. 'It's a tempting thought, Madge, but I'm going to be strong for both of us. If I married you on that basis it would dog me for the rest of my days – a kept man.'

'But Ricky, once we're married you'll be able to go ahead with those marvellous ideas of yours, putting the doughnuts in coloured bags and things.'

I shook my head sadly. 'I have to be honest with you, Madge. There's always a risk in business – for instance, let's suppose that my ideas didn't work out. There's always that possibility, you know.'

She came to me and spoke softly. 'Yes, Ricky, but we'd be married.'

I gulped another drink to disguise the spasm of revulsion that must have swept my face. I tried another tack. 'Look, Madge, if I was an ordinary sort of bloke – you know, Mr Average, dull, mundane – I'd marry you like a shot, because let's face it, Madge – you're a good catch.'

Hat looked over her shoulder at me, but apart from that she just stood by and listened to me digging a big pit for myself. Madge just sat stony-faced.

I began to pace up and down in the hope that somebody else would say something. Why didn't I just come right out and say, 'I'm sorry, Madge, forget the marriage'? But I wasn't sure of her reaction, and I'd already felt that grip of hers; if it became more physical I could be marked for life, on top of which all my schemes of selling doughnuts to the jet set would come to nothing. As I thought about this I realized that already I was going lukewarm on the idea. I tried again.

'Look, Madge, marriage isn't just a question of saying I do and handing over a couple of quid to the registrar. There's more to it than that. There's emotions involved.'

Hat gave an 'Oh my God' look at the ceiling, but Madge still sat there, mouth set like a tiny minus sign.

I slumped into a chair, feeling very old. I thought about my marvellous scheme with distaste. Who wants to fly about all over the place, living out of a suitcase, eating foreign food? I had better things to do with my life than dashing from door to door with a bag of doughnuts. My thoughts

went longingly to the factory – the banter and comradeship of the lads, the fun we had with the packers, who weren't a bad lot. I took another swig of my whisky, and I thought of the day the foreman took me to see the nursing sister when Clydesdale dropped that monkey wrench on my foot – fatherly but firm, as a good foreman should be, and the board room – they were a pretty decent lot, and it wasn't their fault they happened to be in management. I realized that Madge was talking.

Above: Eric with Anna Quayle in Johnny Speight's Spate of Speight *for Thames TV, 1969.*

'Well, Ricky, what is it to be? A wedding, or is this it?'

'Madge,' I started, but she was in no mood for reasonable debate.

'I want to know, Ricky, because if the wedding's off I'll have to phone cousin Rupert.'

The name hit me in the stomach. I'd seen Rupert several times, but only in the newspapers, either full face and wanted, an identikit picture suspect, or being hustled into a side door with a blanket over his head. Madge often brought him up in the conversation and talked as if she was a bit ashamed of him, but I reckoned if you were ashamed of something you kept quiet about it, and I figured she used him as a deterrent. I felt trapped.

'What's your cousin Rupert got to do with it?' I asked, although I knew the answer.

She blushed a little. 'I don't have much family, so I felt I had to ask him to the wedding,' she said.

'When?' I asked.

'Just before I came out I phoned him.'

Hat turned from the window. 'And what date did you have in mind for the wedding?' she asked in a strange voice.

Madge shrugged. 'Well, I don't know how long these things take. I mean the registrar was very nice, and took our names and things –'

I struggled to my feet. The whisky was making me reckless. 'You gave our names?' I said. 'I don't mind you giving your name, but you've no right to give mine – it's private.'

Madge looked at me helplessly. 'Well, he asked me, didn't he? And you have to give him names. I mean, he can't stand up with a blindfold on and say "Do you, Mr X, take Miss Y for your lawfully-wedded wife".' She spread her hands and appealed to Hat, then she came over to me and smiled. What I mean is, I assumed she was smiling but her face was slightly out of focus, and it was the kind of look one has when one is trying to unscrew a tight bottle top. Her voice came from a long way off. 'You'll thank me when we're sunning ourselves on the beach at Majorca.'

'Majorca –', I repeated, with effort.

Again her voice floated to me from outer space: 'Week in Majorca for our honeymoon. I'll get the tickets tomorrow.'

I began to get angry. 'You haven't been dragging your feet, have you?' I said.

Madge's amicable expression fell off, and I had a quick flash of Rupert coming up the street with a couple of heavies, but the whisky kept me going.

'Well, good grief, Madge. I just shop into your pop to talk about –' I stopped suddenly. I realized that I'd said 'shop into your pop' and I hoped they hadn't noticed it. I carried on

Above: Not the sort of partnership Eric had in mind – Sykes And A Marriage, *1975.*

carefully. 'I pop into your shop this afternoon to talk about doughnuts, and all of a sudden I'm an old married man.'

Hat spoke nonchalantly: 'Adam took the apple.'

I swung my gaze round to her. It passed her slightly, then swung back and docked. 'Don't give me that. I'm a very eligible bachelor, whereas Adam didn't have a lot of choice, did he? So don't start quoting the scriptures to me, madam. Don't forget I was the one who nearly went into a monastery.'

Hat stifled a smile. My thoughts tumbled back to that period in my life when I was about to reject society. In fact I'd already written off to Newton Abbot, but then I saw a TV documentary where they showed the monks getting up at four o'clock in the morning, and that put me off. I realized that Madge was talking again.

'What's it to be, Ricky?'

I slumped down in the chair. 'OK, Madge. You want an answer, and I'll give you one. I'll agree to marriage only on certain terms.'

'Oh, Ricky,' she gushed. 'Anything you say,' and knelt down in front of me, which was a reckless thing to do because I was in no condition to help her up again.

'Right, Hat. Get a notebook and pen and you'll be a witness. OK?'

Hat took a notebook out of the drawer and sat down next to me rather anxiously.

'One,' I said. She wrote down 'one'. 'My sister Hattie will come with us on our honeymoon.'

Hat glanced sharply at Madge, then wrote it down.

Madge gaped. 'Oh, Ricky. I've only arranged tickets for two.'

'Well then, you and Hat go,' I said.

Hat protested, but I held up my hand for silence.

'It'll do you good. You need a change.'

Madge struggled to her feet like an elephant with Cyril Smith in the howdah. She straightened her skirt. 'If you don't go, I'm not going either,' she said.

Below: 'Ronnie Fraser, a very funny man, in a scene from The Merchant Of Venice . . . or maybe it was something else. Whatever, it's certainly Ronnie Fraser.' – E.S.

The Marriage

I looked at Hat. 'OK, Hat, it's you and me. We could do with a holiday.'

'I won't be a party to it,' snapped Madge.

'OK then, baby. That's the marriage out. Now, any other business?'

Madge was contrite. 'No, I mean we'll just cancel the honeymoon. We don't have to have one.'

I realized she was backing down and my confidence increased. I turned to Hat: 'No honeymoon.' She dutifully jotted it down. I looked up at the ceiling for inspiration. 'Clause two . . . ,' I waited till the pencil stopped. 'Although Madge Kettlewell and I the above-mentioned will be married . . . ,' I waited to let Hat catch up. 'Although Madge etc. etc. will be married, I will continue to live here with my aforementioned sister Harriet.'

At this they were both at me. 'Oh, no', 'Wait a minute', 'Hang on', etc.

I held up my arms. 'OK, OK. I'll amend that to four nights a week.'

Hat looked at Madge, and Madge said: 'Four nights a week?'

'Yes, and that doesn't include club night and bingo.'

'Oh, Rick.'

Hat wrote 'club night and bingo'. I was beginning to focus better and I had the feeling I was in complete command of the situation. 'Clause three' – Madge was pacing up and down now so I pressed on quickly. 'During which times I shall be domiciled at Madge's etc. etc. we shall have separate bedrooms.'

Madge stopped in her tracks. 'Separate bedrooms?'

'Separate bedrooms,' I replied, 'and with locks.'

Hat stared at me in amazement. She's always thought of me as a kindly gentle person. It wouldn't do her any harm to glimpse the tiger in me now and again.

Madge stepped forward: 'No woman in her right mind would accept these terms.'

I eyed her coldly for a moment. 'Well, Madge. That's it.'

Her fists clenched and the veins came up on her neck.

'That's it, is it?' she hissed. 'That's it.' Her voice strengthened. 'No honeymoon, sleep here, club nights and bingo.' She flounced to the door and flung it open, and she turned, breathing heavily, her big chest going up and down. I wondered how the buttons in front managed to hold things together. In a sarcastic tone of voice she said: 'Will it be alright if I give you a kiss on the cheek every Christmas?' Then she went and slammed the door so hard that two pictures fell down.

We sat in silence for a moment, then Hat started to pick up The Stag at Bay. 'Well,' she said, 'you got out of that', and I felt there was a note of admiration in the way she said it.

I stood up and smiled grimly at her. 'Don't worry, Hat, you have to be up early to get one over on this kiddie.' I swirled the whisky in the glass and drained it. 'She doesn't frighten me with Rupert,' I said. 'I'm not a violent man, Hat, but you've never really seen me when I'm roused.'

She looked at me over her shoulder. I put the glass down and thumped a fist into the palm of my hand. 'Let Rupert come the old GBR with me, and it'll be Goodnight Vienna.' I went to do a karate kick but unfortunately my foot caught in the rug and I fell over the settee.

Hat looked at me gravely. 'Eric, you're drunk,' she said.

'I'm not drunk. If you will leave rugs lying about all over the floor –Then the phone rang. Hat said: 'Hello? Oh hello, Madge.

'Yes, but . . . yes, but – ' She put the phone down, then turned to me slowly. 'Madge has agreed to your terms.'

I lay back on the rug and groaned, and that's where I found myself in the morning with a blanket over me.

So three weeks later I found myself sitting in the front pew at St Bartholomew's in a morning suit, and heavily sedated. Corky sat next to me in his number one uniform, a row of medals and white gloves. He was to be my best man. It had been a twilight three weeks blurred by scotch, although I vaguely remember two escape attempts and an appeal to the doctor to have me certified medically unfit for marriage. Nevertheless here I was in the condemned seat – pale, aloof, half-cut and holding onto a billiard cue. That night I was in the semi-finals of the snooker competition

and I intended, come what may, to stick rigidly to my contract, and tonight at eight o'clock I'd be hot favourite to go into the finals. The vicar looked at his watch, then sauntered over with his white wedding face on. He coughed discreetly and asked me wouldn't I be more comfortable if I left the cue in the vestry, to which I replied no I wouldn't. I could imagine the spotty choirboys belting the living daylights out of each other, which would scarcely do the cue much good.

He smiled apologetically. 'They're usually a bit late,' he said. 'A bride's prerogative.' He coughed discreetly again, and withdrew.

I fervently hoped she was late. I had a sudden vision of the headlines: 'The late Miss Kettlewell on the day she was to be married . . . Miss Madge Kettlewell stepped under a bus while making her way to church.' I broke off the thought guiltily, but my thoughts had a habit of escalating . . . 'Her bridegroom-to-be, Mr Eric Sykes, amateur snooker

Above: Valentine Dyall with Eric and Hattie in Sykes And A Hypnotist, *1964.*

champion, was heartbroken. Condolences have been pouring in: Cliff Thorburn said "I hope it doesn't affect his game", whilst Hurricane Higgins is reported to have said "He was always a hard man to beat, and I know he will bear his great loss as the champion he will undoubtedly become."' I was in the middle of a eulogy from Ray Reardon when I realised that Corky was speaking.

'The bride's always late,' he said. 'It's part of the trick, you see. They can't wait to get you to the altar, then the minute you're there, wallop, the shackles go on and you work to their tempo.'

I ignored him. It was at Madge's insistence that he was best man – it was insurance against me skiving off, and I know for a fact that had I shown the slightest inclination to scarper he wouldn't have hesitated to use the handcuffs. In return he's on the 'free' list at Madge's bread shop. How can I respect a man who'll sell out his friend for a handful of doughnuts? On top of all this, I wasn't impressed by his performance at our house before we left. It was about 2.30, and I was sitting there washing down a few Librium with a glass of whisky, when there was a knock on the door, it was a knock I didn't recognize – it wasn't Madge's coy tit-tit, and it wasn't Corky's jocular rat-tat-tat-tat-tat-tat-tat, nor Mr Brown's peremptory command. This was two thumps with the side of a fist that jarred the glass against my teeth. Hat timidly opened the door and in came this man, not all that tall, but chunky. His face had had more stitches in it than my old trousers.

He nodded expressionlessly. 'Rupert,' he said.

I slowly got to my feet while Hat introduced herself. Then she told him who I was. He just nodded and sat down.

Hat gulped: 'Would you like a cup of tea?' she asked tentatively.

To my great, surprise, he nodded again. 'Lebbod wid doh sugar,' he said.

'Lemon?' said Hat, startled. He just looked at her and she scurried into the kitchen.

Immediately I felt embarrassed with my glass of scotch, and the bottle on the table. I motioned towards it. 'Medicine,' I said, with an apologetic smile. 'It's for my leg.' Then I limped to another seat as far away from him as possible.

His eyes never left me and I noticed several bulges in his double-breasted jacket – a revolver? rope? a hatchet? He could have anything concealed in there, or perhaps he was just a lumpy person. Hat came in with the tea. He nodded at her and took the cup, which looked the size of a thimble in his hand.

The silence was broken by rat-tat-tat-tat-tat-tat-tat, and Corky arrived. 'Well, well, well! And how's the happy bridegroom today?' He smiled hugely and rubbed his gloved hands together.

As soon as Rupert saw the uniform he casually got up and pretended to poke the fire, which incidentally wasn't even lit. All the time he was watching Corky through the mirror over the mantelpiece.

Hat smiled nervously. 'You haven't met Madge's cousin Rupert, have you?'

Corky smiled. 'I haven't had that pleasure, sir.' He stepped forward a pace, then stopped dead in his tracks as if he'd walked into an electrified fence. 'Rupert', he croaked.

Rupert turned and evidently decided there was no threat, so he put the poker down and resumed his seat.

Corky was white and dithering, and seemed to be having difficulty in knowing what to do with his hands. 'Pleased to know you,' he flushed. 'Course I'm not in your line. Traffic control, me.' He smiled nervously. 'All the lads at the station have a great respect for you – professional, that's what you are, and they all respect that. And if there's anything I can do anytime I – er,' he floundered and wiped his mouth on his handkerchief. 'Anything at all, Constable Turnbull's the name, and your cousin Madge she'll tell you, always keep a special eye on her shop, don't I, Hattie?'

Hat turned away. Even she couldn't stand this abject grovelling. I'm sure if Rupert had said 'Lie down while I walk all over you', Corky would have said 'certainly, sir', and not only would he be smiling as Rupert walked over him, he'd be guiding his feet.

'Anybody round here will tell you I'm more of a father figure than a constable.' He wiped his lips again. 'Don't forget, anything I can do, if you're ever in this district, park where you like, I'll sort it out and if there isn't a place give us a ring and I'll have somebody towed away.'

I looked at him searchingly. He wasn't joking – if Rupert parked anywhere in this district, when he returned to drive away the car would not only be ticket-free, but washed, waxed and polished. Fortunately the wedding car arrived at that moment, which saved the constable further embarrassment, and here we were now at St Bartholomew's

Meanwhile at 28 Sebastopol Terrace Madge was parading up and down in her wedding dress, a glass of gin in her hand

and a flush to her cheeks that showed it wasn't her first.

'Do you like it?' she primped.

Rupert, on his fifth cup of tea with 'lebbod', put a finger inside his collar impatiently.

'It looks lovely, Madge,' said Hat, 'but I really think we ought to go now.'

'Oh, he'll wait a bit. I've waited long enough.' She drained her glass and poured another one.

Hat looked at the clock: five past three – they were twenty minutes late already. 'It's all very well, Madge, but you don't know Eric. He'll only wait so long.'

Madge smiled secretly. 'And you don't know me,' she said. 'Constable Turnbull's looking after him, and he knows which side his bread's buttered on. Ricky will be there when I arrive if the constable has to nail his feet to the floor.'

Rupert fidgeted. 'Cub od, Badge. I've got work to do.'

Hat nodded. 'Yes, come on, Madge. How do you think Eric feels sitting there?'

Madge pondered, then she knocked back the gin and poured another. Rupert and Hat exchanged glances and she giggled. 'He'll be all right,' said Madge. 'I'll make it up to him this evening. We'll have a lovely party.'

Hat was on her feet. 'Oh no, Madge. You can't tonight, it's his club night.'

Madge's face fell. 'He's not going to abide by those stupid rules, is he?'

Hat looked at her straight. 'Well, he will tonight. He's in the semi-finals of the snooker championship.'

Madge appealed to Rupert. 'But he can't play snooker tonight.'

Rupert looked away. 'I like sdooker.'

Three miles away, at St Bartholomew's, Corky and I had just sat through our third wedding. The vicar came back up the aisle, brushing confetti from his surplice. He cleared his throat. 'I wonder – shouldn't you give your bride a ring?'

Corky patted his breast pocket. 'Don't worry, vicar. I've got that here.'

The vicar was perplexed for a moment, then he pulled

Above: Corky about to arrest Eric for murdering another fine tune.

himself together. 'No. I mean, shouldn't you telephone and see what's happened?'

'Oh,' smiled Corky. 'I thought you meant the ring. Yes, of course. I'll phone right away.'

But as he rose I pushed him back in the pew: 'Let sleeping dogs lie,' I said, and he gave me a worried nod.

At home the gin bottle was reaching the end of its life, and Madge was beginning to feel the effects. She had a pale sheen of sweat over her face, and her hair had collapsed.

The Marriage

Hat patted her hand. 'Come on, Madge,' she said. 'It's five o'clock. We really should be making a move.'

Madge dabbed away the tears. 'It's stupid,' she cried. 'I mean – what's more important, me or the snooker?'

Hat took a strand of hair from Madge's mouth. 'Well, look at it this way,' she said. 'You've got the rest of your life.'

Madge rounded on her. 'Yes, apart from four nights a week he spends here. Then there's club nights and bingo.' She turned to Rupert for support.

''e's a 'ard bad. Wud of the lads, 'e is', he said, admiringly.

Madge looked at him in amazement. 'But I'll hardly ever see him,' she wailed.

Hat stepped in. 'Well, knowing Eric, I think that could prove a blessing.'

Madge sat there for a moment, then her hand flew to her mouth. Hat helped her upstairs to the bathroom.

In my reverie at St Bartholomew's I had just put away the blue and pink, and I was about to pot the black when somebody jogged my elbow, I shot upright to appeal, and found myself staring into the vicar's face. I looked about me. What was I doing here in church? Was somebody dead?

Then the vicar spoke. 'I really don't think your bride will be coming now,' he said. 'It's after 9.30.'

I stared at Corky. '9.30 at night?' I said.

He nodded.

'I don't think she'll be coming now,' repeated the vicar gently.

I stared at him. Corky helped me to my feet, and he walked me down the aisle. He said: 'Shock, you know.'

The vicar nodded sadly.

Corky went on: 'I've seen it happen often in my business – the police, you know.'

The vicar's eyes widened as if it had suddenly dawned on him that Corky was a constable. It's the same look when the governor comes in and says 'your reprieve's come through.' The vicar nodded uncomprehendingly, and watched as we left the church.

Corky took me as far as our gate, then said he had to change to go on duty, but I knew he was dead scared of meeting Rupert again. He needn't have worried – Rupert had gone hours ago. There was Hat sitting on the settee with Madge wearing her dressing-gown. As I closed the door behind me, Madge got up and rushed over.

'Oh, Ricky,' she cried. 'Can you ever forgive me.'

I looked over her shoulder at Hat, and Hat heaved a big sigh. I threw my top hat on to a chair and walked to the whisky bottle. 'You might have sent a note round to the church,' I said.

'I'm sorry, Ricky. I know how you must be feeling.'

I poured a glass of scotch. 'How can you know how I feel?' I said. 'You haven't the foggiest idea. Everything I've worked for, strived for, dreamed about – just wiped away like that.' I made a sweeping motion with my hand, and gulped down the whisky.

'Oh, Ricky,' sobbed Madge. 'I didn't know you felt as strongly as that.'

I turned on her. 'Oh, you didn't? Oh, my one chance, and you cancel it out like that.' Hat stared at me.

Madge touched my shoulder. 'I've said I'm sorry, Ricky.'

'It's a bit late now, isn't it, Madge? Good grief, I could have beaten Tom Butterworth easy.'

'Tom Butterworth.' said Hat.

'Yes, you know him. He's no good under pressure, and if I could have got a couple of early reds and blacks he'd have gone to pieces.'

The penny dropped. Hat nodded. 'Oh yes, you've missed the semi-finals.'

'What did you think I was talking about?' I snapped.

Madge turned away. 'Well, I'll go and get dressed, then,' she said in a small voice, and Hat went upstairs with her.

That's two months ago now, and Madge is back to her normal suffocating self, and I'm still one of the cogs in industry, but water never flows over a rock without leaving a deposit. Rupert is back in the Scrubs, but every month Hat packs a parcel of goodies and sets off on a visit. Perhaps my troubles are just beginning.

Opposite: 'Just another party.' – E.S.

Episode Guide

SYKES –Episode Guide

SERIES ONE (5 Episodes) (1960)
(All Episodes Black & White)

Episode One: Sykes And A Telephone
Script by Johnny Speight
Plot: Eric and Hattie try to get used to a new telephone, and try to cope with their new neighbour, Mr. Brown.
Broadcast: Friday 29th January 1960 (8.30pm)
Guest Cast: Arthur Mullard

Episode Two: Sykes And A Burglary
Script by Johnny Speight
Plot: With burglaries happening around the neighbourhood, Eric invests in a guard dog that's far from friendly.
Broadcast: Friday 5th February 1960 (8.30pm)
Guest Cast: Percy Edwards

Episode Three: Sykes And A New Car
Script by Johnny Speight
Plot: Eric's pride at owning a new car is deflated by Hattie's cynical attitude.
Broadcast: Friday 12th February 1960 (8.30pm)
Guest Cast: Deryck Guyler

Episode Four: Sykes And An Uncle
Script by Johnny Speight
Plot: Mr Brown's attitude towards Eric changes when he finds out how well-placed his uncle is.
Broadcast: Friday 19th February 1960 (at 8.30pm)
Guest Cast: Campbell Cotts, Sidney Vivian

Episode Five: Sykes And A Lodger
Script by Johnny Speight
Plot: When Mr Brown has work being done on his house, he decides to move in with Eric and Hattie.
Broadcast: Friday 26th February 1960 (8.30pm)
Guest Cast: None Noted

SERIES TWO (6 Episodes) (1960)
(All Episodes Black & White)

Episode One: Sykes And A Movie Camera
Script by Eric Sykes
Plot: Mr Brown is among the guests invited round by Eric and Hattie to watch their home movies.
Broadcast: Thursday 11th August 1960 (8.30pm)
Guest Cast: Deryck Guyler

Episode Two: Sykes And A Library Book
Script by John Antrobus
Plot: Eric falls foul of a cantankerous librarian when he visits the local library.
Broadcast: 18th August 1960 (8.30pm) Guest Cast: Deryck Guyler, Cameron Hall

Episode Three: Sykes And A Holiday
Script by Spike Milligan
Plot: Eric and Hattie plan to have a break and get away from it all, but that's when things start to go wrong.
Broadcast: 25th August 1960 (8.30pm) Guest Cast: Jacques Cey, Keith Smith

Episode Four: Sykes And An Egg
Script by Spike Milligan
From An Idea by Johnny Speight
Plot: (No Information Available) Guest Cast: Richard Waring, Hugh Lloyd

Episode Five: Sykes And A Brave Deed
Script by Eric Sykes
From An Idea by Johnny Speight
Plot: (No Information Available) Guest Cast: Bernard Hunter, Arthur Mullard

Episode Six: Sykes And A Cheque Book
Script by John Antrobus
From An Idea by Johnny Speight
Plot: A spending spree is in the air for Eric and Hattie.
Broadcast: 15th September 1960 (8.30pm)
Guest Cast: Richard Caldicot, Hugh Lloyd

SERIES THREE(1961) (6 Episodes)
(All Episodes Black & White)

Episode One: Sykes And A Window
Script by Eric Sykes
From An Idea by Johnny Speight
Plot: Window smashing plagues Sebastapol Terrace.
Broadcast: Wednesday 4th January 1961 (8.30pm)
Guest Cast: (No Information Available)

Episode Two: Sykes And A Salesman
Script by Eric Sykes
From An Idea by Johnny Speight
Plot: Eric becomes a salesman, but he's far from successful around the neighbourhood . . . Especially when he tries Mr. Brown.
Broadcast: Wednesday 11th January 1961 (8.30pm)
Guest Cast: Bruno Barnabe

Episode Three: Sykes And A Fancy Dress
Script by Eric Sykes From An Idea by Johnny Speight
Plot: Mr Brown decided to do the neighbourly thing and invite Eric and Hattie to a fancy dress ball.
Broadcast: Wednesday 18th January 1961 (8.30pm)
Guest Cast: Deryck Guyler, Robert Atkins, Hugh Lloyd

Episode Four: Sykes And A Bath
Script by Eric Sykes
From an idea by Johnny Speight
Plot: Panic ensues when Eric gets his big toe stuck in one of the taps on the bath . . .
Broadcast Wednesday 25th January 1961 (8.30pm)
Guest Cast: Deryck Guyler, John Bluthal

Episode Five: Sykes And A Marriage
Script by Eric Sykes
From An Idea by Johnny Speight
Plot: Hattie actively sets about finding an eligible batchelor to marry, which makes Eric panic as he doesn't want her to go.
Broadcast: Wednesday 1st February 1961 (8.30pm)
Guest Cast: Gladys Henson

Episode Six: Sykes And An Ankle
Script by Eric Sykes
From An Idea by Johnny Speight
Plot: Disaster follows Eric's attempts to take out the rubbish. It all starts to go wrong when it blows in Mr Brown's garden.
Broadcast: Wednesday 8th February 1961 (8.45pm)
Guest Cast: (None Noted)

SERIES FOUR (6 Episodes) (1961)
(All Episodes Black & White)

Episode One: Sykes And A Mission
Script by Eric Sykes
Plot: Eric and Hattie get an idea to help the poor and needy.
Broadcast: Friday 14th April 1961 (8.00pm)
Guest Cast: Arthur Mullard, John Bluthal

Episode Two: Sykes And A Stranger
Script by Eric Sykes
Plot: After decades at sea, a childhood sweetheart of Hattie's 5 returns to claim her hand, as he promised he'd do when they were ten.
Broadcast: Friday 21st April 1961 (8.00pm)
Guest Cast: Leo McKern

Episode Three: Sykes And A Cat
Script by Eric Sykes
Plot: Tiddles, a four week old kitten, gets stuck on Eric and Hattie's roof.
Broadcast: Friday 28th April 1961 (8.00pm)
Guest Cast: Jvor Salter

Episode Four: Sykes And A Bandage
Script by Eric Sykes
Plot: Hattie ropes Eric into volunteering as a victim for her to practice her First Aid on.
Broadcast: Friday 5th May 1961 (8.00pm)
Guest Cast: Fabia Drake

Episode Five: Sykes And A Suspicion
Script by Eric Sykes
Plot: Eric sets out to save England from being undermined by enemy agents.
Broadcast: Friday 12th May 1961 (8.00pm)
Guest Cast: Hugh Lloyd, Arthur Mullard

Episode Six: Sykes And A Suprise
Script by Eric Sykes
Plot: (No Information Available)
Broadcast: Friday 19th May 1961 (8.00pm)
Guest Cast: David Horne, Patrick Cargill and Wallas Eaton

SERIES FIVE (8 Episodes) (1962)
(All Episodes Black & White)

Episode One: Sykes And A Gamble
Script by Eric Sykes
Plot: A simple game of cards, which he loses spectacularly to Hattie, leads Eric to an encounter with the Mafia.
Broadcast: Tuesday 30th January 1962 (8.00pm)
Guest Cast: Bill Kerr, Alan Simpson

Episode Two: Sykes And A Job
Script by Eric Sykes
Plot: A factory boss takes on Eric and Hattie to work a pair of machines, but quickly lives to regret it.
Broadcast: Tuesday 6th February 1962 (8.00pm)
Guest Cast: Dick Emery, Campbell Singer

Episode Three: Sykes And A Boat
Script by Eric Sykes
Plot: Eric and Hattie take to the river, using a borrowed boat that they're under strict instructions to look after.
Broadcast: Tuesday 13th February 1962 (8.00pm)
Guest Cast: Charles Lloyd Pack

Episode Four: Sykes And A Journey
Script by Eric Sykes
Plot: When Eric and Hattie get a train from Newcastle to London, Hattie faints and Eric ends up wandering the streets of Darlington in his pyjamas.
Broadcast: Tuesday 20th February 1962 (8.00pm)
Guest Cast: Graham Stark, Hugh Lloyd

Episode Five: Sykes And An Elephant
Script by Eric Sykes

Plot: Sykes becomes rather attatched to an Indian elephant, much to Hattie's despair.
Broadcast: Tuesday 27th February 1962 (8.00pm)
Guest Cast: Deryck Guyler, Joan Hickson and Barma The Elephant

Episode Six: Sykes And A Rolls
Script by Eric Sykes
Plot: Eric takes on a job as a chauffeur, and can't believe his luck when he gets a Rolls Royce to drive.
Broadcast: Tuesday 6th March 1962 (8.00pm)
Guest Cast: Martita Hunt

Episode Seven: Sykes And A Haunting
Script by Eric Sykes
Plot: Strange things start to happen when Eric and Hattie find a trunk in the attic, which belonged to Uncle Edwardo – The Greatest Escapologist In The World.
Broadcast: Tuesday 13th March 1962 (8.00pm)
Guest Cast: Dick Emery

Episode Eight: Sykes And A Dream
Script by Eric Sykes
Plot: Eric's dream is just over five feet tall, with titian hair and green eyes . . . But there's a problem; Hattie.
Broadcast: Tuesday 20th March 1962 (8.00pm)
Guest Cast: Moira Redmond, Patricia Hayes

CHRISTMAS SPECIAL (1962) (1 Episode)
(Episode In Black & White)
Episode: Sykes And His Sister
Script by Eric Sykes
Plot: Eric and Hattie settle down at home, intent on celebrating Christmas quietly in front of the television.
Broadcast: Christmas Day 1962 (7.15pm)
(This was a ten minute sketch shown during the BBC's annual CHRISTMAS NIGHT WITH THE STARS show) Guest Cast: (None noted)

SERIES SIX (1963) (8Episodes)
(All Episodes Black & White)

Episode One: Syke And A Fog
Script by Eric Sykes
Plot: Eric gets lost in the fog, much to Hattie's concern.
Broadcast: Thursday 21st February 1963 (8.00pm)
Guest Cast: Cardew Robinson, Molly Weirand and Arthur Mullard

Episode Two: Sykes And A Phobia
Script by Eric Sykes
Plot: Eric becomes paranoid about getting his head stuck between the railings on his bed.

Broadcast: Thursday 28th February 1963 (8.00pm)
Guest Cast: Ronald Fraser

Episode Three: Sykes And A Camping
Script by Eric Sykes
Plot: Eric and Hattie try to cope with life in a tent, after placing a bet that they can with their milkman.
Broadcast: Thursday 7th March 1963 (8.00pm)
Guest Cast: Jack Smethurst, Bill Rhodes

Episode Four: Sykes And A Picture
Script by Eric Sykes
Plot: Hattie takes up painting and persuades Eric to model for her.
Broadcast: Thursday 14th March 1963 (8.00pm)
Guest Cast: Martin Miller

Episode Five: Sykes And A Mouse
Script by Eric Sykes
Plot: Eric turns Sherlock Holmes as he tries to track down a mouse that's at large in his home.
Broadcast: Thursday 21st March 1963 (8.00pm)
Guest Cast: Martin Miller, Victor Platt

Episode Six: Sykes And A Walk
Script by Eric Sykes
Plot: Eric walks all the way to Brighton.
Broadcast: Thursday 28th March 1963 (8.00pm)
Guest Cast: Deryck Guyler, Eric Phillips

Episode Seven: Sykes And A Referee
Script by Eric Sykes
Plot: A football match between the Sebastopol Rangers and WoodLane Athletic goes horribly wrong with Eric as Referee.
Broadcast: Thursday 4th April 1963 (8.00pm)
Guest Cast: Martin Miller, Kenneth Wolstenholme and Janet Brown

Episode Eight: Sykes And A Pub
Script by Eric Sykes
Plot: Eric and Hattie try to cope with running a public house.
Broadcast: Thursday 11th April 1963 (8.00pm)
Guest Cast: Norman Mitchell, Brian Rawlinson

SERIES SEVEN (1964) (7 Episodes)
(All Episodes Black & White)

Episode One: Sykes And A Box
Script by Eric Sykes
Plot: Eric becomes a reporter, but when Hattie tries to help, things go from bad to worse.
Broadcast: Tuesday 25th February 1964 (8.00pm)
Guest Cast: Ronald Adam, Donald Pickering

Episode Two: Sykes And A Plank

Episode Guide

Script by Eric Sykes
Plot: After putting his foot through the floor - boards in a neighbours house, Hattie helps Eric go to collect a replacement plank.
Broadcast: Tuesday 3rd March 1964 (8.00pm)
Guest Cast: Deryck Guyler, Felix Bowness

Episode Three: Sykes And A Search
Script by Eric Sykes
Plot: Problems confront Eric and Hattie that make them wish they'd never got out of bed.
Broadcast: Tuesday 10th March 1964 (8.00pm)
Guest Cast: Sheila Steafel

Episode Four: Sykes And A Following
Script by Eric Sykes
Plot: Eric and Hattie get jobs as the driver and conductress of a bus, and they determine to make it more than just a bus ride for the passengers.
Broadcast: Tuesday 17th March 1964 (8.00pm)
Guest Cast: William Kendall, Harry Locke

Episode Five: Sykes And A Menace
Script by Eric Sykes
Plot: The menace in the lives of Eric and Hattie comes in the shape of a sweet ten year old girl.
Broadcast: Tuesday 24th March 1964 (8.00pm)
Guest Cast: Melanie Parr, Garfield Morgan

Episode Six: Sykes And A Log Cabin
Script by Eric Sykes
Plot: Eric becomes fascinated with pioneers, and how they survived in cabins in the wilderness.
Broadcast: Tuesday 31st March 1964 (8.00pm)
Guest Cast: Ronnie Barker, Derek Nimmo

Episode Seven: Sykes And A Band
Script by Eric Sykes
Plot: Eric's desperation to play the drum in a brass band leads to police intervention.
Broadcast: Tuesday 7th April 1964 (8.00pm)
Guest Cast: Wensley Pithey

SERIES EIGHT (6 Episodes) (1964)
(All Episodes Black & White)

Episode One: Sykes And Two Birthdays
Script by Eric Sykes
Plot: Eric and Hattie - respective twins - try to plan something special to celebrate their joint birthday.
Broadcast: Friday 30th October 1964 (8.00pm)
Guest Cast: Jeremy Longhurst, Gerald Campion

Episode Two: Sykes And A Hypnotist
Script by Eric Sykes
Plot: Eric and Hattie go to the theatre and encounter a surprisingly effective hypnotist.

Broadcast: Friday 6th November 1964 (8.00pm)
Guest Cast: Robert Dorning, Valentine Dyall

Episode Three: Sykes And A Protest
Script by Eric Sykes
Plot: Eric decides to protest to the highest authority when it's announced that a block of flats is going to be built in Sebastapol Terrace.
Broadcast: Friday 13th November 1964 (8.00pm)
Guest Cast: Campbell Singer, Arthur Mullard

Episode Four: Sykes And A Bird
Script by Eric Sykes
Plot: When Eric adopts a pet bird, Hattie threatens to leave home.
Broadcast: Friday 20th November 1964 (8.00pm)
Guest Cast: Fabia Drake, John Arnatt

Episode Five: Sykes And A Cold War
Script by Eric Sykes
Plot: Eric becomes convinced that spies are living next door.
Broadcast: Friday 27th November 1964 (8.00pm)
Guest Cast: Dick Emery, Dandy Nichols

Episode Six: Sykes And A Gold?
Script by Eric Sykes
Plot: Eric becomes convinced he could win an Olympic medal.
Broadcast: Friday 4th December 1964 (8.00pm)
Guest Cast: Peter West

SERIES NINE (1965) (7 Episodes)
(All Episodes Black & White)

Episode One: Sykes And A Mountain
Script by Eric Sykes
Plot: Eric and Hattie get stuck climbing during a Bavarian holiday.
Broadcast: Tuesday 5th October 1965 (7.30pm)
Guest Cast: Anthony Sharpe, Arthur White

Episode Two: Sykes And A Deb
Script by Eric Sykes
Plot: After going to an army reunion, Eric ends up getting engaged to a beautiful debutante, but Hattie is suspicious of her.
Broadcast: Tuesday 12th October 1965 (7.30pm)
Guest Cast: Sally Bazley

Episode Three: Sykes And A Business
Script by Eric Sykes
Plot: After a visit to a psychologist to help Hattie find her 'true self', she ends up opening a roadside cafe with Eric.
Broadcast: Tuesday 19th October 1965 (7.30pm)
Guest Cast: Hugh Paddick, Bill Treacher

Episode Four: Sykes And A Golfer
Script by Eric Sykes
Plot: In Eric's dream, he gets to play golf with Peter Allis, the Ryder Cup Champion.
Broadcast: Tuesday 26th October 1965 (7.30pm)
Guest Cast: Peter Alliss

Episode Five: Sykes And A Big Brother
Script by Eric Sykes
Plot: Eric contemplates the future of wage earners, such as himself and Hattie.
Broadcast: Tuesday 2nd November 1965 (7.30pm)
Guest Cast: Kenneth J. Warren, Campbell Singer

Episode Six: Sykes And A Uniform
Script by Eric Sykes
Plot: Eric and Hattie have problems on a night out in London, when every 'uniform' they encounter causes trouble for them.
Broadcast: Tuesday 9th November 1965 (7.30pm)
Guest Cast: John Junkin, Pat Coombes

Episode Seven: Sykes And A Nest Egg
Script by Eric Sykes
Plot: While Eric takes up astrology, Hattie decides the time is right for her new boyfriend to move in with them.
Broadcast: Tuesday 16th November 1965 (7.30pm)
Guest Cast: Bill Nagy

SERIES TEN (1972) (16 Episodes)(Colour)

Note: A revival of SYKES was set up by the BBC during the Spring of 1972, and it was quickly agreed that the series would be both colour and far longer than any of the past seasons. With 16 episodes to fill, it was also agreed that Sykes could basically rework old plots to fulfil the new quota. While many elements remained the same, new factors had to be taken into consideration, such as the return of Richard Wattis, who now became a regular cast member again, and the improvements in special effects, which allowed far more scope for Sykes's creativity than before. So, to regard them as remakes would be wrong. They're the same stories, but retold for a new audience.

Episode One: Burglary
Script by Eric Sykes
Plot: After a burglar strikes the neighbourhood, Eric buys a guard dog.
Broadcast: Thursday 14th September 1972 (8.00pm) Guest Cast: (None Noted)
(Reworking of Season One/Episode Two)

Episode Two: Uncle
Script by Eric Sykes
Plot: Eric makes a fool of himself at the Golf Club Guest Night, and Mr Brown's attitude changes when he finds out who Eric's uncle is.
Broadcast: Thursday 21st September 1972 (8.00pm)
Guest Cast: John Le Mesurier, Roy Kinnear
(Reworking of Season One/Episode Four)

Episode Three: Walk
Script by Eric Sykes
Plot: When Eric takes up walking, he decides to enter the Olympics, but Mr Brown is sceptical.
Broadcast: Thursday 28th September 1972 (8.00pm) Guest Cast: Deryck Guyler
(Reworking on Season Six/Episode Six)

Episode Four: Menace
Script by Eric Sykes
Plot: Amanda (aged 10) arrives for the weekend, and Eric can't believe that she's as innocent as she looks.
Broadcast: Thursday 5th October 1972 (8.00pm)
Guest Cast: Annabelle Lanyon
(Reworking of Season Seven/Episode Four)

Episode Five: Boat
Script by Eric Sykes
Plot: Mr Brown lends Eric his new boat, so he takes to the water with Hattie.
Broadcast: Thursday 12th October 1972 (8.00pm)
Guest Cast: (None Noted)
(Reworking of Season Five/Episode Three)

Episode Six: Stranger
Script by Eric Sykes
Plot: Eric and Hattie are visited by a stranger, who's returned to fulfil a childhood promise to Hattie.
Broadcast: Thursday 19th October 1972 (8.00pm)
Guest Cast: Peter Sellers, Deryck Guyler
(Reworking on Season Four/Episode Two)

Episode Seven: Football
Script by Eric Sykes
Plot: The local football team make a mistake when they ask Eric to be their referee.
Broadcast: Thursday 26th October 1972 (8.00pm)
Guest Cast: Joan Sims, Deryck Guyler
(Reworking of Season Six/Episode Seven)

Episode Eight: Job
Script by Eric Sykes
Plot: Eric and Hattie join a local factory.
Broadcast: Thursday 2nd November 1972 (8.00pm)
Guest Cast: Graham Stark, Jimmy Edwards
(Reworking of Season Five/Episode Two)

Episode Nine: Ankle

Script by Eric Sykes
Plot: As Eric takes the rubbish out, a gust of wind blows it over Mr Brown's garden, with disasterous results.
Broadcast: Thursday 9th November 1972 (8.00pm)
Guest Cast: (None Noted)
(Reworking of Season Three/Episode Six)

Episode Ten: Mouse
Script by Eric Sykes
Plot: Eric and Hattie find they've got a mouse in their home, and after failing to get rid of it themselves, they call in an exterminator.
Broadcast: Thursday 16th November 1972 (8.00pm)
Guest Cast: Sam Kydd
(Reworking of Season Six/Episode Five)

Episode Eleven: Dream
Script by Eric Sykes
Plot: Eric is bitten by a dog and goes to the doctor, but suddenly he gets hit by something that's far more difficult to treat.
Broadcast: Thursday 23rd November 1972 (8.00pm)
Guest Cast: Joan Hickson, Frank Thornton
(Reworking of Season Five/Episode Eight)

Episode Twelve: Marriage
Script by Eric Sykes
Plot: Hattie advertises for eligible batchelors, but Eric doesn't want her to go.
Broadcast: Thursday 30th November 1972 (8.00pm)
Guest Cast: Gretchen Franklin
(Reworking of Season Three/Episode Five)

Episode Thirteen: Cat
Script by Eric Sykes
Plot: Hattie's kitten, Tiddles, gets stuck on the roof of Major Crombie-Crombie's house, and he loathes cats.
Broadcast: Thursday 7th December 1972 (8.00pm)
Guest Cast: Deryck Guyler
(Reworking of Season Four/Episode Three)

Episode Fourteen: Journey
Script by Eric Sykes
Plot: Eric and Hattie go on holiday with Mr Brown, and head home on the nightsleeper from Glasgow. That's when the trouble begins.
Broadcast: Thursday 14th December 1972 (8.00pm)
Guest Cast: Deryck Guyler, Chick Murray, Bill Maynard
(Reworking of Season Five/Episode Four)

Episode Fifteen: Lodger
Script by Eric Sykes
Plot: Mr Brown has the decorators in, so he decides to stay next door with Eric and Hattie.
Broadcast: Thursday 21st December 1972 (8.00pm)

Guest Cast: (None Noted)
(Reworking of Season One/Episode Five)

Episode Sixteen: Cafe
Script by Eric Sykes
Plot: Eric buys a transport cafe, and decides to go all earthy when customers start to disappear.
Broadcast: Thursday 28th December 1972 (8.00pm)
Guest Cast: (None Noted)
(Reworking of Season Nine/Episode Three)

SERIES ELEVEN (1973) (15 Episodes)(Colour)

Episode One: An Engagement
Script by Eric Sykes
Plot: An army reunion leaves Sykes feeling worse for wear next morning, but then a beautiful girl calls and Eric can't remember what happened the night before.
Broadcast: Monday 10th September. 1973 (6.40pm)
Guest Cast: Fiona Gaunt, Ballard Berkley
(Reworking of Season Nine/Episode Two)

Episode Two: Bus
Script by Eric Sykes
Plot: Eric and Hattie go to work for London Transport, and decide to revolutionise it by running their bus like an airline…the depot manager's far from impressed.
Broadcast: Monday 17th September 1973 (6.45pm)
Guest Cast: Deryck Guyler, Bella Emberg
(Reworking of Season Seven/Episode Four)

Episode Three: Spy Ring
Script by Eric Sykes
Plot: Eric and Hattie's new neighbours drink vodka and pay for things with crisp new notes. So, in Eric's mind, it stands to reason that they're up to no good.
Broadcast: Monday 24th September 1973 (6.45pm)
Guest Cast: Deryck Guyler, David Battley
(Reworking of Season Four/Episode Five)

Episode Four: Golf
Script by Eric Sykes
Plot: Eric's golf mania makes Hattie decide to have a go as well, and she ends up coaching the world's number one golfer.
Broadcast: Monday 1st October 1973 (6.45pm)
Guest Cast: Tony Jacklin, Richard Caldicot
(Reworking of Season Nine/Episode Four)

Episode Five: Rolls
Script by Eric Sykes
Plot: Eric gets a job as Chauffeur to Lady Dorothy, but the only driving lessons he's had must have been a crash course!

Episode Guide

Broadcast: Monday 8th October 1973 (6.40pm)
Guest Cast: Deryck Guyler, Sonia Dresdel
(Reworking of Season Five/Episode Six)

Episode Six: Peeping Tom
Script by Eric Sykes
Plot: Eric gets his head stuck in the garden railings.
Broadcast: Monday 15th October 1973 (6.40pm)
Guest Cast: Deryck Guyler, Campbell Singer
(Reworking of Season Six/Episode Two)

Episode Seven: Fancy Dress
Script by Eric Sykes
Plot: Eric and Hattie go to a fancy dress ball with
Mr Brown - Eric as Caeser, Hattie as a Police
woman.
Broadcast: Monday 22nd October 1973 (6.40pm)
Guest Cast: Deryck Guyler, Raymond Huntley and
Arthur Howard
(Reworking of Season Three/Episode Three)

Episode Eight: Window Smasher
Script by Eric Sykes
Plot: Only Eric's house seems immune to a spate of
window smashing in the neighbourhood...Could
this be a clue to the identity of the culprit?
Broadcast: Monday 29th October 1973 (6.40pm)
Guest Cast: Deryck Guyler, Joan Sims, Richard
Caldicot and Ronnie Brody
(Reworking of Season Three/Episode One)

Episode Nine: Gamble
Script by Eric Sykes
Plot: Eric can't even beat Hattie with a marked
deck of cards, and when junior mafia-man Luigi
shows up, things get worse.
Broadcast: Monday 5th November 1973 (6.40pm)
Guest Cast: Deryck Guyler, Freddie Earlle
(Reworking of Season Five/Episode One)

Episode Ten: Uniform
Script by Eric Sykes
Plot: Eric and Hattie try to enjoy a night out, but
they keep crossing the path of authority.
Broadcast: Monday 12th November 1973 (6.40pm)
Guest Cast: Deryck Guyler, Rita Webb, Pat Coombs
(Reworking of Season Nine/Episode Six)

Episode Eleven: Bird
Script by Eric Sykes
Plot: Hattie is being driven mad by Eric's pet bird,
but he chooses the bird when she gives him an ulti-
matum over who goes.
Broadcast: Monday 19th November 1973 (6.40pm)
Guest Cast: Deryck Guyler, Peter Reeves
(Reworking of Season Eight/Episode Four)

Episode Twelve: Protest

Script by Eric Sykes
Plot: Eric decides to go to extraordinary lengths to
protest about a block of flats being built in
Sebastapol Terrace.
Broadcast: Monday 26th November 1973 (6.40pm)
Guest Cast: Deryck Guyler, Campbell Singer and
Bill Pertwee
(Reworking of Season Eight/Episode Three)

Episode Thirteen: Salesman
Script by Eric Sykes
Plot: Eric becomes a salesman, and determines to
get a buyer at every home in the street... But, things
don't always work out as planned.
Broadcast: Monday 3rd December 1973 (6.40pm)
Guest Cast: Deryck Guyler, Henry McGee
(Reworking of Season Three/Episode Two)

Episode Fourteen: Haunting
Script by Eric Sykes
Plot: Uncle Edwardo - The Greatest Escapologist In
The World - leaves Eric and Hattie a legacy that
makes them more dependant on each other than
ever before.
Broadcast: Monday 10th December 1973 (6.40pm)
Guest Cast: Deryck Guyler, Blake Butler
(Reworking of Season Five/Episode Seven)

Episode Fifteen: Nest Egg
Script by Eric Sykes
Plot: Hattie wants her new boyfriend to move in,
but Eric's far from happy about that prospect.
Broadcast: Monday 17th December 1973 (6.40pm)
Guest Cast: Deryck Guyler, Lionel Murton
(Reworking of Season Nine/Episode Seven)

SERIES TWELVE (1974) (8 Episodes) (Colour)

Episode One: The Stolen Bentley
Script by Eric Sykes
Plot: Eric gets involved with the Police when a
brand new Bentley goes missing.
Broadcast: Thursday 17th October 1974 (8.00pm)
Guest Cast: Deryck Guyler, Anthony Steel
(Reworking of Season One/Episode Three – 'Sykes
And A New Car')

Episode Two: Holiday In Bogsea
Script by Eric Sykes
Plot: All Eric and Hattie want to do is enjoy a quiet
holiday, but everything conspires against them.
Broadcast: Thursday 24th October 1974 (8.00pm)
Guest Cast: Deryck Guyler, Clive Morton and
Sheila Steafel
(Reworking of Season Two/Episode Three)

Episode Three: The Pub
Script by Eric Sykes
Plot: Eric and Hattie get involved with running
their local pub.
Broadcast: Thursday 31st October 1974 (8.00pm)
Guest Cast: Deryck Guyler, Sam Kydd and Queenie
Watts
(Reworking of Season Six/Episode Eight)

Episode Four: The Band
Script by Eric Sykes
Plot: Eric decides that he wants to play a drum in a
marching band, no matter what the Police say about
him practicing.
Broadcast: Thursday 7th November 1974 (8.00pm)
Guest Cast: Deryck Guyler, Bernard Bresslaw and
John Bluthal
(Reworking of Season Seven/Episode Seven)

Episode Five: Two Birthdays
Script by Eric Sykes
Plot: Eric and Hattie, being twins, share the same
birthday, and they decide to celebrate it in style.
Broadcast: Thursday 14th November 1974 (8.00pm)
Guest Cast: Deryck Guyler, John Blyth
(Reworking of Season Eight/Episode One)

Episode Six: A Bandage
Script by Eric Sykes
Plot: Eric quickly begins to regret agreeing to be a
'Victim' for Hattie's first aid practice.
Broadcast: Thursday 21st November 1974 (8.00pm)
Guest Cast: Deryck Guyler, Fabia Drake
(Reworking of Season Four/Episode Four)

Episode Seven: Log Cabin
Script by Eric Sykes
Plot: Eric becomes fascinated with how to survive
in the wilderness.
Broadcast: Thursday 28th November 1974 (8.00pm)
Guest Cast: Deryck Guyler, Frederick Peisley
(Reworking of Season Seven/Episode Six)

Episode Eight: The Fog
Script by Eric Sykes
Plot: Eric gets lost in the fog, much to Hattie's
distress.
Broadcast: Thursday 5th December 1974 (8.00pm)
Guest Cast: Deryck Guyler, Jerold Wells
(Reworking of Season Six/Episode One)

SERIES THIRTEEN (1975) (7 Episodes) (Colour)

Episode One: Commercial
Script by Eric Sykes
Plot: Eric becomes intrigued by the power of
advertising.

Broadcast: Friday 24th October 1975 (8.00pm)
Guest Cast: Deryck Guyler, Arthur Howard

Episode Two: Ski-ing
Script by Eric Sykes
Plot: Eric wants to try out a sport that will surely become a dangerous one in his hands.
Broadcast: Friday 31st October 1975 (8.00pm)
Guest Cast: Deryck Guyler, Eric Pohlmann

Episode Three : Caravan
Script by Eric Sykes
Plot: When Eric and Hattie set off for a caravan holiday, they get stuck in traffic.
Broadcast: Friday 7th November 1975 (8.00pm)
Guest Cast: Deryck Guyler, Sonia Dresdel

Episode Four: Reporter
Script by Eric Sykes
Plot: Eric gets a job as a reporter, and lives to regret Hattie's attempts to help.
Broadcast: Friday 14th November 1975 (8.0Opm)
Guest Cast: Deryck Guyler, Corbett Woodall
(Reworking of Season Seven/Episode One)

Episode Five: Marriage
Script by Eric Sykes
Plot: Eric contemplates settling down and starting a family.
Broadcast: Friday 28th November 1975 (8.0Opm)
Guest Cast: Deryck Guyler, Sheila Steafel

Episode Six: Night Out
Script by Eric Sykes
Plot: Eric and Hattie are determined to enjoy themselves during a night out on the town.
Broadcast: Friday 5th December 1975 (8.00pm)
Guest Cast: Deryck Guyler, Joan Sims

Episode Seven: Christmas Party
Script by Eric Sykes
Plot: A traditional Christmas in Eric and Hattie's household? It turns out to be anything but.
Broadcast: Friday 12th December 1975 (8.00pm)
(This Episode was postponed from 21st November)
Guest Cast: Deryck Guyler, Joan Sims and Neil McCarthy

SERIES FOURTEEN (1976) (8 Episodes)(Colour)

Episode One: Home Movies
Script by Eric Sykes
Plot: Eric and Hattie invite friends round to see some of their home movies.
Broadcast: Thursday 11th November 1976
(7.4Opm) Guest Cast: Deryck Guyler, Robert Keegan

(Reworking ofSeason Two/Episode One)
Episode Two: Fishing
Script by Eric Sykes
Plot: Eric has plans for a peaceful fishing trip, but then Hattie decides she wants to go with him.
Broadcast: Thursday 18th November 1976 (7.40pm)
Guest Cast: Reginald Marsh, Reg Lye

Episode Three: Lodgers
Script by Eric Sykes
Plot: When Eric and Hattie take on lodgers to help with their finances, things do not go according to plan.
Broadcast: Thursday 25th November 1976 (7.40pm)
Guest Cast: Deryck Guyler, Brenda Cowling

Episode Four: Holiday Camp
Script by Eric Sykes
Plot: Eric and Hattie's plans for their annual holiday more than live up to their past track record.
Broadcast: Thursday 2nd December 1976 (7.40pm)
Guest Cast: Deryck Guyler, Pippa Page and Nosher Powell

Episode Five: Inventions
Script by Eric Sykes
Plot: Eric has an idea for an invention that he's certain will revolutionise life as we know it.
Broadcast: Thursday 9th December 1976 (7.40pm)
Guest Cast: Deryck Guyler, Derek Francis, Joy Harington

Episode Six: Flashback
Script by Eric Sykes
Plot: Corky and Mrs. Rumbelow find Eric and Hattie in a rather strange situation.
Broadcast: Thursday 16th December 1976 (7.40pm)
Guest Cast: Deryck Guyler, Joy Harington

Episode Seven: Squatters
Script by Eric Sykes
Plot: Eric and Hattie come back from holiday, only to find an old Irish tramp has taken up residence in their house.
Broadcast: Thursday 23rd December 1976 (8.00pm)
Guest Cast: Deryck Guyler, Roy Dotrice, Michael Ward

Episode Eight: Bath
Script by Eric Sykes
Plot: Chaos ensues as Eric gets his big toe stuck in the tap while he's having a bath.
Broadcast: Thursday 30th December 1976 (8.00pm)
Guest Cast: Deryck Guyler, Joy Harington and Gordon Kaye
(Reworking of Season Three/Episode Four)

SYKES - CHRJSTMAS SPECJAL (1977)
(1 Episode) (Colour)
Script by Eric Sykes
A one off variety show, structured losely around Christmas with Eric and Hattie. Apart from Deryck Guyler, who performed his legendary washboard musical act, and Joy Harington, the special guests were Sylvia Peters and Jimmy Edwards.
Broadcast: Thursday 22nd December 1977 (8.3Opm)
-A copy survives in colour in the BBC Film Archive.

SERIES FIFTEEN (1978) (6 Episodes)(Colour)

Episode One: The Hypnotist
Script by Eric Sykes
Plot: Eric and Hattie go to the theatre and encounter a remarkable hypnotist...
Broadcast: Wednesday 4th January 1978 (6.50pm)
Guest Cast: Deryck Guyler, Gerald Flood, Joy Harington
(Reworking of Season Eight/Episode Two)

Episode Two: Picket Line
Script by Eric Sykes
Plot: Eric gets political and comes to the aid of a picket line.
Broadcast: Wednesday 11th January 1978 (6.50pm)
Guest Cast: Deryck Guyler, Joy Harington, John Blythe and Michael Ripper

Episode Three: Football Match
Script by Eric Sykes
Plot: Eric's simple appreciation of football leads to problems.
Broadcast: Wednesday 18th January 1978 (6.55pm)
Guest Cast: Deryck Guyler, Robert Dorning

Episode Four: Decorating
Script by Eric Sykes
Plot: Eric and Hattie decide that it's time to change their surroundings and decorate.
Broadcast: Wednesday 25th January 1978 (6.55pm)
Guest Cast: Deryck Guyler, Sam Kydd

Episode Five: End Of The World
Script by Eric Sykes
Plot: Hattie becomes convinced that the world is about to end, but Eric won't believe a word of it.
Broadcast: Wednesday 1st February 1978 (6.50pm)
Guest Cast: Deryck Guyler, Joy Harington and Joan Sims

Episode Six: Television Film
Script by Eric Sykes